A SEAL'S DEVOTION

By Cora Seton

Author's Note

A SEAL's Devotion is the seventh volume in the SEALs of Chance Creek series, set in the fictional town of Chance Creek, Montana. To find out more about Curtis, Hope, Boone, Clay, Jericho, Walker and the other inhabitants of Base Camp, look for the rest of the books in the series, including:

A SEAL's Oath

A SEAL's Vow

A SEAL's Pledge

A SEAL's Consent

A SEAL's Purpose

A SEAL's Resolve

A SEAL's Desire

A SEAL's Struggle

A SEAL's Triumph

Also, don't miss Cora Seton's other Chance Creek series, the Cowboys of Chance Creek, the Heroes of Chance Creek, and the Brides of Chance Creek

The Cowboys of Chance Creek Series:

The Cowboy Inherits a Bride (Volume 0)

The Cowboy's E-Mail Order Bride (Volume 1)

The Cowboy Wins a Bride (Volume 2)

The Cowboy Imports a Bride (Volume 3)

The Cowgirl Ropes a Billionaire (Volume 4)

The Sheriff Catches a Bride (Volume 5)

The Cowboy Lassos a Bride (Volume 6)

The Cowboy Rescues a Bride (Volume 7)
The Cowboy Earns a Bride (Volume 8)
The Cowboy's Christmas Bride (Volume 9)

The Heroes of Chance Creek Series:

The Navy SEAL's E-Mail Order Bride (Volume 1)
The Soldier's E-Mail Order Bride (Volume 2)
The Marine's E-Mail Order Bride (Volume 3)
The Navy SEAL's Christmas Bride (Volume 4)
The Airman's E-Mail Order Bride (Volume 5)

The Brides of Chance Creek Series:

Issued to the Bride One Navy SEAL
Issued to the Bride One Airman
Issued to the Bride One Sniper
Issued to the Bride One Marine
Issued to the Bride One Soldier

The Turners v. Coopers Series:

The Cowboy's Secret Bride (Volume 1)
The Cowboy's Outlaw Bride (Volume 2)
The Cowboy's Hidden Bride (Volume 3)
The Cowboy's Stolen Bride (Volume 4)
The Cowboy's Forbidden Bride (Volume 5)

Visit Cora's website at www.coraseton.com
Find Cora on Facebook at facebook.com/CoraSeton
Sign up for my newsletter HERE.
www.coraseton.com/sign-up-for-my-newsletter

CHAPTER ONE

"**C**HEER UP," CURTIS Lloyd said. "Boone will find you a bride if all else fails."

Anders Olsen followed the big, burly man up the steps to the bunkhouse, the informal headquarters of Base Camp, the sustainable community they were both helping to build. Curtis's dog, Daisy, threaded through their legs, as eager as they were to get inside. It was mid-December, cold and dark.

"I want to find my own bride." Anders had a little over a month to do so, or he and everyone else who lived here would lose their homes. That was one of the rules. A wedding every forty days, or Martin Fulsom, the billionaire funding the project—and the reality television show documenting their progress—would give the entire property to a developer and show them the door. Anders didn't want to be the one who spoiled it for everyone else. Six of the ten men who'd started the project had already found wives. Two had children on the way. That was a lot of people who'd be homeless if he didn't do his part.

He didn't want to leave Base Camp in any case. He was dedicated to the cause of promoting sustainable living, and the men and women he lived with here had come to feel like family. It had been a long time since he'd had this kind of home. He wasn't like Curtis, whose family may have disagreed with some of his choices but loved and doted on him just the same. Anders was alone in this world—or had been until he'd arrived here in Chance Creek, Montana, last spring. Now it was getting close to Christmas, and he'd come to feel like he belonged here.

"It'll all work out." Curtis pushed open the door, filled the entryway and blocked the light for a minute before continuing into the bunkhouse, pulling off his woolen cap and unzipping the heavy jacket he wore.

Anders doubted it would be that easy, but he followed Curtis inside and shrugged out of his coat, too. He was as tall as Curtis but not as broad in the shoulders or chest. That didn't bother him. His many years in the Navy SEALs had proven beyond a shadow of a doubt he could hold his own against other men.

Not that he'd ever fought Curtis or even argued with him. They'd gotten along since the first day they'd arrived at Base Camp, neither of them really knowing what they were getting into. Both had answered an ad searching for candidates to help build a sustainable community. They'd known they would need to make a commitment to the job—and the lifestyle. Neither had anticipated the project turning a reality television show with a host of unusual rules, however.

Only last week Curtis had been the one desperate to find a bride. He'd almost run out of time when Hope Martin crashed her car at the end of their lane on the way to delivering her friend Raina to Bozeman for Raina's wedding. Curtis had come to the rescue and gotten both women there, even though a blizzard had made that journey quite an adventure. Along the way, he and Hope had fallen in love.

Anders had no idea where he would find a wife. He hadn't met anyone in Chance Creek, and so far dating apps had been a bust, too.

He'd find her, though. Failure wasn't an option. A long time ago, before his mother had died, while he was still too young to realize what his father's business entailed, he'd had a family and home he loved. He'd promised himself one day he'd have that again. He wasn't going to leave Base Camp if he could help it.

He nearly bumped into Curtis when the man stopped abruptly several feet into the large, overwarm room.

"What the hell is Fulsom doing here—again?"

Anders leaned sideways to get a look and saw Martin Fulsom deep in conversation with Renata Ludlow, *Base Camp*'s director, and Boone Rudman, another member of the community. Fulsom was a fit, energetic, silver-haired man in his late sixties, whose outsized personality filled any room he entered. Renata was a trim woman in her thirties, her raven-black hair tucked into a bun, her professional clothing finally modified from her usual pencil skirts and aggressive white blouses to slacks and sweaters because of the cold weather. She was even wearing winter boots instead of the stiletto heels she had favored well into November.

Beside them stood a man Anders vaguely recognized but couldn't quite place. A rangy, sandy-haired, smug-faced man who was watching Renata in a way that spelled trouble.

"Who's he?" Anders murmured to Curtis.

"Hell, isn't he that guy from that show? The one where they stalk everyone?" Curtis asked.

Greg Devon, one of the other unmarried members of Base Camp, a serious man with a shock of black hair, edged closer to them. "His name is Clem Bailey. He's the host of *Track the Stars*," he said in an undertone. "Fulsom's siccing him on Renata."

"What do you mean?" Anders asked.

There wasn't time for Greg to answer before Boone, who acted as the de-facto leader of their community since the whole thing had been his idea, called out, "Everyone sit down. Mr. Fulsom's got something to say."

Anders knew he wasn't the only one biting back a groan. Fulsom had a penchant for drama. He liked to come and tell them exactly how they were screwing up. If things got too quiet in California where he lived, he came looking for trouble here.

Fulsom stood at the front of the room and looked at each of them in turn, as if making sure every one of them was paying attention. They were, since all their futures depended on him. Fulsom was the one who'd bought the ranch they were building Base Camp on. He was the one who'd organized the television show and made sure it got the publicity it needed to remain one of the top-rated programs in the nation. He was a thorn in their sides but one they couldn't ignore.

"I am sick of your bullshit!" Fulsom boomed suddenly.

Anders looked around at the others. They were all long past responding to the billionaire's histrionics, except maybe Hope, who had only been at Base Camp for a handful of days. This was the way Fulsom began most of his speeches. There was always a complaint, followed by a demand.

An outrageous demand.

"I told you I wanted action," Fulsom went on. "Adventure. Controversy. SEX! And what happens?" He turned on Renata. "You and nearly the entire film crew abandon your posts because of a little snowstorm last week, and you"—he pointed at Curtis—"try to leave the one remaining crew member behind when you embark on the adventure of the century. Which means Byron here"—he pointed to a young cameraman—"had to chase after you and managed to total a very expensive four-by-four in the process, along with everything inside it. That means this week's episode is entirely filmed on outdated, insufficient camera equipment, and it very nearly wasn't filmed at all. What is this? Amateur hour?"

Anders settled in. This could take a while.

He was right. Fulsom droned on in a similar vein while Renata glared at Byron, and Byron did his best to fade into the woodwork. All the while Clem's smug smile grew wider.

When Fulsom finally calmed down, he gestured the newcomer forward. "This is Clem Bailey. He's come to lend a hand to this production. Clem knows how to spice up a television show. He's got ideas. Big ideas! And he's got the balls to see them through. Plus, he knows how to keep a bunch of puissant, know-nothing, self-absorbed actors in line!"

Actors? Anders straightened. So did the other men in the room.

None of them were actors.

They'd all fought for their country as Navy SEALs. Survived situations Fulsom could only dream of—

"Yeah, now I've got your attention," Fulsom said. "You're supposed to be men of action, so get out there and do something worth filming, for God's sake. And you!"

Anders recoiled when Fulsom pointed at him, caught himself and straightened again. He should have known this was coming.

"It's your turn to marry, so do it—spectacularly. Got it?"

"Got it." But Anders had no idea where to start.

"I UNDERSTAND YOU thought you were going to save the world, but you don't seem to be very... effective... at it." Laura Wright tucked her shoulder-length honey-blonde hair behind her ear. Only a moment ago, she'd placed her napkin on the table and pushed her dinner plate a fraction of an inch away from the edge, signaling an end to the meal.

Evelyn Wright tried not to flinch at her mother's harsh assessment of her career so far. It was true she'd arrived back in Virginia on crutches a year ago after being medevaced out of rural Angola when she'd broken her leg in two places, but she had healed quite nicely. She might not make it up Mt. Everest, but that had never been on her agenda anyway. She was already on the hunt for a new job at an NGO overseas.

"You're still in debt," her father, Wayne, added. "Now, of course we were happy to step in and help the daughter we love cover her unexpected bills, and we appreciate how hard you're working to make your repayments on time, but we hoped you'd stretch to pay them faster. At your age, you should really be saving up for a down payment on a house."

"I'm trying—" Life in Richmond wasn't cheap, and she hadn't been able to drive for the first six months she was home. Taxi fare added up, as did everything else. Still, a pang of guilt twisted inside her. Her parents had paid her exorbitant medical bills up-front when she couldn't cover them. Now she was paying them back.

Slowly.

Her mom was right; she didn't have much to show for her efforts so far.

"We've been thinking," Laura said.

"A lot," Wayne put in.

"You're not exactly the marrying kind; that's clear."

Ouch, Eve thought. Not the marrying kind? That was

harsh. For one thing, she was only twenty-nine, and there was plenty of time for her to find a soul mate. For another, she thought she had found a potential husband until three months ago—when she'd confessed to her boyfriend, Heath, she was looking for a new overseas job, and he'd texted her two days later to say he was leaving her for a systems engineer named Claire who had just finished her dissertation. "I need someone like me. Someone who wants to live in Virginia," he'd said. "Claire doesn't flutter around the world like you do. She sets goals and stays in one place long enough to accomplish them. So do I. You and I just aren't compatible."

That accusation still stung. Weren't opposites supposed to attract?

"You've worked for AltaVista for seven months." Her father broke into her thoughts. "I think that's your longest stint with any company, isn't it? You like… variety. But variety doesn't get you a retirement fund."

Retirement fund?

Eve tried not to sigh. Her parents loved to talk about retirement. They were getting close to retiring themselves, so she supposed it was natural it was on their minds, but again, she was twenty-nine. Plenty of time to—

"Honey, the thing is—you're really blowing it," her mother said flatly.

Eve straightened. "That's not fair. I've got a great job at AltaVista—"

"A great job for someone who didn't finish school," her father said, "but you're not going to climb the ladder any further there until you get your bachelor's degree, at a minimum. You know you need a master's to get anywhere."

So this was to be a conversation about school, their other favorite topic. She'd done a semester at the University of Richmond right out of high school, which was where she'd met Heath, but then she'd gotten involved with Amnesty International and ended up traveling around the world for several years, moving from NGO to NGO—until her ignominious return home in pieces.

After a couple of months on her parents' couch, she'd been hired by AltaVista Imaging as a receptionist. Since then she'd moved into the quality control department. It turned out she had a good eye. Her boss had begun to hint there might be work in management for her—someday.

If she was willing to do the schooling.

"Getting your degree is going to take a lot of time if you're working, too," Laura said. "Meanwhile, you're not making any progress toward owning a home."

"A home is the cornerstone of any retirement plan," Wayne added.

Eve stifled a groan. They'd hit upon a guilt trifecta: retirement, homeownership, higher education. Not necessarily in that order.

"Honey, it's time to grow up," her mother said. "And grown-ups have a degree, they own their own home, and they have a plan for later in life." She sat back. "It's obvious to us you're making no progress toward any of that."

Which made her what—a kid? Sometimes she felt like a kid. But she was a world traveler, Eve reminded herself, lifting her glass of water to her lips in order to buy time. She'd fought for better living conditions, equality and safety for people in multiple countries. She was supporting herself now, too. Maybe she was living in an efficiency apartment, and maybe her savings account was languishing as she paid down her debts, but—

"Here's our offer, kiddo," her father said. "We will pay for school if you move home—"

Move home? Eve nearly choked on the water she'd just swallowed. She was not going to move home. "But—"

"And," her mother said, holding up a hand to forestall her protestations, "we will also loan you enough money to cover building costs for a tiny house. We've chosen a spot for it near the fence in our backyard."

Tiny house? Eve swallowed again. Her parents were going to help her build a tiny house in their yard? Years ago, when she'd graduated from high school, she'd proposed the idea, wanting to go straight into activism instead of college. They'd shot it down.

"You'll have to do most of the work yourself, and of course you'll have to pay us back for it," her father cautioned her, "plus nominal pad rent once you're all settled in. Once you pay us off, however, you'll own the tiny house. Later, if you want to buy land of your own, you can move it with you."

Despite her frustration, Eve realized her parents were doing their best, trying hard to make their vision of her future palatable to her particular wants and needs. They'd been listening to her all these years, after all. They wanted her to be happy.

"Since you're single, and likely to remain so, you won't need much square footage," her mother said. "Which is good. We don't want the neighbors complaining."

"But if the right fellow comes along, you can always sell your tiny house and upgrade to something bigger," her father said jovially.

Eve looked from one to the other and had another realization. This was the heart of their concern, wasn't it? All three of her siblings were married and settled, something her mom and dad had made clear they wanted for all their children.

But they were giving up on her.

"A tiny house. A chance to go to school. A way to get ahead in life. What do you think of that?" her father asked.

"It sounds… great," she managed to say, but it didn't sound great at all. It sounded like they no longer expected her to achieve… anything.

Did they really think she'd spend her life alone?

Eve had the sensation of standing on sloped ground and losing her footing, beginning to slide down, down, down.

"There's one more condition." Her mother adjusted the position of her plate again. "Valley Community

College starts up again the third week of January. If you want that tiny house, you need to be enrolled and ready to go to class."

"That's… barely more than a month from now," Eve protested. "I'm not even registered at Valley."

"Actually"—her father cleared his throat—"you are. Here's a course catalog." He handed her a slim brochure, and she took it, stunned. They'd been planning this awhile, hadn't they?

"And here's a company that specializes in tiny house plans. You can buy materials and your frame from them. Just pick which one you like. I've circled three that fall within the proper square footage."

Eve took a second brochure from her mother.

"School. Home ownership. The first steps on your way to a settled, proper life," her father said. "It's all set. All you have to do is say yes."

"And stick to your decision," her mother said firmly. "No backing out when times get a little tough, okay?"

"That's right. No backing out. You make a commitment to us, and we'll make a commitment to you," her father said. "When we get back from Europe in February, we expect you to be hitting the books hard. We'll get your tiny house going as soon as winter ends. In the meantime, you can stay in your old room."

"Well?" her mother prompted. "What do you say?"

The slide down the slippery slope began to feel more like a tumble. Eve didn't want to disappoint her parents, but she hated being tied down to plans. Her ability to pivot was one of her best characteristics.

And her worst, she admitted. Her parents were right; she didn't tend to stick with things, and they were currently paying the price for her pivot to Angola. Back when she'd ended up on their couch, they'd almost cancelled their big trip to Europe, unsure how long her recovery would take. Thank goodness she'd convinced them to move forward on it.

Eve took a deep breath. It wasn't like she had a better option. No one had offered her a new position abroad, and she'd been feeling at loose ends ever since she'd come home. She liked her job at AltaVista okay, but her parents were right; it wasn't really a career.

Time to make a decision and stick to it, as her father liked to say. For once, she'd buckle down, and she wouldn't change her mind three weeks in. She would act like a grown-up. Plant her feet and grow some roots.

"Okay."

"CLEM, GOT A few words you want to say?" Fulsom gestured for him to take his place.

The sandy-haired man took center stage, his smugness still rankling Anders.

"You heard Fulsom. We're going to shake things up around here. Starting tomorrow morning." He stood before them with his legs spread, his hands behind his back. Did he think he could fool them into thinking he was their superior officer?

"What an ass," Curtis murmured.

"Expect the unexpected from here on in. We're going to give the audience what they want—juicy, exciting information about you. That's my specialty, so don't think you can hide from me. That's all. Dismissed."

Everyone exchanged puzzled glances before standing up and putting away their chairs. Anders wondered if he was the only one feeling overexposed already. He knew everyone had parts of themselves they'd rather not share with a national audience, but he had more than most.

His secrets could get him tossed off the show.

"They could cut us a little slack once in a while." Curtis put an arm around Hope and kissed the top of her head. "Bet you're glad you joined Base Camp."

"I'm glad," she said with a grin. "Even if I can't hide from Clem."

"Renata looks pissed," Greg said. "If I was that guy, I'd sleep with one eye open tonight."

"Do you think Clem's here to replace her?" Renata was a ball-buster, but Anders was used to her, at least. They had enough problems at Base Camp without infighting among the crew.

"Maybe." Curtis nodded toward the door. "You and I had better do one last plow of the lane so Fulsom and his people can get out. It's snowing again."

"Sure thing." Anders crossed the room and got his outer gear back on while Curtis gave Hope another kiss.

"…back at our house in a minute," Anders heard him say as Curtis turned toward the door.

Newlyweds.

Would he feel like that about the woman he married?

"Has Boone pestered you about backup brides yet?" Greg asked, joining him near the door.

"We talked about them. I'd rather find my own bride."

"Me, too." Greg was watching Renata talk to Fulsom. The director was gesticulating, making her displeasure clear. "I don't trust anyone else to make a decision like that."

Anders didn't answer that. If he ran out of time, he'd have to marry anyone who would have him. "See you later" was all he said.

"Yeah, see you." Greg pulled a jackknife and a small piece of wood out of his pocket. He was always whittling something. He dragged one of the folding chairs near a window, even though it was dark outside and there wasn't much to see. Was he simply passing time, or was he trying to listen in on Renata, Clem and Fulsom? Anders hoped he passed along any information he gleaned.

Curtis joined him, and together they went outside where the cold air made plumes of their breath. Snow was falling softly, a slow accumulation rather than the crazy amount they'd gotten just days ago. They'd made a habit of keeping the lane as clear as possible, though, in case of an emergency. The state plows had a way of blocking the end of the lane as they passed, and often he and Curtis had to shovel it out by hand.

"Greg seems worried," Anders remarked as they made their way to the truck.

"I'm worried, too. Don't like the look of that Clem

guy, and what did he mean we can't hide from him? We've got enough to do without him throwing us curve balls."

"Yeah, I've got to figure out how to marry *spectacularly.*"

Curtis grunted. "Let Boone get you someone."

"I can do it myself." What kind of woman answered an ad for a husband, especially when a TV show was involved? Someone after her fifteen minutes of fame? Someone who might up and leave when she got bored? He wasn't interested in a relationship like that.

Anders was ready for something real. He wanted to plant his feet, draw a line in the sand and make his stand right here at Base Camp. He wanted a partner who could see what was happening in the world and felt fighting for change was worthwhile, even if it was hard.

He wanted someone to love.

Where did you find a woman like that?

If only Fate would deliver him a wife—like it had delivered one for Curtis. A wife he could marry in a spectacular way, to appease Fulsom—and keep everyone else from finding out what he'd been hiding all this time.

"Come on. Let's get this done," Curtis said.

"KEVIN? WE HAVE a problem." Eve stood in the doorway to her boss's office, waving a hand to get his attention. Kevin, a plump man in his sixties with round blue eyes and a habit of running his hand through his stiff, dark hair until it was mostly standing on end, was staring off into space. This wasn't the first time she'd found him woolgathering, and Eve was beginning to think something was wrong, but she didn't have the kind of relationship with him that would allow her to ask personal questions.

"What kind of problem?" He snapped to, focused on her and tapped a finger on the desk impatiently, as if whatever had occupied his mind a second ago was far more important than anything she could show him.

Eve wasn't sure about that. What she'd just seen was... big.

"I need to show you something." She held up a printout. AltaVista Imaging created digital images taken from satellites. Its clients were generally corporations, government agencies, municipalities, farmers and the like. Many of the images were to be used as proof that they were following environmental guidelines.

Eve crossed to Kevin's desk. "May I?" When he nodded, she unrolled the sheet and laid it in front of him. "Take a look at this."

Kevin heaved a sigh but bent forward to examine the image. "This is..."

"Hansen Oil. Tailing ponds."

Kevin straightened, all his previous lethargy gone. "Hansen Oil? What are you doing with the Hansen account? That's Mark's."

"He's on vacation. Deb and I split his work, re-member?"

"Not the Hansen account." Kevin stood and rolled up the large sheet of paper so quickly he knocked his phone off his desk. "You forward me all those files. Now. And you send me a list of the other accounts you got from Mark, got it? Tell Deb to do the same."

Eve was taken aback. She was still a junior member of the quality control team, but she'd been doing excellent work. "But the tailing ponds—"

"I'll take care of the tailing ponds." Kevin considered her with far more attention than he had in weeks. "Hansen Oil is one of our biggest accounts. If they've got a problem, they have to hear it from me, not you. We can't get this wrong."

I'm not wrong, she wanted to say, but Eve could see that wouldn't help her cause.

"I'm glad I brought it right to you," she said instead. "They'll want to know about the issue immediately. Looks like the runoff might be getting into the—"

Kevin had turned to stow the roll of paper with others on a side table, but the way he snapped around to face her made her shut her mouth. Something was wrong. He'd never behaved like this before, and now he looked—angry.

"The runoff might be getting into the what?" he asked. When she hesitated, he braced his hands on his desk.

Instinct told her not to finish the sentence the way she'd meant to. The runoff looked like it was heading into Terrence Creek, part of the Terrence watershed, which fed into an aquifer that ultimately supplied drinking water to the town of North Run. She'd looked it up, familiar with watershed issues from her work in

Angola. Something told Eve the situation wasn't new. She'd bet her life chemicals had already leached into the water supply.

"Into what?" Kevin asked again.

Eve had heard that tone of voice before but never in the United States. Usually it emanated from a man holding a gun, backed by other men holding more guns, in some Third World outpost where she was advocating for people's rights. She'd never expected such cold anger from her mild-mannered boss in his small, tidy office.

His meaning was clear. He knew what she was going to say, and he didn't want to hear it.

Eve thought fast. "Into an area that's probably home to wildlife," she amended. "I don't know Texas well, but remember the ducks that got into the tailing ponds up in Alberta a few years back? There's a lot of empty land around North Run. I bet there are animals and birds there, too. You know environmentalists will make a fuss."

Usually Kevin was on the side of environmentalists and would have taken her to task for talking about them like that. This time was different.

Some of the tension eased from his body. "I'll be sure to look into that right away," he said. "Good work bringing the images straight to me. Now make sure you forward everything else to do with Mark's accounts to me."

"Will do," she said as cheerfully as she could. Back in her own cubicle, however, her mind raced. She sent a quick text to Deb, a coworker who'd become a friend and whom she chatted with outside of work as well as at the office. She didn't want a record of their conversation through their work emails. A personal text was safer.

Kevin's on the warpath. He wants all of Mark's files. We're not to work on any more of them.

Why not? Deb quickly texted back.

Should she mention what had happened? Eve had a feeling Kevin wouldn't want her to, but he hadn't said she couldn't, either.

I found a problem at Hansen Oil. Showed it to him. He wasn't pleased.

Deb's answer was swift. *Shit, Eve. If it's Hansen Oil, keep your mouth shut. Erase these texts, too. I mean it. Say nothing—to me or anyone else.*

But there's a problem with the tailing ponds.

ERASE EVERYTHING. Don't text me again!

Eve sat back, stared at her phone and then did as Deb asked. Deb wasn't the kind to get hysterical over nothing. Eve thought she understood. Oil companies like Hansen didn't operate only in the United States, after all. She'd come up against their representatives overseas, who sometimes acted like dictators when they could get away with it.

"Eve? Where are those files?" Kevin called from his office.

"I'm sending them right now." She got to work forwarding everything that Mark had passed on to her, then went to erase them, but when she got to the

Terrence tailing pond images, instinct kicked in again. She rummaged around in her purse until she found a memory stick, slotted it into one of the USB drives on her computer and made a copy. Glancing around to make sure no one had noticed, she dropped the USB stick back into her purse.

There were only two reasons to hide an image that revealed a problem like the one she'd seen. One, because you didn't want anyone to know you'd made a mistake. Two, because you had no intention of fixing it. If Hansen Oil didn't want its reputation smeared while it worked to fix its tailing ponds, she could live with that, she supposed. But if it didn't intend to fix them at all, she needed to do something.

Fast.

CHAPTER TWO

"I'M ALREADY ON a bunch of dating apps." Anders faced off with Clem outside the chicken coop. Despite the cold weather, a flock of chickens were clucking and scratching a patch of ground where he'd cleared the snow away in their mesh-sided pen.

"That's not good enough. We've polled the audience, and they want to be more involved in the process. We'll put your wife-wanted ad on the show's website, and make the responses public. People can vote on them—"

"That's nuts!"

"That's good showmanship," Clem countered.

"Haven't you ever read the comment sections on the website?" Anders challenged him. "People are brutal. You let them comment on women's responses to the ad, and they'll tear them apart."

"I hope so," Clem said happily. "If anything controversial happens, we'll air it on the show."

"But—"

"Don't you get it?" Clem kicked at the wire mesh

where a chicken was reaching through to peck something outside its pen. The chicken squawked and beat its wings, making a hasty retreat. "Fulsom's getting bored with your show. And when Fulsom's bored, it isn't good. You want to do what it takes to make him happy. Got it?"

"What if I find my own wife first?" Anders opened the door to the outside pen, stepped inside and began to scatter feed for the chickens. They crowded around him in a frenzy while Clem looked on in disgust.

"You find your own wife, and we'll shut down the ad, but I'm not holding my breath. You've been in Chance Creek for months, and you haven't scored yet. Am I right, or am I right? And by the way—on your intake form you left the name of your high school blank. Why is that?"

The sudden question came from so far out of left field, Anders struggled to keep up. "High school?" he repeated. He'd left that question blank because he didn't want anyone snooping into his past.

"Yeah, high school. Big building. Boring classes. Lots of stupid kids," Clem prompted.

"I… didn't graduate," Anders lied.

Clem frowned. "Didn't graduate? What kind of a hick are you?"

Anders's phone buzzed in his pocket, and he pulled it out gratefully, then nearly groaned when he saw who it was. "I've got to take this." He turned his back on Clem pointedly, wondering if it would work.

To his surprise, it did.

"Whatever." Clem wandered off. Anders waited until he was out of earshot before he accepted the call.

"What do you want?"

"That's a hell of a way to greet your father."

Anders spread the rest of the feed on the ground, exited the pen and shut the door tightly. This was the part of his past he didn't want anyone to know about. He walked off toward the pasture where their herd of bison ranged.

"I'm not interested in how I greet you, and neither are you. Say what you called to say."

Anders hadn't had a close relationship with his father since his mother died. His father, Johannes, had always been too busy running his business to be around much, and he had spent even more time away from home after Anders's mother passed away. A series of nannies and housekeepers had looked after Anders, and those first years had been rough. For all his faults, Johannes had loved his wife, and looking back, Anders realized that losing her to cancer when she wasn't even forty had been a real blow. He couldn't fault his father for grieving for his mother, but he didn't think his father ever realized that meant Anders ended up grieving for both his parents at once.

When Johannes eventually moved on to other women, he chose ones who were the opposite of Anders's mother. Women who had little time for children. Who wanted expensive presents and exotic trips. Anders had learned not to expect anything from his father. They had remained cordial to each other, however, until Anders had walked away from all of it and changed his name.

"It's time for you to come home."

Anders's grip on the phone tightened.

"Well?" Johannes demanded when he didn't answer. "What do you say to that?"

"Not going to happen." Might as well nip this right in the bud. His father's company stood for everything he was against. Johannes wanted him for only one reason—to groom him to take it over. Johannes was the kind of man for whom legacy meant everything.

"Of course it's going to happen. You've had your fun. You've seen the world. Time to grow up and settle down. You're wasting your life."

"Have you watched TV lately, Pop? I'm saving the world."

"Saving the world," Johannes scoffed. "By being on TV? You can do better than that."

"How? By following in your footsteps? How much of our country's carbon footprint are you responsible for? Do you ever think about that?"

"My company helped this country keep its place on the global stage. You remember that!" his father snapped. Johannes must have a cold or something, Anders decided. His voice lacked its usual vigor, and he'd hesitated a fraction of a second before his outburst. His father never hesitated.

"Your company could be leading the charge to a better future." Anders broke off. They'd had this discussion too many times before. He wouldn't change his father's mind. He couldn't help himself, though. "You're missing out on a lot of profits by refusing to change your ways. You should look at what's happening in Europe. Green companies are booming. Someday you'll be sorry you didn't jump on the bandwagon early on."

He braced himself for one of his father's snappy comebacks, but to his surprise, Johannes didn't take the bait. "Taking Hansen Oil into the future is your job, not mine. You've been gone more than a decade. Why don't you get back here and do it?"

Anders wasn't falling for that. If he came back, he'd be his father's lackey. Johannes had his hand in every pie at Hansen Oil, and none of those pies had anything to do with making environmentally sound choices.

"You got something new to say to make me want to?" Anders asked tiredly.

"I'm not going to be around here forever," Johannes said after another hesitation. He sounded just as tired. "You've got a lot to learn before you're ready to run a company this large. You need to start now—"

"I don't want to run your company," Anders said. "How many times do I have to say that? Base Camp is my home now. I'm ranching bison and—"

"Ranching bison." Johannes's tone was acid. "Living with a bunch of do-gooders who know nothing about the real world, or business, or how hard it is to keep things afloat—"

"Gotta go." Anders ended the call. He knew how the rest of the conversation would play out, and he had no time for it. The men and women of Base Camp actually listened to him. They supported him. Were helping him create a home. He wasn't going to leave them.

Unless he had to.

HANSEN OIL IS bad news.

Eve read the text from her friend Melissa Ryder, nodded and wrote back. *Tell me about it.*

The minute she'd made it into the front door of her tiny apartment, she'd started texting. She'd known Melissa since high school, and unlike Deb at work, Eve knew Melissa would hear her out and help her figure out what to do.

They'd met when they were fourteen while working on a campaign to put solar panels on their high school's roof, and they'd been fast friends ever since, although Melissa had graduated from college and became a social worker while Eve had traveled the world. If Eve was a kite, Melissa was the person holding the string that tethered her to the earth, reeling her back in when storms brewed up. One advantage to living in her parents' backyard, Eve had decided, was that Melissa lived a half mile away.

No one ever wins against Hansen Oil, Melissa texted. *What makes you think you can?*

I have to try, right?

What about Operation Grown-up?

Eve wished she hadn't told Melissa about her parents' plans for her—or about her acquiescence to them.

Twenty-four hours in, *Operation Grown-up*, as Melissa had named it, was already chafing. Her mother kept emailing her about the tiny house plans and whether she should go ahead and place an order for bulbs for the flower garden she was sure Eve would want to plant in front of it.

Eve wasn't sure she was ready for a flower garden. That wasn't just a grown-up thing to have. That was a *settled* grown-up thing to have.

I have over three weeks until Operation Grown-up starts. Class doesn't begin until mid-January.

Can you handle classes on top of work?

Guess I'll have to. She was trying not to think about it. School had never been her thing. Getting things done was her thing.

So you're going to take down Hansen Oil in the next three weeks?

Exactly.

Hey—it's time. Is your TV on?

Eve quickly grabbed the remote and flicked on the TV. Rousing music announced the start of *Base Camp*, her favorite reality show, and she watched the opening sequence, which showed all the participants one by one, along with shots of the bunkhouse, pastures, gardens, greenhouses, the huge bed-and-breakfast some of the women ran and of course the tiny houses some of the inhabitants lived in.

I'm watching, she texted Melissa.

Good. This could be the last one if Curtis doesn't find a wife.

He'll find a wife—they always do.

Look at all that snow, Melissa texted.

Eve was glad she lived in Virginia. Winter in Montana looked brutal.

OMG—look, Melissa texted.

Eve was looking. Curtis and Anders Olsen had been plowing the lane from the bunkhouse to the main road. Now there was camera footage of a car stuck in the ditch at the end of the lane. The film cut to the inside of the bunkhouse, where two women were being introduced to the inhabitants of Base Camp.

Despite her own problems, she was sucked into the action onscreen. Hope and Raina had crashed on the way to Raina's wedding. Now they were stuck in Chance Creek.

Lucky women! Melissa texted. *Why didn't we think of crashing our car in front of Base Camp? You could have married Curtis.*

You know it's Anders I want, Eve wrote back. She'd picked him way back when she'd watched *Base Camp*'s first episode. His Scandinavian name was belied by his dark hair and eyes, but even though he wasn't blond, he was handsome in an intelligent, outdoorsy way that appealed to something basic in Eve. Maybe she should show her parents a photo of him and see if they could line up someone similar for her to marry, since they were already taking care of her classes and housing situation.

With a shake of her head to clear her thoughts, Eve focused on what was truly important. She'd been researching Hansen Oil and found a site that listed court cases brought against the company over the years. Dozens of them. All settled out of court. All complaints silenced.

The people who crossed Hansen Oil didn't seem to fare too well. There were rumors of bankruptcies, jobs lost, houses foreclosed on, loans called in.

Johannes Hansen, owner and CEO, was apparently used to getting his own way—and he had the kind of clout that could spell financial ruin to his adversaries. Was she putting her future in danger by crossing him?

Would he come after her family? Her parents were quite financially secure. They owned their home outright and never bought anything on credit. They'd be hard to mess with. She, on the other hand, would be an easy target.

She clicked on footage of him addressing an industry convention. He oozed arrogance in a way that made her hate him on principle. How could she ever stand up to that?

Curtis to the rescue! Melissa texted.

Eve looked at the screen, where Curtis was loading a truck full of equipment. She laughed when he got Hope and Raina into it, sent Byron, the young cameraman, back to the bunkhouse to fetch something and then drove off without him.

The men of *Base Camp* were far more effective in their lives than she was. She supposed self-confidence came with the territory if you were a Navy SEAL.

If only she had someone like that to stand beside her as she confronted Johannes Hansen. Anders wouldn't be afraid of the tycoon. She'd always noticed his quiet strength. His insistence on doing the right thing. Why didn't she meet men like him in real life?

Most men belittled her aspirations to do good in the world. Some told her flat-out it was pointless to care as much as she did. Others, like Heath, grew bored waiting back home for her.

The worst were the ones who pretended they were activists, too—just long enough to try to get her in bed.

Anders wasn't like that, she mused. He'd given his life to Base Camp. Was willing to marry—fast—in order to keep his sustainable community going.

She looked up again to watch a montage of daily life footage at Base Camp. Boone and Riley Rudman sharing a kiss, Jericho Cook keeping the solar panels free of snow, Kai Green working in the kitchen with his wife, Addison, Anders and Greg throwing snowballs at each other, and Nora Pickett smoothing her hands over a barely-there baby bump.

Eve envied them. It would be far more fun to live in a community of tiny houses than in one parked in her parents' backyard. The men and women who lived there would understand her penchant for environmental causes and wouldn't berate her for not having a retirement plan.

If only she could move there.

You didn't get a tiny house on *Base Camp* unless you were married, though, and according to her parents that was never going to happen to her. Too bad she didn't have someone like Boone to find her a backup husband, the way he was always trying to find backup brides for the men on the show.

She'd take Anders if he was available.

Now she was being silly, Eve told herself sternly. She'd never meet Anders Olsen, and even if she did, she doubted he'd look at her twice. He had his act together, he was a true activist who was accomplishing something big and he'd want an equally accomplished partner. Not someone who'd gotten shipped home from Angola on crutches—and had worked a desk job ever since.

A chirp from her phone announced another text.

What if you sent the information to a newspaper? Let them do the work.

That had been her first instinct. Then she'd looked more deeply into Hansen Oil's past. Newspapers had reported the company's transgressions dozens of times.

Still Hansen Oil kept on breaking the rules.

It would take more than a newspaper article to stop it. People didn't care about oil spills these days, let alone other mishaps that were harder to explain or comprehend. They needed some compelling human-interest story to catch their attention. *Base Camp*'s directors obviously understood that. Why else would they focus so much on the participants' social lives rather than spending whole episodes on the science behind solar panels, good ranching practices and the like?

Her gaze flicked to the TV, where a frantic Curtis was flagging down a snow-plow operator. Somewhere along the way to Bozeman their vehicle had gone off the road—because one of the cameramen, pursuing them, had plowed into them—and now they were all on foot. She shook her head. Week after week the men and women of *Base Camp* met their challenges with such fortitude and togetherness. They'd know what to do with the information she'd discovered.

Anders would know. He'd think through the problem patiently, like he always did. Come up with a plan and carry it out, even if there was a problem or two. Just like his friend Curtis was doing in this episode.

She was really too old to have a crush on a TV star, she reminded herself. At least no one knew—

Are you still watching? Melissa texted.

Of course.

Lusting after Anders? He's not getting much screen time this episode.

Okay, so Melissa knew, but she wouldn't tell anyone.

Not nearly enough, Eve agreed. *They need to do an episode that's all Anders, all the time.*

He's got to get married sometime. Only 4 guys left to go, Melissa texted.

Eve was dreading that. She knew her crush on Anders Olsen was just that—a crush. He was a guy on TV, and although she was a bleeding heart when it came to environmental causes, she wasn't silly enough to think her crush would come to anything. It would still hurt to watch him marry some other lucky woman.

Raina's going to make it to her wedding!!!!! Melissa texted.

Eve watched one snow plow whisk Raina to her wedding, while Curtis turned back to get Hope, who had fallen behind while he rushed ahead with her friend. A few minutes later, another snow plow gathered them up, too, and carried them to Bozeman.

When they reached the church, and Hope raced for the door, hoping to be in time to see her friend's wedding, Eve got a little misty. Onscreen, Curtis looked a little misty, too. It was obvious he'd already grown to care about Hope.

He'd seized on his chance when he'd met her and done what it took to be able to woo her. That's what life was about: taking chances. At least, that's what she used to think. Going back to living at home, even if it meant getting a tiny house and a chance to go back to school, somehow felt like losing ground.

Once she'd been so ready to meet life head-on. Now her goals were getting smaller and smaller. Who was she to think she could take on Hansen Oil? Maybe it was time to notify some environmental activism groups and hope they could find an effective way to blow the whistle on the company.

Eve did another online search and confirmed what she already knew. Every time a case against Hansen Oil neared completion, the company settled—for far less than it was assumed they would have been fined in court if the ruling had gone against them.

Eve clicked on a few more links desultorily. She supposed a grown-up would say that's just how the world worked.

On her TV screen, Hope and Raina were reunited.

"You made it!" Raina cried.

Curtis was beaming. You could almost read his thoughts: he'd done it. Gotten Raina to her wedding and Hope there in time to be her bridesmaid. It was satisfying to make a difference in someone's life.

She used to know that firsthand.

OMG, Curtis is in love with Hope, Melissa texted.

I know. They'll definitely get together, Eve texted back.

This is so romantic I can't stand it.

Eve focused on her laptop again. She typed *Base Camp* into her browser. Watched as the television show's page came up. There were all the men of *Base Camp*—and the women, too.

There was Anders.

The photograph was a portrait shot, close up and clear. Anders had serious eyes and dark hair. A strong jaw and a firm expression.

Her gaze flicked to the television screen. She'd missed several scenes. Now everyone was back at Base Camp, and Curtis was preparing to marry Hope, getting into a Revolutionary War–era uniform, the traditional outfit all the Base Camp men wore at weddings. Anders came to congratulate him, and her heart sped up. Damn, he was handsome. So composed. So sure of himself. They all were. Curtis hadn't told Hope and Raina they couldn't get through that blizzard—he'd simply persevered until he delivered them to the wedding—on time.

She bet Anders was the same. He'd never walk away from a mission just because it was tough.

So why was she prepared to give up the battle against Hansen Oil before she'd even tried?

On TV, Boone entered the room full of men preparing for the wedding.

"You know what time it is," he said.

They're drawing straws! Are you watching? Melissa texted.

I'm watching, she wrote back. As if she could turn away. It was her favorite part of the show—when the remaining single men found out who would marry next.

"Let's see who's up next!" Boone said onscreen. "Anders, Walker, Angus, Greg, come on down."

All the men gathered around, the married men laughing and teasing the holdouts.

"It's got to be Walker's turn," Clay said.

"I bet it's Greg. It's the quiet ones who surprise you," Kai put in.

"All right, Walker, you pick first. You always hang back, and you always get away with waiting another month."

The big man shrugged, considered the straws in Boone's fist and picked. Held up a long one. "Not me."

Groans came from all around.

I swear Walker has to be cheating, Melissa texted. *How on earth hasn't he picked one of those straws yet?*

Eve knew what she meant, but she was too busy watching the television to respond.

"Greg, you're up," Boone said.

Greg drew, too, and got another of the long ones.

Clay drummed a beat on his thighs. "It's down to Anders and Angus."

"Hell, I'll go next." Angus grabbed a straw testily. Eve bit her lip. *Please let it be Angus,* she willed. When

Angus held up his straw and it, too, was long, she let out a gusty sigh. "Thank you!" Angus called up to the ceiling.

Damn, Eve thought.

That was that.

Boone passed Anders the final straw—the short one. Anders took it. He looked straight at the camera for an instant, and Eve's breath caught. It was as if he'd seen her, but of course he hadn't.

EVE—it's Anders! He got the short straw! Melissa texted.

Anders would marry in forty days. She was going to have to watch another woman fall in love with him.

Suddenly her future stretched out in front of her, blank and boring. Going to AltaVista every morning and pretending she didn't know the firm was covering up environmental disasters. Going to school at night, slogging through course after course to get a practical degree. Living in a tiny house, which was great—in her parents' backyard, which was not quite so great, even if she loved her family dearly.

Choosing the safe path. The responsible path.

Eve, did you see that? Anders pulled the short straw! Melissa texted again. Any minute her phone would ring, Eve knew.

I saw, she texted back quickly. She was unprepared for the pain that squeezed her heart. Anders was just a TV personality. He probably wasn't even like the persona he played on the show. Who knew how much of what he said was scripted?

She wasn't sad about losing a man she'd never met, she decided. She was sad about losing herself. About the choices she was making. The ones dooming her to a plain Jane existence rather than the boisterous, interesting, inspiring life Anders and his future wife would lead.

The other men were teasing him. He was going along with it, but for the first time she glimpsed insecurity in his expression. Was he... afraid... he might not be able to pull this off?

Anders—afraid?

No.

But the possibility made her heart squeeze. She wished she could reach out to him and tell him she was afraid, too. She wished she could tell him about AltaVista and Hansen Oil, and ask his advice. She wished she could find a man like Anders to partner with her as she went through life. Someone who would bolster her courage and help her be her best self.

On the TV screen, Curtis's wedding to Hope progressed quickly, and soon the happy couple trailed off to spend their wedding night in their brand-new tiny house. The reception wound down.

The show ended with a shot of Anders climbing into one of Base Camp's trucks and plowing the lane out to the road—alone.

OMG—he's so hot! Melissa texted.

She was right. Anders was hot, and he wouldn't be alone for long, would he? He needed to marry within forty days. Sooner, she amended. There had to be some delay before the show was aired.

Eve blinked back the tears that suddenly stung her eyes.

He was going to marry, and she was going to go on with her little life.

And no one would stop Hansen Oil.

This is what growing up looked like. This was what it meant to make practical choices.

ANDERS needs a WIFE, Melissa texted.

As if Eve didn't know that. As if she hadn't daydreamed a hundred times while watching the show that she'd be his choice when the time came.

Just as she predicted, her phone rang. She debated not answering, but Melissa was like a bulldog and would keep calling all night if she had to.

Eve took the call.

"Are you crying?" Melissa demanded.

How could she possibly know that? "No," Eve lied.

"Yes, you are, because you're miserable."

"I'm not miserable, I'm just—"

"You are miserable, and you've been that way ever since you got home. If I didn't know you so well, I'd take it personally," Melissa went on. "You're not going to be happy in your parents' backyard even if I am living a half mile away, and you're not going to be happy not exposing what Hansen Oil is doing."

"It's no use—"

"Who stole my best friend and left this—wimp—in her place?" Melissa demanded. "The Eve I know would never give up without a fight!"

"I promised my parents—"

"You promised you'd settle down in time for classes. That gives you over three weeks to stop Hansen Oil."

"But how—?"

"Did you watch the show or not?" Melissa didn't wait for her answer. "Anders needs a wife. You need a way to tell the world what's happening at Hansen Oil—a compelling way."

"You want me to marry Anders?"

"Marrying Anders would be a bonus, but we can't count on that."

That was Melissa all over: practical to a T. Her parents loved Melissa.

"Ouch," Eve said.

"You just have to get on the show long enough to blurt out what you know. To make a splash. If you expose what's happening at Hansen Oil while you're on *Base Camp*, the news will pick it up, and people will talk about it on social media. You'll seem so mysterious and interesting coming out of nowhere with this proof of wrongdoing, the audience will eat it up, and people will start sleuthing on their own. It will be like crowdsourcing an intervention against Hansen. In three weeks you can expose it and nail your fifteen minutes of fame. Then you can come home and start school, and hang out with me, all the while knowing you've already contributed greatly to society. What do you say?"

"How on earth would I even get on the show?"

"I think I have an idea, but it's not a very practical one..."

CHAPTER THREE

"MAYBE YOUR WIFE will simply show up, like mine did," Curtis said two days later when they were preparing to plow the lane again.

Anders had spent the evening wading through women's profiles on online dating apps—without any luck. If he was honest, he was finding it hard to figure out what he was looking for.

"Not many women crash their cars in the ditch at the end of our lane," Anders pointed out. "So far that's only happened once."

"You've got over a month," Curtis added. "It's not quite time to panic yet."

Anders was panicking. Somehow he'd thought it would be easier than this to find a wife. As a teenager in Texas, he'd always had a girlfriend. With a family name like his and a fortune to inherit as soon as he came of age, Anders had rarely entered a room without some pretty girl sidling up closer, as if proximity could work a spell on him and make him hers.

Even when he'd changed his name and joined the

Navy, he'd done fine with women he met in bars and restaurants near his military bases. No one broadcasted their Navy SEAL status, but women who lived near bases always seemed to know, as if there were an underground information network among them.

Since coming to Base Camp things had been different.

He'd been different.

He'd known he needed to find a wife, which was a lot different from finding a girlfriend. If he was going to share his life with a woman, he needed to be able to be honest with her. That meant telling her about his past. About his father's business.

Which would leave him exposed.

That hadn't stopped him from signing on, though. He'd wanted what Base Camp stood for far too much to back down. Now he admitted to himself it had been a stupid move.

What if he got close to a woman, confided in her, and she blew the whistle on him? What if she left, and he wasn't able to convince anyone else to marry him?

What if he ruined things for everyone?

He'd thought he'd escaped his father's sins when he left home at eighteen, but he'd been wrong; they'd followed him all the way to Montana.

Anders had no idea how Johannes lived with himself. Like any other person his age, he couldn't remember a time when the words *climate change* weren't a part of the nightly narrative on the news, but his father's response to that narrative had never been interest or concern—or a desire to do something to fix the problem.

His father's response had been rage.

Rage at the implication that climate change existed. Then, when its existence was proven beyond a shadow of a doubt, rage at the idea that human beings could influence it at all. He was adamant their family business certainly wasn't to blame.

After his mother's death, his father's rage had become far more personal, until Johannes became like a Medieval princeling, building rhetorical walls around his little fiefdom, patrolling them morning and night and bristling at any interlopers who might lay the blame about crumbling environmental conditions at his door.

Like all children, Anders accepted his father's worldview without question, and little outside thought had penetrated his sheltered world. His wasn't the only family in town to make their fortune in oil. Even the people on the news shows they watched talked in the same language his father did and declared the entire idea of climate change preposterous.

Anders was nearly fourteen when his science teacher played a movie he later found out most people in the country had seen many years earlier. It took two and a half periods over the course of several days for them to watch the whole thing. Anders still remembered the silence in that classroom as his peers took in information that contradicted everything they'd learned at home. The confusion. His wasn't the only family who regularly debunked this kind of theory, but as the movie's narrator—a man who'd once run for president but lost to the conservative candidate all their families had voted for—explained on screen with charts and graphs and photographs and film footage what was happening in their world, Anders felt the walls of his father's fortress crack, and for a moment, a scathing, searing light shone in.

That's all that would have happened if not for Thomas Craig, a skinny, bespectacled boy Anders knew only because they'd been in Cub Scouts together years before. After the third class, when the movie had reached its conclusion, Anders had met up with him by chance in the boys' bathroom. While both of them gave their hands a cursory wash before heading to lunch, Thomas had glanced his way.

"It's true," he said. "All of it. My dad's been talking about climate change for years. Not in this town, obviously," he went on with a glance over his shoulder as if they'd been discussing the overthrow of the city council. "When he goes to international symposiums, it's all anyone's talking about, all around the world. Scientists, politicians, economists, you name it."

Anders vaguely knew Mr. Craig was a scientist, but he couldn't have said what kind. He wasn't sure what economists even did, and everyone knew you couldn't trust politicians. Still, another crack breached his father's theoretical fortress. The problem was, Anders had a scientific bent himself, and the movie rang true in a way his father's arguments against climate change didn't.

Thomas moved to pump the handle of the paper

towel dispenser, ripped off a handful and dried his hands. "Dad says he'll die before the worst of it hits, but you and me—we're going to see big changes. We should have kept the oil in the ground."

He pitched the paper towels into the trash and left. Anders, alone, braced himself against the countertop, his stomach as unsettled as if the earth were shifting and roiling beneath him. *Should have kept the oil in the ground.* He looked up and met his own gaze in the mirror. Keeping oil in the ground was heresy. It ran contrary to everything the Hansen family stood for.

Which was why Anders's last name wasn't Hansen anymore. He'd changed it to Olsen when he'd left home, going up the branches of his family tree to find an offshoot that had no stake in the oil business. He'd spent four years researching the situation and arguing with his father, first urging him to watch the movie, then to change the family business from the ground up.

At eighteen he conceded defeat, walked out the door and never went back. The judge who allowed him to start over with a new name didn't comment on his petition but shook his head in a way that Anders had recognized even then. It was foolish to turn your back on a fortune, no matter where that fortune came from.

That fortune would have come in handy here at Base Camp, but he wouldn't go back and change things even if he could. He shuddered to think what his friends here would say if they knew the truth about him.

He knew one thing for sure—Boone would have flat-out rejected his application to become a part of this place. Base Camp's goal was to run 100 percent on renewable energy sources. An oil baron's son wouldn't be welcome.

Anders joined Curtis in the cab of the truck. Plowing the lane was easy, but as he'd predicted, the drift at the end of it was harder going. In the end, they had to park the truck and pull out their shovels. A moment later, a horn honked and an SUV came down the lane from the direction of Base Camp, its cab steaming in the frosty air. Renata and some of the crew members filled the vehicle. She rolled down her window.

"This going to take long?"

She'd been as cranky as a wet hen since Clem had arrived at Base Camp, and with each passing day her mood was deteriorating.

"Just a few minutes. Where's Clem?"

Renata's features hardened. "Staying at Base Camp tonight. Thinks maybe you all are getting up to something exciting after hours. Byron's staying, too." She closed her window before he could ask any more questions. Anders got to work, his unease increasing. They were supposed to get a respite from filming at nighttime. He hoped Renata had made that clear to her new co-director.

When they'd cleared half of the pile, he and Curtis stepped aside to let the waiting truck past. Once it was gone, quiet descended.

Anders appreciated the brief reprieve. He dreaded going back and facing Clem again. As the next one in line to marry, he knew he was already being tracked by the camera crews even more than usual. If Clem wanted drama, it would be coming his way, most likely.

"That's that," Curtis said fifteen minutes later, throwing one more shovelful of snow onto the bank. "Let's call it a night. God knows we'll be back out here in the morning, doing it all over again."

"Sure thing."

Anders hesitated, looking down the road in both directions. Not a car in sight. They were alone out here, and he savored the peace. Snow drifted down quietly, landing on his skin in brief, cold pinpricks. In a minute he'd be back in the bunkhouse, settling down for the night in a sleeping bag on the floor with the other single members of Base Camp. There was always someone around there. Always talk and jokes. Just for a moment it was nice to be—

Anders squinted, peering through the dark and slowly falling snow. "What's that?" He pointed to a shape making its way slowly toward them. It was small figure. A child?

No, not a child.

"I don't see anything." Curtis moved to his side.

"There." The shape stopped. Wavered. Then it was coming at them again. "Is that—?"

Curtis swore and began to run. A second later, Anders sprinted past him. He covered the hundred and fifty yards in record time, lunged forward—

Just in time to catch the woman who fainted into his arms.

"...IN SHOCK. WE'VE got to get her warm."

"...ridiculous shoes, no jacket—how'd she make it this far?"

"...come on, come on, wake up..."

Eve listened to the voices spilling over her, having done her best to keep still while Curtis and Anders lugged her inside a building and set her gently on the floor.

Thank God everything had gone according to plan so far. If she'd had to wait much longer, she would have frozen to death for real out there. She'd been hiding in a thicket of bushes down the road from the lane that led to Base Camp for nearly an hour—without the benefit of winter outer gear. She'd known she needed to make this as realistic as possible, and several previous episodes of the show had established that Anders—either with Curtis or alone—always plowed the lane just before bedtime if it was snowing. After a whirlwind twenty-four hours of planning, she and Melissa had landed at the Chance Creek airport this morning, rented a car, set up headquarters at a local motel and waited to see if the forecasted snow came.

It had, and they'd put their plan into motion. It had taken a lot of arguing to get Melissa to drop her off more than a mile down the road and head back to town to eliminate the chance that anyone might see them.

"If you wind up dead in a ditch, I'm going to kill you," Melissa had said. "At least wear a jacket."

"I can't. I have to look like I've been through hell."

"Don't overplay this," Melissa had retorted. "Keep

to the script."

"I swear I'll keep to the script," Eve had intoned. "Thank you—for everything. This is a brilliant idea."

"I hope so." Melissa hadn't looked so sure anymore. Her first uncharacteristic bout of enthusiasm for this venture had worn off within hours, and it had been up to Eve to keep them on track ever since. Before Melissa could call it off completely, Eve had shut her car's door, waved Melissa away and stood there until her friend turned around and drove back to town.

Then she'd started walking.

She was wearing a ridiculous pair of blue flats that were utterly ruined now. The cold wind had bitten through her thin clothing and started tears tracing down her cheeks. She was almost soaked through from the falling snow. Halfway to Base Camp she'd had to admit Melissa was right—she could die before she made it.

She'd kept going until her feet were so cold she couldn't feel her toes. When she'd drawn near to the lane that led to Base Camp, she'd taken cover in the bushes and waited for headlights.

By the time they finally approached, she was shivering so hard she could barely put one foot in front of the other, but she'd broken into an unsteady run. When she collapsed into Anders's arms, she'd barely been acting.

Now her feet and nose and the tips of her ears were burning. Eve hoped she hadn't gone overboard and given herself frostbite.

"Miss? Can you say something? Do you know where you are?"

Eve pretended to struggle to open her eyes, although really, a nap would have been nice. So far, it was all going to plan. Curtis had fallen for Hope when her car crashed in front of Base Camp. Anders should fall for her. Men liked to save women, after all.

She'd made herself utterly save-able.

When she opened her eyes, she took in the knot of men clustered around her. Above them, a wooden ceiling. Below her, a rough floor. Her fingers slid over wide planks, quarter-inch gaps between their up-curled edges.

The bunkhouse.

Eve blinked. Shut her eyes and opened them again, as if she didn't know what was happening. A true victim would be wondering how she'd made her way onto a television show. Base Camp didn't advertise its location, but it hadn't been all that hard to track down.

She wondered where the rest of the men and women were. Only a handful were present.

"…she's coming around."

"…should get a doctor—"

"Look. She's awake!"

Eve pretended to try to sit up. Groaned when the room actually spun and allowed hands to lay her back down. Hell, she'd pushed it too far, hadn't she? She was cold to the bone.

"What's… going on?" she made herself murmur. The shiver in her voice was all too real.

"We found you walking up the road. You had no jacket, no gloves or hat. You're soaked. Your shoes are wrecked. It looks like you were walking a long time. Do you know what happened?" Curtis asked. Behind him she saw Hope, his new wife.

Eve felt a momentary pang of guilt and prayed this gambit wouldn't cause trouble for the members of Base Camp. Hansen Oil might try to retaliate when the show aired the images she'd brought. On the other hand, Base Camp was backed by Martin Fulsom, a billionaire in his own right. He'd be hard for Johannes Hansen to push around.

"Start with something simpler," Anders said to Curtis. Behind him stood Greg Devon and Angus McBride. It was uncanny seeing all these people in real life after watching them on TV for months. "Miss, can you tell us your name?"

Anders Olsen was talking to her, just like she'd daydreamed about—

She stifled an urge to laugh. This wasn't a daydream, and she couldn't blow her cover.

Not yet.

"Evelyn. Eve," she managed. She didn't give them her last name. Instead she got into the act, looking around wildly. She and Melissa had worked on her story the whole way here. "Where am I?" She surged up again.

"Woah, woah!" Anders held her shoulders and gently lowered her down. His touch made her breath catch and her stomach do a funny little flutter. "It's all right. Whatever happened out there, you're safe here. Understand?"

She read true concern in his eyes. A fierce protectiveness in the lines of his muscular body. For a moment she was disconcerted. Her heart squeezed like it used to when she'd watched him on the television.

It was as if he actually cared.

He was a Navy SEAL, she told herself firmly. All the men here were. They were programmed to help people; it went no deeper than that.

She was nothing to Anders.

"We should get you to a hospital," Curtis said.

"No!" This time she refused to stay lying down. "No, I can't go to the hospital." If they handed her over to the authorities, she'd have no reason to come back. She shivered, her soaked clothing chilling her to the core.

Anders searched her face. "Why not? What happened out there?"

"I—" Eve broke off, finding it hard to hold her train of thought when he was so close. Suddenly her mission to fight Hansen Oil didn't seem so important. She wanted to spend time with this man. To get to know him—

"We should call the sheriff," a woman said.

Eve turned. Avery Lightfoot. The last of the women from the beginning of the show who was still single. Where was Walker, the man she so obviously loved? The one who somehow never drew the short straw?

There. In the corner of the room, sitting on the edge of a large wooden desk watching them.

Boone's desk.

Eve swallowed, fighting vertigo. Everything was just like it was on television. All the single members of Base Camp must have been getting ready to bed down in the bunkhouse for the night, just like they did on the episodes. All the married couples must already be in their tiny houses—except Curtis and Hope. At least there weren't any camera crews present.

Then Avery's words penetrated her brain. *Call the sheriff.*

No. Absolutely not.

Her fingers flexed involuntarily, her nails trying to dig into the wooden floor. Eve found her voice again.

"No sheriff! Please—" She'd practiced this part with Melissa over and over again. "I had a fight with my boyfriend. I jumped out of the car and ran." She let her head fall forward, as if feeling faint. Anders caught her, his arm strong around her shoulders.

"We won't call anyone," he said. "Not until you ask us to. Take a deep breath. One thing at a time."

"Did he hurt you?" Greg asked.

She shook her head. If she pretended to be abused, these people would want to get the police involved. Her story wouldn't stand up to that kind of scrutiny.

Her boss had been suspicious enough at her sudden request for time off so close to Christmas. "If you're unhappy here, you'd say so, right?" Kevin had asked yesterday morning when he'd summoned her into his office. "Usually people give more than a day's notice when they want a vacation. I don't have to say yes, you know."

"I know. I hoped you'd understand. I haven't taken any time while I've been at AltaVista, and a good friend asked me to visit last minute," she'd lied.

"If this is about Hansen Oil—"

"It's not." She'd kept her gaze steady, but inside butterflies had played havoc with her nerves.

"I don't want to hear you're taking a job with one of our competitors," he'd said, and she'd relaxed a little. If that was all he was worried about, she was okay.

"I won't take another job," she'd assured him. "I just want to see my friend. Get out of town for a bit."

"Guess I can't blame you. The weather has been dismal this past month."

She'd practically run out of his office when he'd dismissed her.

Now she faced the men and women of Base Camp. She'd have to tell a lot more lies before she was done.

"Eve, did your boyfriend hurt you?" Anders pressed.

"No." His concern nearly undid her. Up close, she could see the laugh lines at the corners of his eyes. The stubble on his jaw. She wanted to touch him—to confirm he was real. "He just gets so angry." She allowed her voice to break on the last syllable. "He was driving fast—to scare me. He said—" she broke off. "He said he hated it when I argued with him." Thank goodness Melissa had helped her come up with a backstory about "James," her fake boyfriend. Eve had dated some losers in her time but never anyone who scared her.

"What were you arguing about?" Avery asked.

"His parents. We're supposed to be visiting them—so they can meet me," she explained. "The whole time I've known James he's told me stories about how controlling his dad is. How he'll lose his temper and break things or punch holes in the walls. I was already pretty nervous about going, and James kept picking on me." She took a breath. It was a lot harder to lie to these people than she'd thought it would be. Before they'd just been participants on a show. Now they were flesh and blood. "He said I should have worn a dress, but it's so cold out! He said it's disrespectful I wore pants. That I'm always disrespectful. I said, 'What is this? The sixties?' James really lost it. He said he hates it when I make fun of him. Suddenly I knew what was going to happen. He was taking me to meet his parents because he's planning to propose. He's been hinting about it for months, and it's nearly Christmas. He was going to make that his present to me."

"He must love you," Anders ventured.

"No," Eve told him. This was the genius part. Melissa had come up with it, basing it on a movie she'd seen. Eve made sure to hold Anders's gaze as she spoke. "No, he doesn't love me. He only wants to control me. He's exactly like his father—I don't know why I never saw that before."

Anders winced. She wondered why. Had someone tried to control him?

"I had to get out of there," she said.

Anders nodded. "Of course you did."

"How did you get here?" Greg asked suddenly. A good question, Anders thought. He'd gotten so caught up in Eve's story, he wasn't thinking about any of the details.

"Walked. I... I made him stop the car. I got out and started walking. I thought..." She hung her head again, as if too ashamed to go on. "I thought he'd pull over and park. Follow me and apologize. It all happened so fast I didn't have a plan. Then I heard the engine. He—took off."

"And he didn't come back?" Anders was outraged. You didn't leave a person miles from anywhere alone at night—

"Where's your coat?" Greg pressed.

"I—I'd taken it off. It was hot in the car. I put it in the back seat to make room. I didn't think he'd just leave me there," she added. She wouldn't meet any of their eyes, and Anders couldn't blame her. She'd been through a humiliating ordeal.

"We need to get you out of those wet clothes," Avery said, making an end to the conversation. "Sounds to me like you were lucky to get away from a guy like that."

Eve nodded, but she looked unhappy. Anders hoped she wasn't regretting what she'd done. Avery was right; any man who treated his girlfriend like that wasn't going to treat his wife any better. If this... James was here, he'd have a few things to say to the guy.

He wondered if James was looking for Eve right now. He might have driven off to prove a point, but most men wouldn't walk away from a woman like Eve. She was pretty. Athletically built but feminine, too. When she got to her feet with Avery's help, her damp jeans and sweater clung to her figure in a distracting way, and Anders felt a tug of desire low in his gut.

James was an idiot to leave her behind.

"Avery's right. You should get changed," he said. Eve was shivering. She was lucky she hadn't gotten hypothermia.

"Curtis, can you make Eve some tea? Eve, I'll let you borrow some clothing of mine," Avery said. "Can you walk?"

"I think so." Eve limped after Avery, following her first to where Avery stored her clothes and then to the bathroom. When the door closed behind them, Anders exchanged a look with the other men in the room, struggling to tamp down his libido. It wasn't surprising to find himself attracted to Eve. He was looking for a wife, after all, and she was the right age range—and apparently single now.

Bad joke, he told himself. It wasn't appropriate to consider her for the part. She was scared. She'd just been left unceremoniously by a man with whom she'd been in a long-term relationship. She must have been afraid she might come to harm out there in the dark and cold.

"What do we do with her?" Greg asked quietly.

"Send her home, I guess," Anders said reluctantly. He didn't like the idea at all. What if this James guy came at her again?

"Send her home?" Curtis, on his way to the kitchen, came right back. "Are you kidding?" When Anders shrugged at him, he lifted his hands skyward. "The Universe—it heard you. You need a wife—there she is!"

"We know nothing about her," Greg pointed out.

"We know she's been dumped, she's freezing and she needs help," Curtis countered. "She's the perfect candidate for a quick wedding."

Hope, who'd watched the entire proceedings curiously but so far had said little, sent him a sideways look. "Was that what you thought when you met me?"

"Pretty much. Along with, wow—she's hot." Curtis leaned down and kissed her. "I was running out of time, and suddenly this gorgeous, interesting woman crashes her car at the end of my lane. Of course I thought you might be the one. Luckily, I had a good excuse to spend enough time with you to see if I was right. We need a reason for Eve to stick around long enough for Anders to find out if they're compatible."

"I don't know," Greg said. "Don't any of you think it's a big coincidence that Clem arrived two days ago— Mr. I Know How to Get Good Ratings—and suddenly Eve turns up on our doorstep, too? What if he's planted her to get you to fall for her—so he can ruin everything when she doesn't show up for your wedding in a few weeks?"

Anders exchanged a look with Curtis. He hadn't thought of that.

"That's... twisted," Curtis said.

"Clem's twisted," Greg countered. "Don't tell me he

doesn't want us to fail."

"Thank God he and Byron aren't here—for the moment," Hope put in.

Anders had been wondering about that. "Where are they?"

"Up at the manor. He wanted to stay and see what we do at night. Then he realized we don't have beds squirreled away somewhere for important people like him to sleep in, so he had the bright idea that he could commandeer a room at the B and B. I told them there are guests staying tonight, but he wouldn't listen. Riley will send him packing when he gets there, and he'll be back to torment us."

Anders figured she had that right. "We'd better warn Eve. She might want to leave sooner rather than later."

"Forget warning her to leave. How are you going to get her to stay?" Curtis persisted. "I don't buy that Clem planted her," he told Greg.

Anders was torn. She could be a plant. But Curtis was right; if he let Eve slip away without even trying to connect with her, he'd regret it. He turned to Hope. "What do you think?"

"I think you should ask her what she wants to do. If she's got an angry boyfriend trying to track her down, she might want to lie low for a while. This would be the perfect place."

"And if she's working for Clem?" Greg challenged her.

"Anyone working for a sleazy guy like Clem will

show their cards sooner or later. Who could keep their story straight with all of us asking questions?" Hope went up on tiptoe to kiss her husband. "Come on, let's get that tea for Eve."

Shortly after they had disappeared into the kitchen, the bathroom door opened, and Eve and Avery came out. Avery looked pleased with herself. Eve looked self-conscious. She was dressed like Hope and Avery in a Regency-era gown, but it didn't fit very well. Anders couldn't help the smile that tugged at his mouth. He'd noticed the same thing with all the women; the old-fashioned clothing softened them. Made them look younger. More naive. He'd learned the hard way, though, that no matter what they wore, the women of Base Camp were fierce, smart, modern women. Not to be underestimated.

Still, Eve looked—sweet. And delicious, too. The lacy tops of her modern bra cups peeked out over the low neckline of her gown. Avery must not have had an extra set of old-fashioned undergarments. Eve had pulled her hair into a simple braid, but tendrils had come free and spiraled into curls. His body came awake with a strength that surprised him all over again.

Maybe Curtis was right; maybe he needed to persuade her to stay.

"Eve is going to spend the night," Avery announced, as if she'd heard his thoughts. "James has got her purse and her money along with her luggage and outerwear. She needs to cancel her credit cards and get some sleep. Time enough in the morning to figure out her next move."

"Do you have your phone?" Greg asked Eve.

Eve nodded and pulled it out. "It's dead, though. I don't have a charger."

"I've got one." Avery bustled off.

"Do you want to borrow my phone to get in touch with your boyfriend?" Greg asked.

"Greg," Anders warned. He wished he could march the man outside and knock him into a snowbank. Curtis and Hope reappeared from the kitchen, Curtis gingerly carrying a cup of hot tea.

When Eve shook her head, Anders let out the breath he was holding. "Absolutely not. The way James was acting—I never want to see him again. I'm not going to spend my life with a man who belittles me. Who thinks he can tell me what to do."

Curtis met Anders's gaze over her head and waggled his eyebrows.

"Where do James's parents live?" Greg asked suddenly.

She frowned. "I—uh—Bozeman."

"Where in Bozeman?"

Eve blinked. "I don't know the street. I've never been to Montana before."

"Stop interrogating her." Avery took the cup of tea from Curtis's hands, gave it to Eve and ushered her back to her folding chair. "I swear they can't help it. Once a Navy SEAL, always a Navy SEAL."

"Won't your in-laws be worried when you don't show up?" Greg followed them.

Was he determined to ruin everything? Anders followed, too.

"They aren't my in-laws. Not now. Not ever." Eve took a sip of her tea, and Anders noticed her hands were still shaking. Was she cold? Or nervous? Finding herself here must be overwhelming.

"Don't you think you should call them?"

"Why would she call them?" Avery turned on Greg. "Let James explain what he did when he shows up at their place without her."

Eve stood up suddenly, tea sloshing from her cup. "I'm intruding," she said. "You don't need this kind of drama here. You don't know me, and I'm taking up too much of your time. As soon as my phone is charged, I can call an Uber—"

"You're not going anywhere tonight—and Chance Creek doesn't have ride sharing yet." Avery turned on Greg. "Everyone's going to back off, let you drink your tea and get a good night's sleep. Tomorrow we'll sort out what to do next."

Eve shook her head. "I don't want to be any trouble."

Greg had the sense to look shamefaced. "I didn't mean—"

"You are definitely staying," Anders spoke up. "Avery's right; it's too late for you to go anywhere tonight. Drink your tea and then come to the kitchen, and we'll see what Kai has in the fridge. Kai is our cook." He paused. "We haven't really introduced ourselves, have we? I'm Anders Olsen. This is Curtis

Lloyd, Greg Devon, Angus McBride, Hope Lloyd and Avery Lightfoot. That's Walker Norton back in the corner," he added. Walker hadn't said a thing since Eve's arrival. Anders wondered what the quiet man was thinking.

"I know." Color traced through Eve's cheeks. "I watch *Base Camp* every week."

HAD SHE BLOWN it? Should she have pretended not to know them?

No, she decided. That would have been the stupid move. Even people who never watched the show knew the names of the men and women it featured.

"When I opened my eyes and found myself here," she added quickly, "I thought I was dreaming—but my feet hurt so badly I knew it couldn't be a dream."

Did they know she was lying? They had to. She felt like her cheeks were burning, and in a minute, if she wasn't careful, she'd start stammering. She hated pulling one over on these kind people.

It was only for a little while, she reminded herself. Just until she could find a way to get on camera and present the images she'd taken from AltaVista. First she needed to charge her phone. She'd had to let it run out, or everyone would have wondered why she didn't simply call a cab when she found herself out on the street. Once charged, she could access the image files. Then she'd have to figure out how to present them while the show was being filmed—in a way too compelling to edit out.

Melissa would be wondering what was happening, too. As soon as her phone charged—and she had a minute alone—she'd text her to let her know she was okay.

Somehow all of it had seemed possible when they were dreaming up the plan. Now Eve figured it would be a miracle if she lasted the night before she tripped herself up and everyone saw right through her. She wasn't sure why she'd made an immediate enemy in Greg, but she had. That didn't bode well.

"It's no dream—" Anders had just started to reassure her when the door to the bunkhouse burst open and two men strode in. Eve yelped at the sudden interruption and clapped a hand to her chest. Who were these people? She didn't recognize either from the show.

The taller of the two strangers immediately honed in on the sound. "Who's this?" he demanded and crossed the room toward her. To Eve's relief, Avery blocked him. She noticed the second man was carrying a video camera.

Hell. These were crew members.

"Eve needs rest. Anders and Curtis rescued her. She's had a rough night—" Avery held out her hands to stop the second man from filming, but the first pushed past her.

"A rough night?" He turned back to the cameraman. Clapped his hands twice. "Byron, hurry up and get this. Now we've got a story we can run with." He gestured to Anders. "Navy SEAL desperate for a wife saves woman desperate for—" He looked at Eve. "What are you desperate for?"

She gaped at him, unable to keep up. What was she desperate for? Justice against Hansen Oil? She couldn't say that yet. "S-safety?" she managed. She was supposed to be on the run from her boyfriend.

"Clem—" Avery began.

"Saves woman desperate for safety." Clem grimaced. "Too repetitive. We need something better." He looked her up and down again. "Navy SEAL desperate for a wife saves woman desperate for *love*. That's how we'll frame this episode. What do you say, little lady? Give the SEAL a kiss, would you?"

Eve's mouth dropped open. Normally, she'd be happy to give Anders a kiss, but she doubted he wanted one, and she wasn't going to assault him, especially not on the say-so of this guy.

Anders's fingers balled into a fist. Curtis grabbed his arm. "Don't punch the director," he cautioned. "No matter how much he deserves it."

Director? Eve looked at the man again. Somehow she'd thought the director was the sharp-faced woman named Renata, who did the voice-overs on the show and sometimes interviewed the participants onscreen.

"Clem is new here," Avery explained. "*Very* new."

"Byron, get filming," Clem demanded. "I need an episode that will knock everyone's socks off, and it looks like we've got the start of it. What brings you here, Eve? Lust?" He elbowed Anders. "After all, this guy's up for grabs."

She couldn't think of a thing to say.

How many times had she fantasized about Anders—

"Stop filming." Eve finally found her voice. She wasn't ready for any of this. She'd figured she'd have time to get the lay of the land before they put her on an episode. Now she wondered what she'd been thinking. Of course they would want to film her arrival.

Her cheeks were hot. Was she blushing again? Clem's accusation had thrown her off. What if they guessed she'd come here deliberately? They might throw her out before she had a chance to do what she'd come to do.

Should she say something right now? Talk about Hansen Oil? Tell them about the images?

No.

She couldn't *tell* them. She had to *show* them, which meant she needed to wait until her phone charged.

For now, she had to be careful and dispel any suspicions Clem, or Greg, or anyone else might be harboring.

A woman who'd just been dumped by her boyfriend and found herself at Base Camp wouldn't want to be filmed. She had every right to protest. "Please don't film me," she said again. "You can't put me on an episode."

Clem grinned. "Like hell I can't. Anders, back me up. You need a wife. Here's a candidate."

Anders's hands were still clenched, and Eve couldn't blame him; everything about Clem rubbed her the wrong way, and she'd been here only a matter of minutes.

"What's wrong? You don't like her looks?" Clem elbowed Anders again.

She had to be scarlet. What if Anders didn't—

"I like her looks just fine," Anders said. "I don't like your attitude one bit, though. You need to shut up—"

Eve swallowed hard in a suddenly dry throat. Now she was warm in an entirely different way. Anders liked her looks?

"But maybe she doesn't like you," Clem spoke right over him. "Maybe she hates everything about Base Camp. Maybe she'd like to see you all dead. What do you say, Eve? Are you a terrorist? Are you going to blow up the bunkhouse?"

He sounded downright hopeful.

"No." Eve cleared her throat and tried again. "I'm not a terrorist. I'm an environmentalist."

Clem lifted an eyebrow. "An environmentalist." He chuckled a little. "What did I tell you, Anders? Love at first sight. You two will be married in no time."

Eve didn't mean to look at Anders, but she couldn't help it. She found him looking back at her, his dark eyes assessing her.

What was he thinking?

"You're single, right?" Clem demanded.

A corner of Anders's mouth curved into a smile, flustering her all over again. "I—" Eve started but found she couldn't finish.

The man was lethal when he did that. But she couldn't go down this path—not all the way. Three weeks from now she'd be starting school and waiting for the delivery of her framed-in tiny house. She'd be on her way to becoming a real adult.

"She has a boyfriend," Anders informed the director, and his gaze challenged her to deny it. Clem scowled.

"A boyfriend?" he repeated.

Eve shook her head decisively. "Not anymore," she said. "I can't stay more than a day or two, though."

"Why not?"

"Because I have a job. A life." A woman who'd just washed up at Base Camp wouldn't be in a hurry to accept Clem's proposition. "I'm supposed to be in Montana through Christmas, then go home. Would it be possible… for me to stay just until then?"

That would give her plenty of time to figure out how to expose Hansen Oil on camera, then get away and hide before the next *Base Camp* episode aired.

"Of course," Avery said. "We'd love to have you for the holiday!"

"No," Clem said. "No, no, no."

"Why not?" Anders turned on him. "You just said she should stay."

"I said she should marry you. No dead weight on set."

Eve stiffened. She was about to lose her chance to fulfill her mission. Anders stepped toward the man, but Clem forestalled him. "You heard what Fulsom said. This show is going to the dogs, and it's my job to fix it. I say the only way she stays is if she's considering being your bride. Otherwise, she's out of here."

"That's not fair," Avery said.

"Who gives a damn about fair?" Clem asked her.

"Okay," Eve blurted. She didn't know what else to do. When everyone turned to her, she felt her cheeks heat all over again. Walker, who'd been quiet since she arrived, grinned suddenly, and that unsettled her more than anything else. A moment later, his expression was just as unreadable as ever.

"Okay?" Anders repeated. "You... sure about that?"

"I'm not making any promises," she hurried to add, "but I need a place to stay, and James will never find me here. And who knows?" She lifted her hands, hoping she wasn't going too far. Melissa hadn't prepped her for this contingency. "Maybe the Universe is playing some strange practical joke. Maybe you're the perfect man, Anders Olsen, and the whole reason I was with James in the first place was to get me here. Nothing would surprise me right now."

Was it working—brazening it out like this?

Avery smiled. "I like the way you think."

"Sometimes things just work out." Hope took Curtis's hand.

"What do you say?" Greg asked Anders. "Do you want Eve to stay?" Eve could tell he was still suspicious of her.

Eve looked from him to the others in the room. Clem looked smug. Curtis was nodding. Hope was amused. Avery was happy. Walker was unreadable. And Anders—

Anders was smiling again. "Yeah," he said slowly. "I'd like that."

CHAPTER FOUR

"**T**RY TO GET some sleep, and we'll talk more in the morning," Anders said to Eve an hour later. Clem was finally gone after crowding around her for far too long and asking far too many questions. Finally, the director said since he couldn't sleep at the manor, he'd head back to town, where the production company kept rooms for crew members at a motel. He ordered Byron to stay and film anything interesting that might happen. Byron didn't look too pleased about that.

"I've set up a sleeping bag for you over here," Avery told Eve. "Sorry we don't have fancier quarters, but this is the way it is for now. I've made your bed as comfortable as I can." She and Eve had changed again—this time into pajamas. Anders had heard that initially the women had worn Regency-style nightgowns to go with the rest of the Regency theme, but somewhere along the way they'd relaxed their standards and at night switched to more modern—and, he assumed, more comfortable—sleepwear.

Eve looked at the sleeping bag laid out on the thin

mattress pad on the floor and sighed. "I've watched the show. I know how this works. All the single people sleep in the bunkhouse."

Anders sympathized with her lack of enthusiasm. He had been looking forward to the day he got to move into his own house for a long time now, but never as much as tonight, when he wished he could offer a real bed to Eve.

Not that he was trying to sleep with her. He didn't take advantage of women, despite what Clem obviously wanted from him, but Eve had been through a lot and deserved better than this. And sharing a bed with her—simply to keep her safe and warm—wouldn't be a hardship.

His body had been letting him know all night that he'd spent too much time without a girlfriend. He wondered if he'd sleep at all with Eve so close.

"Good night. You can rest easy; we'll all be looking out for trouble. If your boyfriend comes anywhere near here, we'll take care of him." He wished he could say more to reassure her—and let her know the man was obviously a fool if he'd treated her badly.

"Good night," she said absently but didn't move away.

It must feel strange to bunk down in a room of people you didn't know. "You're safe here," he assured her again. "Your boyfriend can't have any idea where you got to."

"Ex-boyfriend," she reminded him. "I'm so over him."

He believed her anger, but he knew love didn't disappear just because you wanted it to.

"Let's get you to bed," Avery said, interrupting them, leading her toward the women's side of the room.

Anders turned to find Curtis watching him. Hope had already left for their tiny house. Curtis was pulling on his coat.

"What?" Anders asked.

"I didn't say anything." He looked like he was holding back an *I told you so.*

"Don't read anything into the situation that isn't there." Anders kept his voice low, hoping Eve couldn't hear them.

"What if I'm reading something into the situation that *is* there?"

Anders ignored him and made his way to bed.

But not to sleep. Too many thoughts jumbled in his mind, the way they had been these last few days, ever since he'd drawn the short straw and found it was his turn to marry. Eve was certainly pretty. She was scrappy, too. No shrinking violet there, despite her short stature. It had taken guts to run away from her boyfriend and keep stumbling through the snow until she'd fallen into his arms.

Still, a woman who'd just been dumped by a controlling boyfriend would hardly be in the mood to fall for him—would she? Was there time for them to get to know each other well enough to predict how they'd feel in the future? At some point he'd need to take a leap of faith with someone, he supposed. Unlike Curtis and his new belief in mystical possibilities, Anders was a pragmatist. He figured if he wanted a wife, he needed to make the most of any situation that presented itself. Eve was here, and she'd agreed to stay for a few days. He needed to make a quick judgment about whether he could commit to trying to build a life with her, and if he could, he needed to work even more quickly to convince her to stay long enough to give it a try.

In the end, Base Camp was what mattered most. Doing his part to convince people to take sustainability seriously. He'd marry someone—anyone—so that Base Camp could go on. Even a backup bride Boone located for him.

Anders turned over. Just as he suspected, sleep was eluding him, and now that it was dark and quiet and he knew Eve was only feet away, he was having trouble corralling his thoughts and not letting them wander into more interesting pastures.

What would it be like to get to know Eve better? To share a bed together—or a sleeping bag?

He didn't even have the privacy required to take care of a bout of lust like this. Which is what this was.

Pure lust.

It wasn't like he'd fallen for Eve at first sight.

He hadn't *not* fallen for her, either, though.

Anders turned onto his other side with a sigh and peered through the dark room to where the women were sleeping. Avery blocked his view of Eve, but he could imagine her lying in the dark, her dark hair tousled on the pillow, her eyelashes feathered on her cheeks.

She was a beautiful woman. An intriguing one. Since his libido had already decided they were compatible, would they connect in other ways? After all, they couldn't spend a lifetime screwing.

Hell. Now his mind was really working overtime.

Anders forced his thoughts to more mundane matters. He'd show her around Base Camp tomorrow, he decided. Talk to her about his work. See if they held any interests in common.

Would they share a worldview? After all, she'd announced she was an environmentalist. That was a start.

What about his secret? If he told her who he was, what would she think of him then? Could she see him for himself? Or would she judge him on his father's actions?

He wanted someone who knew him through and through—and wouldn't walk away. A woman who got him—the way his father never had. A woman who wouldn't stand in the way of his goals. Or tell him how dumb he was for not choosing money over his values.

Was Curtis right? Had the universe provided him with a suitable candidate?

Would Eve stay long enough for him to find out?

WHEN EVE WOKE again, it was still the middle of the night and the bunkhouse was bathed in the dim light that seeped through the curtainless windows. She turned over, wincing at the hardness of the floor beneath her mat, and tried to go back to sleep. When she closed her eyes, however, worried thoughts crowded her mind.

What would happen if Anders and the others discovered she was lying to them? Could she really pull off exposing Hansen Oil in the next few days? Would she last at Base Camp that long? What if Anders decided he wasn't attracted to her after all and asked her to leave?

She opened her eyes, looked at Avery's sleeping shape nearby but was afraid to look beyond her to Anders.

But when she shut her eyes again, her thoughts spun and tangled. What if Hansen Oil went after her—or her family? What if it brought a libel suit against her? What if it cleaned up the spill before anyone could investigate?

She supposed that last possibility would be a good thing. She'd weather embarrassment if it meant the company fixed the problem before it poisoned North Run's water supply—if it hadn't already.

She'd managed to text Melissa earlier and let her know everything had gone according to plan. *Only problem is, the director practically ordered Anders to try to get me to marry him.*

That's a problem? Melissa had texted back.

It's a complication. I need to focus on taking down Hansen Oil.

I'm here when you need me. When do you think you'll be able to do the big reveal?

I don't know yet. The new director seems far more concerned with Anders's sex life than sustainability or environmentalism.

Let me know if you need my help.

Will do.

Eve pressed her palms to her eyes. There was nothing more she could do tonight. She had to sleep.

Try as she might, sleep wouldn't come, and now she needed to use the bathroom.

She sat up in her sleeping bag gingerly, climbed out of it as carefully as she could and moved across the room to the bathroom, trying not to wake the others. Afterward, she slipped into the kitchen, hoping to find some chamomile tea. If she didn't sleep tonight, tomorrow she'd be off her game, and she was already having trouble keeping all her lies straight.

In the kitchen, a long room off the side of the main one where she'd been bunked down, Eve moved quietly until she found what she needed.

"Everything okay?"

She jumped when a man's voice sounded behind her, spun around and breathed a sigh of relief when she saw Anders in the doorway. Then her heart kicked up again. He was wearing a pair of pajama bottoms and nothing else. The hard planes of his chest were a sight to behold. The muscles in his arms and shoulders were mesmerizing.

She forced her gaze to his face.

"Couldn't sleep."

"Me, either." Anders joined her in the kitchen, taking the kettle from her hand and setting it on the stove. In a few minutes he served her a cup of chamomile tea, and she took it gratefully, barely able to breathe with him so close. "Bad dreams?"

Neither of them had turned on the light in the kitchen for fear of waking the others, and she was grateful for the dimness. It made it easier to twist the truth. "A few."

"I've dealt with them myself," he said. He took a sip from his own mug. "Sometimes all you can do is stay awake."

She wondered what he had seen during his time with the SEALs. Probably things she couldn't imagine. Things she didn't want to know about. "Why did you join up?" It was a simple enough question, she decided. Anybody might've asked it. She hadn't given away the fact that she was really interested in the answer.

She wasn't sure if she'd ever met a man like Anders before, with his combination of strength and the gentle way he spoke to her. She'd met military guys, of course—there were plenty of them in Virginia—but overall her impression had been of brash, loud, self-important men with places to go and things to do. They hadn't had Anders's watchfulness.

"Needed a way out." He chuckled. "Texas had lost its charm for me."

"Texas, huh?" She hadn't noticed an accent. Maybe he'd done his best to lose it.

"That's right," he agreed. "Where are you from?"

"Virginia."

"Is that where your folks are?"

She nodded.

"I got as far away as I could from what's left of my family," Anders said.

"There must be a story there."

He shrugged. "Not the first guy to disagree with a

parent's choice, I'm sure. Do you plan to settle there? In Virginia?"

"I… guess so." In the dark, in this kitchen so far from home, she was able to admit to herself for the first time that her life wasn't going to work out the way she'd thought it would. In addition to the changes her parents were imposing, she wouldn't have a job when this was over. Might struggle to find a new one after her actions here made her notorious.

"I'm going to stay right here," Anders said. "At Base Camp. No matter what."

"I can see why," she said. "It looks pretty idyllic—on TV anyway."

"You really watch the show?" He made a face.

"Doesn't everybody?"

"I don't think everybody watches it." He grinned. "I'm glad you do, though. Less explaining to do."

"This place is a little weird," she agreed. "For one thing, if I hadn't expected Avery and Hope to be wearing Regency clothing, I would've had a lot of questions."

She had to admit she liked the way Anders smiled. It was pure mischief, and she wondered what he'd been like as a little boy. He sure was compelling as a man. Eve was grateful no one was filming them. It made it easier to focus—to be in the moment.

One of her recurring fantasies popped into her mind. The one where she and Anders found themselves alone in one of the tiny houses the married couples lived in, and Anders took her to the ladder to see the loft bedroom.

Stop it, she told herself. They were a long way from anything like that, even if he was looking at her like he might be thinking something along the same lines.

He had to marry in a few short weeks, after all. It made sense he'd consider any single woman who crossed his path—whether or not Clem forced that path on him.

She took a step backward, bumped into the counter and nearly dropped her teacup. Anders lurched forward quickly, caught it and set it down for her, leaving him even closer.

"Are you all right?"

"I just—"

Eve tried to find some way to finish the sentence without betraying what his proximity was doing to her, but she couldn't. He was so close it was hard not to touch him. She wanted to explore his muscles. Touch his skin—

She held her hands straight at her sides.

"I—" She tried again. "I don't—"

She was going to blow this if she didn't pull herself together. What would a woman do who'd just been left by the side of the road by her boyfriend?

Faint?

She'd done enough of that earlier.

Cry?

She wasn't sure she could do that on cue.

She must have looked stricken, though. Anders stepped even closer.

"It's okay." When he took her into his arms and murmured against her hair, Eve was so surprised she didn't think she could have moved if she wanted to. "James won't find you, I promise. You can take all the time you need here before you go home."

In the circle of his arms, she leaned against his bare chest, allowing him to comfort her. Anders smelled so good. His skin was warm against her cheek. His heart was beating strong beneath her ear.

Anders Olsen, reality TV star, was holding her.

"I don't know why I'm shaking," Eve managed to say. She'd never admit what he was doing to her.

"It's just shock. It's okay," Anders said again, his arms tightening around her.

It wasn't shock, Eve knew.

It was something else entirely.

"YOU NEED TO get off that show and come home," Johannes said.

Anders, leaning against the fence that spanned one of the bison pastures the following morning, shifted his phone to his other ear. Two calls within days of each other. That was unusual. Something had to be up. "We've had this conversation before. I'm not quitting the show. And I'm not coming back to Texas. It hasn't been my home for a long time. We both know that."

There was a long pause. "You can't hold on to old arguments forever. What would your mother think?"

It was Anders's turn to pause. His father hadn't mentioned his mother in years. Why would he do so now?

"Is there something you want to tell me?" Johannes was a tight-lipped son-of-a-bitch. Beating around the bush would get them nowhere.

Maybe his father was missing his mom. Anders did sometimes. Other times he was grateful in a cowardly way she'd passed away before he'd split with his dad. His mom was the daughter of an oilman, too. She'd grown up with derricks in her backyard. He wasn't sure she'd have understood his choices. His combative relationship with his dad had made it easier to walk away, especially after all their arguments. His mother was a quiet woman. She'd never liked fights. He might still be living in Texas if she was there.

"Hansen Oil is your legacy," his father said tightly. "You need to be here."

"I'm making my own legacy." His father's tone bothered him. He sounded drained.

"You don't need to make your own legacy. I've already gone and done all the work! Why won't you come make use of it?"

Something was definitely wrong. Johannes Hansen didn't *use* his wealth; he simply kept acquiring more money, as if there was some magic number that kept edging up and up out of his reach. Anders had always wondered what he was reaching for. He had so much already; surely a little more couldn't make a difference.

"What I'm building isn't about money," Anders said carefully. "It's about doing what's right. About building a community that makes the world better than we found it rather than degrading it."

"You think I set out to degrade my community?"

His father was one step from fury, and driving Johannes over the edge wasn't Anders's intention.

"I'm telling you what I'm trying to do."

"Make me look bad. That's what you're trying to do. You're going to drag me through the mud!"

"Hardly." He was doing his best to keep the link between him and Hansen Oil hidden. If he was exposed, he might very well be kicked out of Base Camp. He couldn't imagine Boone and the others would be pleased there was an oil baron's son on the team. Not quite the image they were trying to put out.

Plenty of people in Texas had to have recognized him, though, even after fourteen years. He'd been lucky no one had spoken to the press so far. That was his father's influence. Back when he'd insisted on changing his name, his father had found a judge willing to keep the proceedings off the record—for a small sum of money, of course. Who knew how much more money his father had spread since then to buy other people off.

"Do you know what will happen if it comes out that a Hansen is advocating for green energy on a major television show?" his father pressed, anger thinning his voice.

"Good thing I'm not a Hansen then." Anders was ready to hang up.

"You can't erase who you are with a court date. You think the media is going to care that you walked away? Hell, they'll eat that up! It'll be in the news for weeks.

Hansen Oil will come under additional scrutiny."

That's what this was about. "What've you done now?" he demanded. Hansen Oil had a less than stellar track record when it came to its operations. He spotted Boone heading his way. "You know what? Forget it. You aren't going to tell me the truth anyway, and I've got to go."

"You get your ass back to Texas pronto—"

Anders clicked to end the call. He never intended to return to Texas.

"Anders—got a minute?" Boone called, approaching from the direction of the bunkhouse.

"Sure, what's up?" He filed away his problems for later.

"Heard you had some excitement last night."

Walker must have brought him up to date on Eve's arrival, since Boone and Riley had long since retired to their tiny house by the time Eve had showed up. Boone and Walker were thick as thieves.

Anders turned to survey the bison grazing far off the snowy pasture. They were tough creatures, able to dig through the accumulated snow with their hooves to reach the grass below. He'd already made his morning rounds to check on all the livestock, slipping out while Eve and the others were still asleep. The snow had stopped overnight. Soon he'd need to help Curtis plow the lane again.

"Eve seems like a good candidate. Maybe marrying you off will be easier than I thought," Boone went on.

"Don't get your hopes up."

"How about your hopes? Are they… up?"

"Too soon to tell," Anders lied. "She's just broken up with her boyfriend. I think… I think she doesn't dislike me." He gave Boone a pared-down sketch of their meeting in the kitchen in the middle of the night, neglecting any mention of how his pulse had pounded when he'd held her. "She was shaking like a leaf," he ended. "She's really upset by what happened."

"Stands to reason. Doesn't mean she won't fall for you, given time."

"Maybe. Maybe not."

"Only one thing for it. Keep her here as long as you can."

"Did Walker tell you what Clem said?"

"That she can stay only if she gives being with you a chance? Yes. Seems like Clem did you a favor there since she agreed."

Anders nodded. "Maybe. I guess we'll see. Could've knocked me over with a feather when she went for it," he admitted. He shoved his hands in his pockets.

"You must have made a good impression. Sounds like she wants to lie low for a few days at least, anyway," Boone said. "Walker said she wants to stay through Christmas."

"Meanwhile, you know damn well Clem's going to be searching for her boyfriend. He'll do whatever it takes to make trouble, including bringing him on the show."

"So give him something better to focus on. And get Eve so hooked on you she won't want her boyfriend if

Clem does find him."

"It's not that simple," Anders protested.

"Maybe it's simpler than you think," Boone countered. "She let you hold her last night. She saw this guy's true colors when he left her in the middle of nowhere."

Anders wasn't sure Boone was right. After Eve had steadied herself last night, she'd excused herself and gone back to bed. She knew he needed a wife—Clem had said so—and she hadn't given him any indication she was interested.

Which was too bad. He was definitely interested.

Holding Eve had turned all his senses up full blast. Suddenly it wasn't about needing anything. It was about wanting a woman—wanting Eve. It took more than attraction to make a marriage work, but Anders figured attraction was a good starting point.

But only if both of them felt it.

"What if you're wrong?"

"I've already got a backup bride lined up."

"Backup bride?" Clem popped in behind them as if Boone's words had summoned him. "What's wrong, Olsen; you scare Eve off already?"

"Hell—" Anders pulled himself together. How much had that weasel heard?

"He hasn't scared Eve off," Boone told him. "You're going to scare her if you go after her boyfriend, though. I heard one of the crew talking about tracking him down—I think that's a really bad idea."

"Nothing like a lovers' triangle to get great ratings." Clem danced back out of Anders's reach. "Hey, watch it."

"Sounds like her boyfriend has an anger management problem. What if he hurts her this time—and she sues you? What's the show's liability then?" Anders challenged him.

"I'm not worried about liability. I'm worried about this show dropping off the air altogether because no one wants to watch it anymore. If you don't want me going after her boyfriend, what are you offering me in return?"

"What do you want?" Boone demanded.

Clem thought about it. When an oily smile spread across his face, Anders's stomach sank. "Anders here is bound to blow it with Eve. When he does, he doesn't get to meet or talk to the backup bride I know you're lining up—until he meets her at the altar. Deal?" he asked Anders. "You bag Eve, or you marry a stranger."

"Deal," Anders said without a second thought. He'd staked his future on Base Camp, and he'd see it through. He'd already pledged himself to marry, no matter what it took. He didn't want a stranger, though. From what he'd learned so far, he'd prefer Eve.

"By the way," Clem said, "who'd you go to prom with?"

Fuck. Anders raced to come up with an answer that wouldn't lead Clem to any discoveries about his real identity. "I already said I didn't graduate."

"You didn't even make it to junior year? What kind of a shit-for-brains are you?"

"The kind of shit-for-brains who didn't have time

for prom. Gotta go." He didn't wait for Clem to answer. The man was definitely trying to trip him up—to find some bit of information to follow and learn about his childhood. Soon Clem would figure out exactly what he was trying to hide.

That would be a disaster.

"I'M GLAD YOU'RE sticking around for a while," Boone told Eve when she exited the bathroom. She'd put on the clothes she'd worn the day before when she'd stumbled up the road toward Base Camp. They'd dried overnight but weren't in the best condition, and she hoped she could borrow something or go to town to shop before the day was over. At least she'd had a shower. Avery had loaned her shampoo and conditioner—along with clean socks and a pair of boots. She'd told Eve she could borrow a gown again, but the one she'd worn last night hadn't fit that well, and she couldn't imagine spending a day in it. "Anders is out tending the bison. I'm sure he'll be back in a minute."

"Okay." Eve felt a little shy. All these people had bought her story about her boyfriend, but what would they think if they knew what she was really after?

They were environmentalists, too. Wouldn't they savor the chance to take down a company like Hansen Oil? Or would they be afraid of the repercussions?

She and Melissa had agreed that the way to ensure her message about Hansen Oil stayed in the show when it was edited and aired was to make her interactions with the others so interesting that the director couldn't stand to cut it. Eve figured that meant allowing Anders to pursue her, among other things.

She found she didn't mind. After the way her body had buzzed with desire when Anders had comforted her in the kitchen last night, this morning she'd decided she deserved one last fling before she went home and really put her shoulder to the grindstone. If the thought of leaving Base Camp already gave her a pang, she just wouldn't think about it.

Boone's words penetrated her spinning thoughts. Bison? Did he say bison?

Eve wanted to see them. She'd forgotten about the herd here at Base Camp. The animals reminded her of one of the more interesting images that had crossed her desk at AltaVista. It had been a set of before-and-after photos showing a large swath of land situated in the great plains where several ranchers had converted from raising beef cattle to bison. The improvement in the health of the vegetation over several years after the switch was remarkable.

"Feeling more like yourself?" Avery entered the main room from the kitchen and handed Eve a cup of coffee. Eve looked up to see Byron was quietly filming her.

"Yes. Thanks. Boone mentioned bison," she said hesitantly, struggling to keep from glancing at the camera again. "I'd love to see them."

"I'll take you right after breakfast. Then we'd better get you to Alice's house."

"Alice. As in Alice Reed?" Eve straightened. "You

mean—for a Regency gown of my own?" All the women at Base Camp wore them, but she hadn't expected to get one herself. She'd be here only a handful of days.

Avery grinned. "Why not? If Clem is going to force you to be on the show while you're here, you might as well get a dress or two out of it."

Eve's spirits rose. A Regency gown would be fun. When the rest of the members of Base Camp trickled into the bunkhouse for breakfast, she enjoyed meeting them. Last night the bunkhouse had been full of men, but now there were more women to balance the numbers. They were interested in meeting her and asked questions, but everyone seemed too well-mannered to quiz her closely about getting left behind by the fictional James.

"If you're staying through Christmas, you'll be here for the Night Sky Bonfire tomorrow night," Nora said. A dark-haired woman with expressive features, she'd held back a little, but Eve had expected that from what she'd seen on the television show. Nora had been attacked by a stalker earlier in the year. She looked like she'd overcome the effects of the attack, but Eve had a feeling she went through life with a certain wariness around strangers.

"We're all planning to go. It's a good excuse to get off the ranch and see other people," Avery chimed in.

"It will cheer you up," Hope said. "The best thing for a broken heart is to keep busy."

"Until then, we'll keep you busy around the ranch,"

Riley said. She was Boone Rudman's wife, a friendly brunette.

"That sounds good," Eve said. "I'd love to go to the Night Sky Bonfire." She remembered her earlier vow to make sure all footage of her was kept in the show and leaned toward the other women. "Will Anders go, do you think?" She could almost feel the cameraman focusing on her.

Riley looked amused. Avery delighted. "Of course he'll be there."

Eve glanced up to make sure Byron had his video camera pointed squarely at her. "Then I'll definitely go."

CHAPTER FIVE

"SO BY CHOOSING bison," Anders concluded, "we're ranching animals that developed in harmony with this particular landscape." He glanced at the sun, realized he'd been talking for quite some time and stopped. "I probably lost you a half hour ago, huh?" Behind Eve the small camera crew following them had begun to shift and stir. He'd definitely lost them a while back.

"No," Eve said. "I mean, yes, you got a little technical, but overall, no. This is important stuff, and it interests me. I work at a satellite imaging company. Did I tell you that?" She touched his arm. Ever since she'd joined him out here, she'd stuck close to him. Maybe Boone was right, and he had made a good impression. Her focused attention on his pet causes was certainly making a good impression on him.

Anders nodded, squashing an urge to tuck a wayward tendril of her hair behind her ear. He couldn't remember another woman who'd lasted half as long when he got going on a favorite subject. Eve hadn't simply listened. She'd asked questions and shared her own opinions once or twice so that he knew she'd thought about the issues at stake long before she arrived at Base Camp.

Who knew a little conversation could be such an aphrodisiac? He was having a hard time keeping his mind on bison and off all the other things he and Eve could do—if they were alone.

But he was putting the cart way before the horse. They'd just met, and they weren't kids at a frat party. He was looking for a wife. Who knew what Eve was looking for? He had to take it slow.

But not too slow.

What had she just said? Something about satellite imaging?

Right. She'd told Avery about her work, and Avery had told everyone else about it.

"Our clients come from all areas of the business sector, including agriculture and the ranching industry. I've seen what overgrazing can do." She sent a quick look over her shoulder at the crew, something she did every couple of minutes. Clem waved his hand at her to stop looking into the cameras. She turned back to Anders.

Anders studied her, surprised. What were the chances a city girl like her would spend a minute thinking about overgrazing? He needed to stop jumping to conclusions and start asking her enough questions to learn who she really was if he was going to get to know her.

"I'd like to see some of those images."

"I can point you to some you can see online, but unfortunately, most of what we do isn't for public consumption. I often think it should be—" She broke off and glanced at the cameras.

Clem made a face and waved his hand at her again.

"You're interested in sustainability, then," Anders guessed, trying to recapture her attention. And his own focus.

"I am. Sometimes people… sometimes they don't know the trouble that's brewing right under their feet." Eve looked thoughtful. They were standing where Anders had loitered with Boone that morning, looking out over the herd grazing in the distance. There was something special about a herd of bison. Anders thought it was because they looked almost prehistoric. You could imagine them roaming the continent before people even existed. Anders thought they belonged to the land in a way he only wished he could.

"True enough." He wasn't doing this right, was he? He was supposed to woo Eve, but until today he'd had no idea how hard it would be to get personal with a camera crew recording your every move. He'd grown used to them filming him at chores or during his interactions with the other inhabitants of Base Camp. This was different, though. Eve might very well decide she wasn't interested in him.

Getting dumped onscreen didn't sound fun.

"What exactly does your job entail?" he asked.

"I work in quality control. I make sure the images

we're sending to the clients line up with their expectation. It's frustrating sometimes. Our clients ask for very specific images, and we give them what they want, which isn't always what they need—or should get."

"In what way?"

Eve's brow furrowed, as if she was wrestling with a problem she'd been wrestling with for some time. She glanced at the cameras but visibly forced herself to look somewhere else.

"Say they want a photo of a forest that was clear-cut and then replanted, but they don't ask us to include the old-growth forest growing around it for comparison, so you can't see how sterile the new growth is compared to the naturally occurring woods. Or they ask for an image of a mountain whose top has been taken off to mine it—without capturing the pristine mountains around it for contrast." She shrugged. "I know they're getting those images to prove a point, whether it's to satisfy their investors or government regulators or watchdog groups, and it makes my fingers itch when I have to leave out the really pertinent information, especially when I feel like those images are being used in a way that's untruthful." She cut off. "I can't possibly know how they're using the information," she corrected herself, "and it's not my job to wonder about it; it's my job to provide the best images we can."

Anders's heart warmed. She believed in the kind of justice that went beyond following instructions, even if she'd ended her statement by toeing the company line. He had no doubt she was parroting something she'd heard a dozen times from her superiors at the imaging company. A business like that wouldn't last long if it editorialized on the images it made for clients.

She was a person who asked questions, though. Someone who didn't believe in keeping her mouth shut if it meant going along with something wrong.

He was the same.

"Are you a photographer yourself?"

Eve laughed. "No. I don't have the eye for that."

"Sounds like you do. Have you always worked for AltaVista?"

"No." Eve grew still. "I jumped around from thing to thing before that."

"Like what?"

"Nothing too exciting." Eve shifted restlessly, and he knew she was ready for a different topic of conversation. He was curious about her past but didn't want to irritate her.

"Come on, let me show you the greenhouses." He crooked his arm, and she linked hers through it gratefully.

"I'd love to see them."

Anders continued to lead Eve on a tour around Base Camp, and she was suitably interested and appreciative, but more than once she grew quiet, and he wondered if she was thinking about her ex-boyfriend. Maybe Hope was right, and the Night Sky Bonfire tomorrow would distract her. The gathering sounded like a fun tradition. A science teacher from the local high school brought telescopes to a dark field, and anyone could come and look through them at the stars and moon. The booster club sold hot chocolate and held a bake sale to raise money for the sports teams. There was skating on an outdoor rink, too. Boone had told them about it earlier in the month, and they'd all decided to go.

They lunched with the others in the bunkhouse, and then Avery came to fetch Eve. "Alice had an errand out this way, so she's coming here to fit your gown. She'll do it up at the manor, where there's more room and privacy."

"I'll come, too," Anders said quickly. He'd enjoyed himself this morning and wasn't in a hurry to leave Eve's company.

"No men allowed," Avery said with a smile. "Just us girls."

"Huh."

"I'll deliver her back in no time," she promised him. "Ready, Eve?"

"Ready."

Anders watched the women slip out of the bunkhouse.

Clem sidled over to him through the crowded room as everyone brought their dishes to the kitchen and prepared to head outside to their afternoon chores. "That's what you call exciting? Showing your girl a bunch of bison and greenhouses?"

"That's what Base Camp is about. She's got to want it if she's going to stay."

"She's got to want *you* if she's going to stay," Clem

corrected. "Show some skin or something, sailor."

"Fuck off," Anders told him.

But Clem was right; he didn't think he'd made much progress so far. He'd acted like a tour guide, not like a potential suitor. Problem was, he wasn't sure how to get from here to there.

"You got to put away your pride and just go for it," Curtis advised him, getting up from his seat, balancing dishes in his hands. "That's what I did."

"No, what *you* did was announce that you planned to marry me," Hope said, taking a cup from Curtis's hands before he dropped it. She smiled up at her husband before turning back to Anders. "I'm serious," she added. "He just up and said it like it was a done deal."

"It *was* a done deal—for me." Curtis kissed the top of her head.

Anders didn't think that would work with Eve.

"Get her drunk and challenge her to a game of quarters," Jericho Cook said, passing on his way to the kitchen. "Worked for me and Savannah."

"Don't look at me," Harris Wentworth said from his seat close by. He was working on a second plate of food. "I just picked Sam here up at the airport and drove straight to the chapel. Have no idea why she went along with it."

"You were irresistible." Samantha, sitting next to Harris, laid her head on his shoulder.

"But you came to Base Camp in order to get married," Curtis pointed out.

"To *you*, not me," Harris baited him.

Curtis waved him off. "Best thing that ever happened to me. No offense, Sam."

"None taken," she said cheerfully.

"Everyone ended up with the person they were meant to be with," Riley put in. "It'll work out for you, too, Anders."

He hoped she was right.

"By the way," Clem said, "when did you start using social media?"

Another trick question. Clem must be struggling to find any information about his life before age eighteen, which is when he'd shut down all his old accounts and opened new ones under his new name. "When I joined the Navy, I guess."

"Late bloomer, huh?"

"You could say that."

"WE ESCAPE UP here sometimes to get away from all the men," Riley confessed as she brought Eve a cup of tea in the manor house kitchen. "Not that we don't love them. We do. But it's nice to do our own thing sometimes."

Eve was enjoying getting to know the women she'd watched on *Base Camp* for so long. Alice hadn't arrived yet, and to her surprise the camera crew that had followed her and Anders all morning so far hadn't trailed them up here.

Eve was about to answer when the back door swung open, letting in a gust of frosty air. A pretty but sharp-faced, dark-haired woman walked in.

"That's Renata—our director. She was here first—before Clem," Savannah whispered hurriedly, bending close. "Renata, how are you?" she said more loudly. "Come have some tea."

"I'm not here for tea. I'm here to work," Renata said shortly.

Eve sighed. She should have known the reprieve was too good to last. It was strange being on this side of things on a television show she'd watched for months. She'd never considered what it would be like for the all the men and women of Base Camp to be constantly filmed. She wasn't surprised they got as much personal stuff done as they could during the moments when the crews were absent.

Everyone straightened as several crew members followed Renata inside, and the easy comradery that had reigned in the kitchen a moment ago disappeared, although Avery made a funny face signifying that this was all just part of the game they had to put up with. Eve had learned that the women of Base Camp were a positive, can-do, artistic lot for the most part. They laughed plenty, teased each other often and seemed happy with their situation.

"Where's Clem?" Riley asked.

"It's just women, remember? That's what you told the guys when you came up here so Clem couldn't follow," Renata said acidly. "Guess I'm still good for something," she added as Byron, the young cameraman, slipped in behind her to set up his shot.

"Byron's not a woman," Sam pointed out.

"He might as well be," Renata said. Byron made a face behind her back. "And it's not like he hasn't filmed you all a hundred times before. Relax."

The women laughed and got back to chatting. Avery handed Renata a cup of tea, and the director accepted it, despite what she'd said before. She sat down in a seat next to Eve, blew on the hot liquid and took a sip.

"Have you worked in television long?" Eve asked her as Byron focused on recording a conversation down the table about upcoming Christmas celebrations.

Renata nodded.

"What do you think about Base Camp—really?" Eve pressed her. Now that she'd had a tour around the place and gotten to see what went on behind the show, she was intrigued. She was beginning to realize how hard all the participants worked around here.

"It's an interesting experiment," Renata said. "I'm not sure how well it translates to the real world."

"Oh?" Eve would have thought Renata would be more of a proponent.

"I think in the end it's going to be consumer-driven technology that drives the way to sustainability." Renata took another sip. "People want things to be cheap. When solar becomes cheaper than fossil fuels—and I believe that day is coming—it'll sweep the country. Pretty soon driverless vehicles will take over shipping— because the efficiencies that make them environmentally friendly also will grant huge cost savings to companies, some of which they'll pass on to consumers. Electric cars are cheaper to maintain than gas-powered ones, so it stands to reason they'll eventually take over, too. It's all about price and efficiency. If scientists and innovators can come up with green technology that saves us money, we'll use it. If not, we won't—unless we're forced to by government regulations. I can't see middle America selling their three-thousand-square-foot houses and living tiny, no matter how well we sell it."

"Why are you doing this, then?"

Renata blinked. Seemed to realize she might have been too candid. "Because… it's still interesting. The people here at Base Camp are testing technologies and practices that might be useful in the larger world. And because… it's what Fulsom wants."

"The billionaire?" He was the one funding the enterprise, Eve knew. He had a way of popping up on the shows from time to time, but she had to admit she found him a little pompous and overblown.

"That's the one."

"I'm not sure I understand."

Renata fiddled with her teacup. "I never meant to be in TV at all. I'm a filmmaker. I wanted to work in Hollywood. Feature films. Fulsom made me an offer I couldn't refuse early on in my career, though. He wanted a documentary made about him, and I needed a chance to shine. Now I've worked with him and filmed him for… years." She sighed. "Then *Base Camp* came up. He put me on the project. It's only temporary."

"Will you go back to filming him now that Clem's here?"

"Maybe." Renata pushed her chair back. "Or maybe this is his way of showing me to the door. Who knows?" She looked as if she might stand up, and Eve hoped she hadn't offended the woman.

"Renata—" She searched for something to say. Remembered Anders's question from earlier. "Do you do any camera work yourself?"

"Not much." To Eve's relief, Renata settled in again and edged closer. "I do a fair amount of editing, though. I enjoy that."

That sounded interesting. "Could you show me? If you have time," Eve hastened to say. She wondered how the equipment differed from the software they used at AltaVista.

"Sure," Renata said after a moment's hesitation. "I could do that."

"Today? After I get my gown?" Eve pressed. It wasn't like she'd be here very long. The Night Sky Bonfire was tomorrow night.

"Why not? Clem's got everything under control, I'm sure."

"Not as good as you would," Eve said loyally.

"That's enough brownnosing."

But Renata looked far more cheerful than she'd been when she arrived.

Eve wasn't the only one questioning her future, apparently. It had been interesting to hear Renata's cynical take on Base Camp. Interesting, but Eve found she saw things differently. She thought the men and women of Base Camp were onto something. From what she'd seen of the planet through the images that crossed her desk, there were changes coming most people weren't prepared for. Downsizing would be the least of the changes they all needed to make. People were going to need to work together more, the way Anders and the others were doing.

She wished she could stay here long enough to learn more about the solutions they were creating, but she had her real life to get home to, such as it was. Going back to school was going to seem like a let-down after this.

ANDERS DIDN'T SEE Eve again until dinnertime, and he was beginning to feel frustrated by the time she appeared with the rest of the women, dressed like them in a pretty, wine-colored Regency gown. Over the top of it, she wore a long thick coat that echoed the lines of her dress, as well as boots, mittens, a scarf and a hat.

"Alice came through in spades," Riley said brightly as they all filed into the bunkhouse. "Doesn't Eve look pretty?"

"She does." Anders nodded his appreciation and hoped Eve could see how much he meant it. He knew the first four women who'd joined Base Camp had taken to wearing Regency garb as a way to remind them why they'd walked away from their jobs and taken a chance on the more artistic pursuits they'd studied in college. He appreciated the fact they'd continued the tradition even as they'd been dragged onto the television show and other women had come to live here, too. He knew the old-fashioned clothes could get in the way of modern pursuits, and recently he'd overheard a funny conversation and learned most of the women were wearing yoga pants under their gowns for the duration of the winter, but the truth was in those clothes they looked—

He didn't even know how to put it. Whatever it was, it tugged on something deep inside him. Something masculine. Anders had served in the military long enough to know that most of the differences people liked to chalk up between men and women were—in a word—bullshit. The women he'd met along the way were every bit as smart, just as good at tactics, just as hard-nosed when it came to making the tough decisions, every bit as good at leading others, and as tough—if not tougher—than the men who served alongside them.

Women were badasses.

They were also—pretty. When they wanted to be. When shit went down overseas, you didn't think in terms of masculine or feminine, pretty or ugly. You just got the job done, and so did they. Here it was different. Things were peaceful. There was time in the day to consider the way a beautiful woman's gown enhanced her figure. The way a sideways glance from under her long lashes sent a zing of desire through him.

Lord knew he was zinging all over the place with Eve so close.

"I thought I'd see you again earlier," he said to Eve and could have kicked himself for sounding so eager when several people around them smirked.

"I spent the afternoon with Renata." Eve hung up her coat with the others near the door.

"Renata?" Greg asked from where he sat near one of the windows, whittling. "What'd you two do?"

Good question, Anders thought. Renata was usually as prickly as a cactus.

"We just… hung out," Eve said airily. "What's for dinner?"

A neat way to turn the conversation, Anders thought some minutes later when everyone had settled down to eat a hearty bison stew. Renata let herself into the bunkhouse partway through the meal. Anders watched her head for the kitchen, wondering again what the women had found to talk about.

He realized Greg was watching the director, too.

"Hi, Renata," Eve called out when she caught sight of her. "Try the stew; it's delicious!"

"Will do," Renata said cheerfully as she passed by.

Anders met Greg's surprised look. Normally the director had little to say to any of them if she wasn't bossing them around.

"Hey, Renata," Greg called out a moment later when he'd recovered from his shock. "There's a chair here for you when you've got your food." He patted one that was near to his.

Renata, just reaching the kitchen door, turned a look on him that could melt tar in the Arctic. "I'm not blind. I can distinguish the empty chairs from occupied ones." She stalked into the kitchen and didn't come out again.

Angus made a crashing and burning sound and

spread his fingers to emulate a big explosion. Greg rolled his eyes and got back to eating.

"Really, what did you two talk about?" Anders asked Eve again when conversation around them turned general and he got the chance.

She pretended to zip her mouth shut. "It's a secret. You'll never get it out of me." She was in an awfully good mood for someone who'd spent part of the afternoon with their cranky director.

"You sure about that?" Anders angled his chair closer to hers and deepened his voice, leaning in to murmur into her ear, "I have my ways."

"Really? Navy SEAL ways?" She shot him an amused glance.

This close he could see a dusting of light freckles on her cheeks. Was she flirting with him? Anders thought she might be.

"They do teach us a lot of different tactics," he teased back.

"Like what?"

She was definitely flirting with him. Anders remembered what his friends had said. Announce your intention to marry her. Get her drunk and play a game of quarters. Pick her up at the airport and drive straight to the chapel. None of the other men had played by the rules to win their women.

Why should he?

"Like this." He leaned in, glanced around to see that no one was looking, brushed a quick kiss over her cheekbone, near her ear, and drew back—

Crossed his arms and looked down at her. "Spill everything you know."

Eve gawked up at him until a smile tugged at the corner of her mouth. "Does that usually work?"

"How do you think we found where Bin Laden was hiding?"

Eve elbowed him playfully. "You're making that up."

"Maybe." He leaned closer again. "Maybe not."

Eve took a bite of her stew. "Sorry, I can't tell you what we talked about. Not yet," she added. "Maybe sometime. But when I'm done eating this, you'll probably be able to persuade me to go back for a second helping." She indicated her bowl.

"You've got it." He didn't push the matter. He'd gotten what he really wanted: a chance to kiss Eve. To joke with her.

To make it clear he viewed their budding relationship as something other than a platonic one.

She hadn't shut him down. On the contrary, she'd kept things going.

That had to mean something, he told himself happily as they got in line for a second helping of food.

EVE WOKE UP to the quiet buzz of her phone and knew Melissa had to be texting. She kept notifications from her on even when she turned everything else off. She slipped out of her sleeping bag and crossed to the bathroom. Once inside, she locked the door and looked at her phone.

Problem, Melissa had texted. *Even if Clem films you all week, he'll still have time to cut you out of the episode after you show the Hansen Oil images. They must have tons of footage from a week's worth of shooting. No one would know you'd ever been there if he decides not to put you in.*

What's the alternative? And why are you awake? Hope texted back.

Stay for more than one week, Melissa wrote. *Once they air an episode with you on it, they'll have to keep going with the footage, even if you blow the whole thing up. The audience would demand to know what happened to you if you simply disappeared. That means you'd better grab their hearts—and their attention— right off the bat. Then during the second week—right at the last minute—you pull out all your information about Hansen Oil.*

It sounded good, but there were two problems. One, she'd need to ask for more vacation time, which might make her boss suspicious. Two, if Kevin saw her on *Base Camp*, he'd definitely know she was up to something.

As soon as my boss sees me, he'll tell Johannes Hansen, she texted. *I'm pretty sure he's afraid of Hansen. Then Hansen will come after me.*

There's a delay, right? You'll be almost through the next week by the time the first episode airs. There would be only a few days before you could make your big splash about Hansen Oil and leave.

Eve didn't like the thought of leaving, but Melissa was right. *Base Camp* aired almost in real time but not quite. Maybe she could pull off staying a little longer. As soon as possible after the first episode aired, though, she'd have to get away.

She had no idea where she'd go then.

Could she return to Richmond and make good on the deal she'd made with her parents? Move into a tiny house in their backyard and start school as if her time in Chance Creek had never happened? Would trouble follow her? What could a company like Hansen Oil do to someone who'd exposed its wrongdoing?

You really think that's a good idea? she asked Melissa.

I think it's the only way to make it work.

You never said why you're awake.

Just couldn't sleep. Better go try some more now.

Me, too.

Later that morning, Eve helped Avery get into her Regency clothes.

"Don't the men mind us hogging the bathroom?" she asked.

"They're used to me hogging it. There are composting toilet facilities located in several places around Base Camp—and outdoor showers when the weather is better. Plus they're a lot less shy about changing in public than I am," she confided. "So… you and Anders… I saw him kiss you yesterday."

Eve was glad Avery couldn't see her face as she did up the back of Avery's dress. "It was just a peck on the cheek."

A brush of his mouth that had set every nerve in her body alight. She'd thought about it over and over since then, spinning out a fantasy of what else could happen between them until the thought of it made her ache.

Every time she tried to corral her imagination, it got away from her again until she was envisioning Anders in her sleeping bag with her. Holding her. Kissing her.

And doing oh, so much more.

She was in trouble.

She couldn't stay away from Anders. Not if she wanted to pull this off.

"We were just joking around," she told Avery.

"Hmm. Then there's Renata. You seem to have made an impression on her, too. I can't believe you got her to smile."

"All you have to do to make Renata smile is talk about her favorite thing. Filmmaking. There, done."

"Your turn."

Eve stood up straight as Avery moved behind her to lace up her corset. It wasn't tight like a Civil War–era corset would have been; it was more of a structural garment that gave her the right shape for her Regency gown.

"Filmmaking is my favorite thing, too," Avery said.

"And you've never discussed it with Renata?"

"No." Avery laughed. "Never even occurred to me."

Eve supposed that was because Renata called the shots around here—or had until Clem showed up. Avery wasn't the only one who seemed a little afraid of the director. Renata didn't frighten Eve, though. She reminded her of her aunt Patricia, an outspoken woman who'd made a career out of advocating for children in the foster care program in Virginia. According to Eve's mother, Patricia hadn't started out so blunt and no-nonsense. She'd become like that when she realized it was what it took to get the job done.

"Can you keep a secret?" she asked Avery.

"Definitely." Avery smiled wryly and shook her head at some private thought. "What is it?"

"Renata started teaching me to edit film yesterday. We're getting together again this morning while Anders is doing his chores. You know I work for a satellite imaging company, but I've never worked on video. It's great." It had occurred to her that maybe she could put together a short video about Hansen Oil to put on the internet after she exposed the company on air.

"I bet. Renata must have some awesome equipment."

"Want to join us?"

Avery looked wistful. "I've got chores to do, and I'd be a third wheel, anyway."

"I'm not *dating* Renata; she's just showing me a few things." Eve hadn't expected Avery to hold back like this. Several times on the show Avery had mentioned wanting to make movies.

"How about this," Avery said. "Let's you and I get some footage. We've got time before breakfast. When you work with Renata, we'll see what you can do with it."

"That sounds great." She could definitely use the practice.

They dressed up in their warm outer gear, and she followed Avery outside.

"Let's start with the kittens," Avery said.

Avery led the way to the barn and took Eve to see what turned out to be the handful of half-grown cats Curtis and Hope had rescued during their fateful trip across Montana.

"They're not much use as barn cats," Avery said. "Everyone's spoiling them rotten. I won't be surprised if they turn into tiny-house cats."

They ended up filming a kitten Olympics, getting footage of the cats jumping for treats, prowling along a "balance beam" and having wrestling matches.

"You could add music and sound effects and put it on the show's website," Avery suggested.

"Evelyn Wright, are you up there?" a man called.

Eve and Avery stiffened.

"Clem," Avery mouthed. Neither said a word.

"For God's sake." Clem's head poked over the top of the ladder a moment later. "I can hear you rustling around. You're needed for an interview. Now."

Eve sighed and followed him down to the ground.

"You can go," Clem said to Avery when she made it down, too.

"I'll stay."

"Fine." Clem waited for the camera crew with him to set up, then asked Eve a string of personal questions she didn't want to answer but felt she had to. They covered her name, age, status, job and other mundane things. Just when Eve thought it would end, Clem leaned closer. "Did you make up that story about your ex-boyfriend?"

"Do I look like the kind of woman who makes up stories?" she managed to say but not before a telling hesitation.

"Some attention-seekers will do anything for an audience."

"I'm not an attention-seeker," she lied.

"What do you think about Anders?"

She wanted to turn on her heel and march out of the barn, but she needed Clem to want to keep her here. *Drama*, she told herself. *Give him drama.* "Anders is… pretty hot."

Clem's eyebrows shot up. He must not have expected that kind of candor.

"So, you like him?"

"What woman wouldn't? Have you seen him without his shirt on?" Too late she realized what she'd just revealed.

"Have you?" Clem moved closer. "Have you two already done the nasty?"

"Done the nasty?" Avery repeated loudly. "Are you in second grade?"

"Bumped uglies. Made the beast with two backs. Done the dirty deed," Clem continued, eyes gleaming.

"No," Eve said shortly. This was embarrassing.

"But you want to."

She bit back a denial, remembering everything she'd seen watching *Base Camp* up until now. The show was about sustainability, but really it was about relationships.

"Yes," she said, lifting her chin. "As a matter of fact, I can't wait to bump uglies with Anders."

Avery laughed. Clem sputtered a moment, trying to regain his smug expression but failing. "I suppose you'll squawk if I tell him you said that."

"Would you tell him?" she asked sweetly. "Because if I have to wait another night for him to slide into my sleeping bag, I think I'll explode." Not far from the truth, she admitted to herself, but she was laying it on so thick Clem would think she was joking.

"You think you're funny, don't you?" Clem gestured to the film crew. "Cut. That's enough. But you know what?" he said to Eve. "I will tell him. What's more, I'll show him. Bet that SEAL will ride you hard and put you away wet tonight." He laughed when her mouth dropped open in shock.

"Ee-ww!" Avery said. "Clem, you're disgusting. Get out of here."

To Eve's relief, he did, trailed by the crew.

"I'm sorry you were subjected to that," Avery said. "What on earth possessed you to rile him up? Or is it true?"

"It's a little true," Eve admitted, making sure no one else was close enough to hear, "but I'll deny that if you repeat it."

"I hope you fall in love with Anders," Avery said. "I like you, Evelyn Wright."

CHAPTER SIX

"T ELL ME ABOUT your home," Anders asked Eve at lunchtime. He'd been disappointed she'd chosen to spend the morning first with Avery, then with Renata, but she'd joined him as soon as she entered the bunkhouse, which he took as a positive sign. Anders leaned back in his folding chair, wishing the weather was warm enough for them to eat around the campfire outside like they had all summer. It was far more idyllic than sitting all squashed together in the bunkhouse.

"There isn't much to tell. I live in Richmond—in an apartment." She ducked her head, as if embarrassed by this. "I have two sisters and a brother. They're all married and have kids."

"You're the baby?" Anders guessed.

"No." She made a face. "No," she said more softly. "I'm second oldest. And before you ask, yes, I do know it's time I thought about settling down."

"You hear that a lot, huh?"

"Sure do. You said you were from Texas? Why don't you have an accent?"

"Lost it in the service."

"When did you join up?" She took a bite of the lasagna Kai had prepared for dinner and sighed with happiness. When she'd realized he'd replaced the noodles with thinly sliced zucchini, she'd expected it to be disappointing. It wasn't. He hadn't stinted on the cheese, and it was delicious. "This is good."

"It is," he agreed. "I joined up as soon as I could when I was eighteen. Spent over a decade with the Navy."

"Didn't like it back home?" She took another bite.

"No. Mom passed when I was eight. Then it was just my dad and me. We never did see eye to eye about much. Luckily, my uncle and I did. I spent a lot of time on his ranch when I was young, but it wasn't enough. I needed a ticket out." He made a show of digging into his meal. He didn't want to get into his past too much.

"The Navy was your ticket?"

"That's right. I learned a lot, saw the world, as they say. Joined up with Boone and the rest of the guys, and here I am."

She took a final bite of lasagna and set her plate aside, wiping her mouth with a napkin when she was done. "What got you interested in the environment—and bison?"

Anders smiled. This was what he wanted to talk about. "I've been an environmentalist since I was a teenager. I saw a lot more to convince me during my time with the Navy, but it was the side trips I took that got me hooked on the idea of saving the world. Some guys spend their leave at home. Some blow their money taking fancy trips, staying at hotels. You know, making up for all the barracks and plain living we do most of the time. I was the opposite. I started going places that were really off-grid. The farther away from civilization, the better. I saw some stuff, believe me."

"I bet."

Anders liked the way she watched him while he talked. Her whole attention on him.

"One thing I noticed was the difference in the environments where hunter-gatherers lived and where farmers or herders lived."

She cocked her head.

Anders tried to explain. "It makes sense that they're really different. When you're a hunter-gatherer, you need your landscape to be as diverse as possible because it has to provide for all your needs. When you farm or ranch, the goal is to make the land produce as much as possible of a small subset of crops or animals. First you clear everything else away and keep it away. Then you direct all your scientific and technological advances toward that end—getting more of a single crop."

"I definitely see that in satellite images. Each crop has a specific color, so you get monotone squares or circles when you photograph them from above."

"Exactly. The United States has run with it. It's far more efficient to monocrop. You can mechanize planting and harvesting. On the downside, you have to add a lot of fertilizer and pesticides to monocrops. They aren't good at defending themselves against insects, and they deplete the soil."

"Where do bison come into all this?"

Her interest in one of his favorite subjects was almost an aphrodisiac. Anders wanted to reach out and trace the line of her jaw. But they didn't have that kind of relationship yet. All he could do was woo her with words.

Was he wooing her? Suddenly worried, he bent closer. Maybe he was boring her.

"Well?" she prompted.

Maybe he wasn't boring her quite yet.

"Bison belong here naturally. They eat what the prairie provides and, in doing so, actually help it regenerate. Their dung acts as a natural fertilizer as they graze. Their hooves mix the dung in with the soil. We don't have to add petroleum-based fertilizers, and we don't have to supplement their feed during the winter, either, like we have to do with cattle. Bison can handle the snow. We're not exactly hunter-gatherers, but we're not exactly ranchers in the traditional sense, either."

"You do grow crops here, too."

"We do. We're experimenting with different processes to learn what's best. This first year we went about things in pretty standard ways, but we intend to try intercropping among other things."

She nodded. "It must be gratifying to know that what you're doing is restoring balance to this area."

"It's just one ranch." Sometimes he wondered if they were pissing in the wind, television show or no television show.

"That's where you start—solving one problem at a time."

As if she knew how to get that done. She'd set off after high school with the best intentions and come home on a stretcher. Had anything she'd accomplished during that time made a difference?

She'd been relieved when she'd realized earlier that despite his threats, Clem hadn't shown Anders the footage of her saying she wanted to sleep with him.

Yet.

She enjoyed talking to him like this—a lot. Sex with Anders would be something special. She was sure of that. Talking was... foreplay. And since the topic interested her, it was interesting foreplay.

She realized she was smiling.

Anders smiled back ruefully. "I get going about bison and don't know when to stop," he said.

"I'm not bored," she said forthrightly. "Not at all. I love listening to you."

Her words registered with him, and he leaned closer. She liked the way his dark eyes searched hers. Anders was a very handsome man, and Base Camp was a very appealing place.

She'd better watch herself.

"You might regret saying that." He chuckled.

"I doubt it."

It had been a while since she'd flirted with someone so openly. She'd been in a bit of a rut back home, Eve realized.

How had that happened?

Her last boyfriend, she decided. The last real one. Heath. James might be a figment of her imagination—a hyped-up character she'd created with Melissa—but Heath had taken what was left of her confidence and stomped on it when he'd dumped her. She'd barely gone out since then.

"Eve? You okay?" Anders asked.

He was close enough their positions felt intimate, even though they sat in a crowded room. Anders's jaw was strong, his eyelashes as dark as his hair.

"Why aren't you blond?" she asked. "Anders is a Swedish name, right?"

"It is, but my mom—"

Eve couldn't help herself. She leaned forward and kissed him.

And kissed him again.

When she pulled away, Anders grinned.

"Sorry," she said.

"What for?" He moved closer, slid a hand under her hair to cup her head and kissed her back, a good, long kiss that left her whole body humming. "It was a good idea," he told her.

She looked up and spotted Clem watching them. And Byron filming them.

"I'm not sure of that. I won't be here long."

Anders studied her, then seemed to notice they were receiving a lot of amused glances and covert looks. "Let's take this one day at a time, okay?"

"Okay," she heard herself say.

"WHAT'S MORE ROMANTIC than looking at the stars?" Curtis asked Anders in an undertone as they climbed out of the truck they'd driven to the Night Sky Bonfire. Hope, Avery and Eve climbed out of the back seat and straightened their long jackets and gowns.

Anders shrugged.

"You'll make big strides with Eve tonight if you play your cards right. I'll try to head off Clem and the crew as best I can. Give you a little privacy."

"Good luck with that." Clem seemed determined to stick close. And ask far too many questions. He'd taken to jumping out at him in odd moments and peppering him with questions about his youth. Where did he go to summer camp? Who was his favorite teacher? Who was his best friend? According to Anders's contract, he was supposed to answer direct questions. He felt like a failed politician with his I don't knows, I don't recalls, and other evasions.

When a string of fireworks went off some yards away, Anders whirled and fell into a defensive crouch before almost immediately realizing what was going on. Speaking of Clem, there he was, and one of the cameramen had caught his defensive maneuver on film.

Perfect.

"Done that plenty of times myself," Curtis said, but he was chuckling. Had Eve seen him? Anders checked, but she was chatting with the other women. Good.

He wasn't the only one surprised by the fireworks. A murmur had run through the gathering when they went off, and Anders spotted Cab Johnson, the local sheriff, threading his way through the throng to find the perpetrators. A moment later, he collared a couple of teenagers and marched them off.

Anders bit back a grin. He could only hope that was the extent of the mayhem committed here tonight. He needed to focus on Eve and give this budding relationship between them a decent chance.

"Hey, Anders," Clem called out. "I've got something here you should see." He held up his phone and beckoned him over. Anders closed the distance between them reluctantly.

Eve turned, and when Clem said, "Watch this. Eve had something to say earlier," her mouth opened and her eyes widened.

Avery turned, too, and bustled over as if she'd grab the phone from Clem's hand, but Avery was petite and Clem was tall. He held it up high in one hand, tapped the screen with the other and turned the sound up loud. Anders made out Eve, Avery and Clem onscreen, standing in the barn.

"Have you seen him without his shirt on?" Eve was asking. Clem had the sound up so loud several other people in the vicinity turned to see what was going on.

Avery jumped again, but Clem reached out, palmed her head and held her down, lifting the phone even higher.

"Clem, that's enough," Anders said, but the footage went on.

"Have *you*?" Clem asked on the tiny screen. "Have you two already done the nasty?"

"Done the nasty?" That was Avery. "Are you in second grade?"

Good question, Anders thought.

"Bumped uglies?" Clem said onscreen. "Made the beast with two backs? Done the dirty deed?"

"No," Eve said on the video.

The real Eve looked like she wanted to sink into the ground. Anders didn't blame her.

"But you want to," Clem said onscreen.

Despite himself, Anders's gaze flicked back up to Clem's phone, and he waited for Eve's answer. Surely she'd denied it.

"Yes," Eve said on the footage. "As a matter of fact, I can't wait to bump uglies with Anders."

Anders laughed, but he couldn't help the images flooding his mind. Getting Eve alone, pushing deep inside her, pumping until—

Hell.

He didn't mean to look at her, but he did and found Eve still wide-eyed, a butterfly caught—pinned and framed—on a wall.

"Clem, you're an asshole," he managed to say.

"Just thought you'd want to know," Clem said gleefully. "Now you can skip all the boring stuff and get right to the action." He ducked when Anders lunged at him, surprising him with his dexterity. "Remember what Curtis said. Don't hit the director!" he taunted as he backpedaled away.

It took three of the men to restrain Anders.

Someday he'd get his revenge.

IF IT HADN'T been for Clem, Eve would have enjoyed this gathering. The weather had cooperated, and the sky overhead was a sea of stars. Part of the field near the high school had been flooded to form an ice rink that was full of skaters. Several telescopes had been set up in a darker patch, and people stood in line to get their chance at a celestial view.

A bonfire burned between the ice rink and a concession stand, where people bought hot chocolate and various baked goods.

She was too busy wishing the ground would swallow her whole to be able to enjoy it.

Why, oh why had she thought it was a good idea to say what she'd said to Clem? Now Anders thought she was the kind of woman who jumped into any warm bed. There wasn't anything she could say to defend herself, either.

That didn't keep her from trying.

"I didn't mean… He was being so obnoxious…" she stuttered when Clem escaped and Boone, Greg and Curtis let Anders go again.

"You don't have to explain," Anders said. "We've all lashed out at the crew at one time or another. I know you didn't mean it."

The thing was, she did. She hesitated, not knowing what to say. When a corner of Anders's mouth quirked up, she closed her eyes.

She opened them a moment later to find he'd moved closer, and the others had melted away into the crowd. She spotted Curtis and Hope getting in line to look through one of the telescopes. Riley and Boone were headed toward the ice rink.

"Maybe you did mean it," Anders said softly. He tilted her chin up with one finger and bent toward her, giving her all the time in the world to move away.

She didn't.

She let him kiss her, lightly at first, and when he captured her mouth with his, wrapped his arms around her and kissed her for real, she kissed him back.

"I've been waiting to do that forever," he said when they came up for air.

"You've known me forty-eight hours," she pointed out unsteadily. "And you kissed me earlier today."

"You mean *you* kissed *me*. Now I want to do it again."

She let him, and he brushed his mouth over hers once, twice, and pulled her closer, deepening the connection until she was weak in the knees.

"Guess we can't do that all night," Anders said when they broke apart.

She nearly asked why not, but he was right. They were in a public place, and she barely knew him, and she was leaving—

"Want to skate?"

"I… sure."

Portable spotlights had been set up around the ice rink. Eve and Anders stood in line to secure rental skates, then sat on a bench near the rink to put them on. Everyone seemed to be leaving their boots where they were, so they did, too, and picked their way through the snow toward the ice.

It had been a while since she'd skated, but she used to go to a local ice rink when she was a child, and she was competent. Anders took her hand, and they started out slowly, increasing their speed as they found their balance.

"It's been a long time," Anders said. "Forgot how much I like this."

"You skated in Texas?"

"Yep. Believe it or not."

He was good, his strokes sure, and he kept her upright a time or two when she would have fallen. The crowd was full of families and children, all having a good time, but it seemed to Eve there was an edge to the festivities. The darkness pushed in at the light. On these long winter nights, the boundary between the worlds was thin, if mythology was to be believed.

She caught sight of Riley and Boone. Then Avery—and even Walker. The tall Native American man looked at ease on his skates, too, and Eve remembered he was a local. Probably everyone in Montana grew up skating.

"All right, folks, time for a little music!" a man called out as loudspeakers crackled to life nearby. "Find your partner and hold hands for a little romantic skating!"

Anders squeezed Eve's hand as a waltz filled the air. Eve curled her fingers around his, and they skated together in time to the music.

"This is kind of fun," she said after a minute.

"A little tame. But not bad."

Eve laughed. "You have to start somewhere."

"True." He sped up a little and whipped her around the turn. Eve shrieked and clung to him.

"If you let go, I'm going to go flying!"

"I won't let go." He slowed a little but kept her arm in his. "Where'd you learn to skate?"

"At a local rink. I took lessons."

"Didn't know they had skating in Virginia."

"It gets cold there in winter. Cool," she amended when he laughed at her. "Not as cold as Montana, I guess."

"You got that right."

"How about you? Where'd you learn to skate?"

"Same. Local rink. I played hockey for years."

"Really? Were you any good?"

"Was I any good?" he growled and pulled her closer. "Hell yeah, I was good." He put his right arm around her shoulder and held her hand with his left. Eve liked the contact. From the satisfied smile on Anders's face, he liked it, too.

They continued on until the music stopped, then glided toward the outer edge of the rink. When they came to a halt, Anders pulled her close again.

Eve met his mouth with her own, resting her hands on his arms, going up on tiptoe in her skates to reach him.

His kiss felt good, and Eve didn't want it to stop. When he broke it off, she steadied herself, still holding on to him, before stepping back as a new song started. He linked his arm with hers and began to skate again.

She kept pace, wondering how she'd ever bear to leave Anders behind when the time came.

She probably wouldn't have a choice. He might like her now, but when she used his show to expose Hansen Oil and unleashed a firestorm of negative attention from the company, he'd realize she'd come here under false pretenses.

She didn't want to contemplate that.

"Is there anything about Texas you like?" Eve asked Anders.

He thought about it. "The sky," he said finally. "The storms. They're something to see."

"I'll bet. You don't mind these kind of winters?"

"Not at all. I like seasons. How about you?"

"I like winter, but I have a feeling it lingers here a little too long for my taste."

Anders was quiet, and Eve remembered he was trying to convince her to marry him.

Or was he?

He hadn't actually mentioned matrimony so far. She imagined he was trying her on for size, in a manner of speaking, but if she kept dissing Montana's climate, he'd think she was telling him she wasn't interested.

"I imagine you get used to it, though," she added hurriedly.

Anders just nodded. "Should we go look at the stars?" he asked a few minutes later.

Eve, who'd been searching for something to talk about, accepted gratefully. "My feet are getting cold," she admitted.

"Can't have that." When they sat on the bench to change back into their boots, Anders took first one of her feet and then the other into his hands and chafed them vigorously. "How's that? Any better?"

Eve had fallen into a daydream about other ways those hands could warm her up and struggled to answer. "G-great." She hurried to put her boots on. She couldn't remember ever being so susceptible to a man's touch before. Had Heath ever made her feel this way?

She didn't think so.

But then Heath wasn't Anders. He wasn't nearly as handsome. Or as gentle. Or as rugged, either, she admitted to herself, remembering the way Anders had gone after Clem.

She was going to miss Anders when she left.

They returned their skates and joined the line for one of the telescopes, and when Anders put an arm around her shoulder and drew her close for warmth, she allowed herself to enjoy it.

Out of the corner of her eye, she spotted Clem and a camera crew, focusing on her.

Better make this good.

Her need to keep Clem's interest was the only reason she was standing on tiptoe and pressing a kiss to Anders's cheek, she told herself a moment later, but when he bent down to meet her mouth with his, she forgot about everything else.

Twenty minutes later, it was finally their turn, and Eve took turns with Anders looking at the stars, moon and other features of the night sky, tutored by an excited man who obviously loved everything about astronomy.

By the time they made their way to the bonfire, she was ready to sit down.

"How about I get us some cocoa?" Anders asked.

"Sounds lovely," she said.

She hadn't seen any sign of the camera crew for at least fifteen minutes and had assumed Clem had gotten bored while she and Anders were stargazing, so when she found a section of log near the fire to sit on, and Clem plunked down on the section beside her, Eve bit back a sigh.

"Having fun?" he asked as if he didn't believe it was possible at an event like this.

"As a matter of fact, yes."

"You're falling for him, aren't you? Starting to think seriously about staying?"

She wasn't sure how to answer that, so she told the truth. "Thinking about it."

"You don't know the guy very well, though. Who knows what he got up to before he came here?"

He was fishing for drama again. Trying to create problems where there were none. "He was a Navy SEAL."

"What else do you know about him?" Clem challenged her.

"He's from Texas."

"Anyone would know that from *Base Camp*'s website. He hasn't told you anything about himself, has he?"

"Sure he has."

"Name one thing you know that the viewing audience at home doesn't."

His insinuating tone bothered her. Anders was taking his time getting to know her, like any normal man would. They hadn't exchanged pedigrees. "He's a hockey player."

Clem straightened. "Hockey player? No one from Texas plays hockey."

"He does."

"Imagine that," he drawled. "Anders has hidden depths. A real mystery man, that one. He popped into the world fully grown, you know," he added conspiratorially.

"What is that supposed to mean?" Could she push him away? Clem had gotten far too close for comfort.

"Look him up. Anders Olsen doesn't exist until he's eighteen. He was never a child."

"I just told you he played hockey growing up."

Clem shrugged. "Look up Evelyn Wright, and you'll find her Girl Scout jamboree picture from when she was nine. Look up Anders Olsen and… nothing."

He stood up and left, striding off like he hadn't a care in the world, leaving Eve puzzled over what he'd said. He was right; she had gone to the Girl Scout jamboree when she was nine. Had Anders managed to keep his childhood off the internet? That was a feat these days. Did Navy SEALs hide their past as a matter of course? Had he simply not been active on social media when he was younger? Lots of people hadn't been, after all. Although, like Clem said, it seemed like lots of older photos ended up online anyway.

"Cold tonight, huh?" A woman sat down near her and broke into her thoughts.

"Yes. Thank goodness for whoever built this fire." Eve turned to smile at the newcomer and did a double take. "Melissa?"

"Shh. Been keeping an eye on you. Looks like things are going well."

"They are. For the most part."

Melissa leaned closer. "Love your dress. I'm totally jealous." She grew serious. "Was that Clem Bailey talking to you a minute ago?"

"You know Clem?"

"I know who he is—it's hard to miss *Tracking the Stars*. Remember my roommate in college? Jana? Her uncle knew him. She got to visit his show once a few years back. Said Clem was a total sleaze. He hit on her—while her uncle was standing right there."

"Yuck. He's directing *Base Camp* now, and he's a pain in the ass. He just said something really weird to me."

Melissa kept a watchful gaze on the crowd. "Directing *Base Camp*? That's strange. I wonder what happened to his gig at *Tracking the Stars*? What did he say?"

"He said Anders didn't exist before he was eighteen. That there's no information about him anywhere. He kept saying I don't know Anders well enough to fall for him—which is true, of course. I'm not here to marry Anders. Clem kept pushing, though. He asked for one thing I knew about Anders that no one else did."

"What'd you tell him?"

"He played hockey as a kid." Eve relayed the conversation.

Melissa looked thoughtful. "So now Clem has a place to start."

"What do you mean?"

"If there's something Anders doesn't want him to know about the past—something he or his parents were hiding by keeping off social media—Clem can find it. He knows Anders's age, right? And that he comes from Texas. Now he can search for hockey team photos from the right era. It could take some doing if lots of schools or towns had teams, which I can't imagine, but it shouldn't be that hard to find him."

"If there were photos, wouldn't Anders's name pop up?"

"Maybe. Maybe not if he wasn't tagged in them."

"Why would Clem bother looking for them when he's got Anders in the flesh to interview?"

"He's probably looking for the skeletons in Anders's closet—and yours. That's what Clem Bailey does—tries to embarrass people."

"Good thing I don't have many skeletons." Did Clem already know about her work for NGOs? Would he tell Anders about it? It's not like it was a big secret, but she'd been downplaying her past because she didn't want anyone to guess her real purpose for being here.

"I'd better go. Hang in there, okay?" Melissa said.

"You, too. You must be so bored at that hotel."

Melissa shrugged. "Not that bored. I… met a guy in

town. A cowboy—a real one. I guess technically a rancher. He owns his own place. We're going out to dinner tomorrow night."

"Really?" Eve perked up. This was an interesting development. She couldn't picture Melissa with a rancher.

"Might as well. When am I going to get another chance to date one?"

"I don't know. Have fun. Send me a photo."

"Will do. You have fun, too. Anders is even better looking in person."

"You're right," Eve admitted.

Melissa frowned. "Don't get hurt, Eve."

"I'm trying not to. See you soon."

Melissa slipped away into the crowd. Eve stood up, looking for Anders. She finally spotted him close to the head of the line at the concession stand and went to meet him. "I'm just going to duck into the bathroom. Be back in a minute," she told him.

Coming out of a stall a few minutes later, she bumped into Avery.

"Holding up all right?" Avery asked as they washed their hands and primped in front of the mirror.

"I'm having fun. I'm not in any hurry to get back out there, though. It's freezing."

"I know," Avery said sympathetically. "But you need a few romantic interludes before we can get to the part where you stay and marry Anders."

Eve, heading to the paper towel dispenser, nearly tripped over her own feet. "That's not a sure thing."

"Why not? He's hot for you."

"It's not like he's got a lot of choices, right?" She hadn't heard a word about any other women in the running. From what she'd seen, Chance Creek was a small town. Anders's only other option was to find a woman online.

She'd yet to see him spending much time on his phone.

Avery, looking in the mirror, straightened her hat. "He took one look at you when you washed up here and fell hard."

"You think?" Eve didn't believe that. He was a man, and she was a woman, and nature was taking its course, but a man like Anders wasn't going to fall head over heels with her at first sight.

In her case, she'd been lusting after him for months. It was only natural her hormones would kick into high gear when she got here.

"Yeah, I think. He's the one whose arms you collapsed in. He's the one who carried you into the bunkhouse. It's Fate. Now get back out there and lure him to the altar."

Eve had to laugh, and when she left the ladies' room, her step was lighter than when she'd gone in. She found Anders where she left him.

"Thanks," she said when he handed her a hot cocoa. "What a night, huh?" They watched a young man walk by in a down jacket and shorts as they made their way to the bonfire.

"I've been people watching," Anders said. "There

are definitely some characters out."

"You got that right." Clem was certainly one of them with his assertions that Anders had never been a child. "Anders Olsen is your real name, right?" she joked.

Anders choked on the drink he'd just taken, coughed and spluttered, and finally found his voice. "What kind of question is that? Is Eve Wright *your* real name?"

Hell. Double hell. If he thought she was interrogating him, he might start interrogating her back. How could she deflect him?

Drama.

"It is for now," she said quickly. "But Eve *Olsen* has a ring to it, doesn't it?"

Anders blinked, and too late Eve realized what she'd done. She'd distracted him, all right, which was good.

She'd also essentially proposed to him.

Whoops.

CHAPTER SEVEN

*E*VE OLSEN.

Anders took a breath, opened his mouth to speak. Closed it again.

Anders Olsen is your real name, right?

He didn't know what to make of her question. Had Eve somehow figured out his ruse, or... did she want to marry him?

She looked almost as shocked by what she'd said as he felt, and Anders didn't know how to answer her. He had to say something, though, or she might guess that she'd just uncovered his secret.

"Eve Olsen," he repeated slowly, buying time. "Yeah. It does have a ring. But—"

"I didn't mean you have to marry me. Shit. Shit, shit, shit," Eve said. "Now you think I'm some desperate celebrity chaser, and I'm not. I swear. I just—it just popped into my head—"

Anders relaxed a little. Her embarrassment wasn't feigned. "I didn't think you were proposing," he assured her. "You just caught me off guard. I always thought I would be the one to pop the question."

"You will be! I mean, I want it to be you. I mean, I don't want—" Eve gave up with a groan that made Anders chuckle.

"I know what you mean," he said.

"I'm just going to curl up on the ground and die," she said mournfully. "Me and my big mouth."

"When it's time to propose—if it's time to propose—I'll do the honors." He nudged her with his shoulder. "Does this mean you're considering it?"

"Marrying you? I don't expect you to want to marry me," she said in a rush, "but with Clem practically dictating that you do, it's hard for me not to at least think about it—abstractly."

"And what do you think about marrying me and living at Base Camp for good—abstractly?" Would she brush off the question or answer it?

Eve looked away. "I don't know," she said finally. "I didn't come here looking for this, you know?"

"I do know. You had a boyfriend."

She blinked, as if she'd forgotten all about him. Good. That was progress.

"I… like it here," Eve said. "I like… you."

"That's a good start."

"WE'RE READY TO head home if you are." Boone caught up to them near the bonfire.

"I'm ready to get warm," Eve told him. "What about you, Anders?"

"Sure thing."

She was grateful their conversation had been interrupted. Good thing it would be time for bed when they got home so she wouldn't have the chance to slip up again and ruin everything. Thank goodness Anders had bought that she was thinking of marriage—and didn't realize she was repeating Clem's insinuations. It had never even occurred to her that questioning Anders's bona fides would get him questioning hers.

That had been a narrow escape. She couldn't afford to mess up like that again.

In the truck, Hope rode up front with Curtis, and Eve was sandwiched in back between Anders and Avery. Anders found her hand in the dark and held it all the way home. She let him, torn between desire and worry.

Back at Base Camp, he detained her when the others trooped inside.

"Just want a minute alone," he whispered before drawing her into another kiss. His mouth moved over hers softly at first but then demanded more. Despite her intentions, Eve gave in and leaned against him in the snow, enjoying every minute of it. When his hands slipped to her waist and he tugged her closer, she nearly moaned. She'd give anything for the chance to be with him.

She was well and truly in trouble.

And she couldn't stop now.

SHE'D HELD HIS hand the whole way home. Kissed him several times.

They'd talked about marriage.

That had to mean something, Anders thought. "I had a good time tonight," he told her.

"Me, too."

It was cold out here, but he didn't make a move to go inside. "Eve—" Anders made up his mind he wasn't going to hold back, even if he was concerned he was moving too fast. He didn't know if it was Fate that Eve landed here when she did, or just circumstance, but he meant to make the most of it. He liked everything about Eve. Her feistiness. Her interest in his work. The way she immediately got along with the others—even Renata, whom no one got along with.

She was intelligent. Caring.

Beautiful.

Until he'd met her, he hadn't realized how much he'd been keeping to himself these past few years. Didn't realize that part of the reason he'd joined Base Camp was because he'd known he'd have to take a relationship deeper than he'd allowed himself for a long time. First his feud with his father, then his time with the service had kept him thinking short-term rather than about marriage.

Now he wanted to find his match.

He wanted Eve.

If only they could be alone for a minute...

Anders considered the situation. "Listen, my house isn't finished inside, but it's got four walls and a roof. We could go there—" He threw an arm up to protect himself from the sudden glare of a floodlight. Clem and a cameraman stood nearby. The camera was rolling. Capturing everything they did.

Everything they said.

How long had they been there?

"By all means, let's go to your house, Anders. Filming inside will be much warmer," Clem said with a shit-eating grin.

Anders stifled a curse. He took Eve's hand and hurriedly ushered her toward the bunkhouse instead. "You've got great timing," he muttered to Clem as he passed.

"Always have. So, Eve…" The man got in Eve's face. "Looks like you've managed to get close to Anders. How long have you been following *Base Camp*? Was Anders always your first choice out of the men on the show? Or would anyone do? Hey!"

Anders shoved Clem into a snowbank and whitewashed his face. The cameraman filmed it all, until Anders spotted him and snarled, "You want to take a turn?"

Byron stopped filming. "I'm good!" He backed away.

Anders turned in time to see Eve slip inside the building.

"Damn it," he said to Clem, who was coughing and sputtering, wiping snow from his face. "Now see what you've done."

"You're going to pay for that, Olsen."

"I already am."

"IT'S NOT USUALLY this bad," Avery said as they got ready for bed in the bathroom. Eve was helping Avery with her gown and corset. "Clem is really trying to stir things up. I'm sorry he said all that to you."

Eve's cheeks still burned from Clem's accusations. "I didn't come here to sleep with Anders," she said again. Maybe she had lusted after Anders in the quiet confines of her own home, but that didn't make her a groupie.

"Don't let Clem get to you."

He had gotten to her, though. Partly because he was right. Until a few days ago, she'd never imagined herself meeting the cast of *Base Camp*, let alone participating in the show, but she had been drawn to Anders since the first episode. He wasn't flashy like some of the other men. He didn't dominate a room the way Boone did when he showed up. He wasn't movie-star pretty like Jericho Cook. He didn't have a Scottish accent like Angus McBride, who'd been keeping a low profile lately because the woman he loved had left the show and gone back to California. Nor was he a joker like Curtis could be.

Anders was… Anders. A serious man with a funny, sexy streak who got things done and cared passionately about what he was doing. It was that quiet passion that had struck her right from the start.

Clem was right; she'd watched the show… and found Anders to her liking. That didn't mean she'd had some creepy crush on him back when she'd been watching him on TV.

Damn the interfering man. If Clem hadn't been around, she'd have gotten the chance to be alone with Anders. She'd wanted to go to his house. Wanted to discover what he'd do next. Would he have kissed her again?

Maybe tried for something more?

She went all warm and liquid inside just thinking about it. Maybe they'd known each other only a day or so. She was attracted to him.

Was that wrong?

Was she a groupie, after all?

"Stop it. I can tell Clem's gotten into your head. Whatever he's been saying, don't listen to him!" Avery insisted.

"He's saying I made this all happen somehow because I wanted to be with Anders."

Avery met her glance in the mirror curiously. "Did you telepathically force your boyfriend to dump you near Base Camp and drive off without you?"

"No!" And she kept forgetting her fake boyfriend. She had to keep her story straight.

"It would be an interesting superpower."

"I don't have a superpower." Eve had to laugh. Avery was right; she was being ridiculous. "Even if I did, I wouldn't use it to get dumped on a country road."

"Exactly," Avery said. "So Fate has thrown you and Anders together. Go with it, if that's what you want."

"I don't know what I want," Eve said, discouraged. "And I'm supposed to go back home to work in a few days." Except she needed to extend her time at Base

Camp without Anders proposing to her—or anyone discovering her true purpose here.

"You should stay through New Year's." Avery stepped out of her gown and into a comfortable pair of pajamas. "No one gets any work done Christmas week anyway. Do you really have to go back before the first?"

"I suppose not. Do you really want me here that long?" Inwardly, Eve perked up. Maybe extending her stay would be easier than she'd thought. Her parents wouldn't be home this year. They were still in Europe and would spend Christmas with relatives in Germany. Her siblings meant to make the most of their absence to stay at home Christmas morning or head to their in-laws' houses. Each of them had invited her to tag along, but she'd demurred, citing the drive times and the fact she had to be back to work. Before all of this had come up, she'd braced herself for a lonely holiday. Luckily, Melissa hadn't had plans, either. Her folks had moved to Florida a few years back, and although she'd been invited to celebrate with them and their new friends, they understood when she chose to do something else.

"Of course I do," Avery said. "Sometimes it gets a little old being the only single one around here."

"What's the deal with you and Walker?" Eve had been curious since she got here.

"Ugh. Go ask him. Anyway, there's a New Year's Eve bash in town we're all going to. You can come along and dance the night away with Anders."

New Year's Eve. A big bash. Eve tried to picture it. Could she arrange things to expose Hansen Oil there—

in front of the whole town? That would sure grab headlines. It would take an awful lot of planning—and a lot of guts, too. Her heart quailed at the thought of disrupting an evening like that and upending everyone's lives here at Base Camp, including Avery's. She had been so kind.

She was here to do a job, though, she told herself firmly, turning her back so Avery could help her with her gown. She had to follow through with it one way or another.

Later that night, back in the bathroom after everyone else had turned in, she checked her phone.

Clem's right; Anders doesn't exist before he's 18, Melissa had texted.

Are you sure?

I'll keep looking.

I think I know when and where to call out Hansen Oil, Eve texted back. *More tomorrow when I've had a chance to think it through.*

Looking forward to hearing your plan. Night.

Night.

Sleep didn't come easy that night. Avery had asked her to stay until New Year's, and she didn't think Anders would object—or Clem, as long as she kept kissing Anders—but things were about to get complicated. She'd quizzed Avery about the show's schedule and had learned that Christmas Eve would mark the end of one week of filming. Avery had explained that behind the scenes, crew members compiled the show's footage as they went, and episodes aired quickly, part of Fulsom's plan to make the show seem immediate to the viewers. This week's footage would make up next Friday night's show. New Year's Eve was three days later, when she planned to spill what she knew about Hansen Oil. Her boss watched *Base Camp* regularly; it was fodder for water cooler chitchat at AltaVista. As soon as he saw her on next week's episode, he'd guess what she was doing. He knew all about her past working for NGOs. Knew she was a sucker for environmental causes. Knew she thought he should have blown the whistle on Hansen. He could put two and two together.

Would he tell Johannes Hansen? Would Hansen believe him? What would happen next? She could only hope that three days was too short a time for anyone to come after her. Of course, even if she ran and hid the moment she did her big reveal, it would be a week before the episode was aired. A week for Johannes Hansen to come after Clem, Renata—and Fulsom—to try to stop them.

Would Clem include her in the episode? Would Fulsom back him up?

There was no way to know.

Then there was the question of Anders's mystery childhood. Under cover of her sleeping bag, she did some internet searches and found Melissa was right; there was no trace of Anders Olsen on the internet until he was eighteen. Then came proof that he'd joined the Navy and received several commendations during his service. Most of the entries on him were from *Base Camp*, most of them fawning fan messages that left her cringing.

When she heard someone turning over in their sleeping bag across the room, her thoughts shifted to the way Anders had kissed her tonight. The way he was making his interest known.

She could fall for him, she admitted to herself.

Maybe she'd fallen for him already.

Did he have something to hide?

She supposed that put them on equal footing.

She finally fell asleep and had some hot and heavy dreams about Anders. When she woke, she was thick-headed and flushed with thwarted passion. She wished she could get him alone, but the bunkhouse was already full of men and women passing through on their way to do their chores or wait for breakfast.

Eve liked the communal meals, but she wasn't sorry not to be in charge of cooking for a crowd like that. That had never been her thing. Kai and Addison managed it quite well, even though she knew Base Camp had been robbed of many of its stored vegetables a few months earlier.

"We're doing okay for now," Kai told her when she asked about the problem during one of her first passes through his food line. "It's next month I'm really worried about. We're going to be heavy on meat and dairy, and light on veggies and fruit by then. Not ideal, but there are worse things that could happen."

Eve had been impressed with his can-do attitude, but then everyone here was like that.

She hurried to find Avery to help her dress in her

Regency clothes. After a quick breakfast, she presented herself to Anders.

"I want to help with your chores."

It was time to get to know Anders better. Those three days between when next week's episode aired and when she outed Hansen Oil at the New Year's bash were going to be critical, and she needed to figure out what would happen if Hansen came after her. Could she count on Anders to help? Or would he push her out of Base Camp?

"I'd be glad to have your help," Anders said. "Dress warm. It's cold out there today."

As far as Eve was concerned, it was cold out there every day, but she'd spent a lot of time in unfamiliar climates and figured she was tough enough to deal with it. They were trailed outside by a small camera crew, par for the course around here. That was good, she told herself. More chances to make herself an integral part of the show. At the barn they met up with Avery and Walker. Eve had finally put it together that Avery had been neglecting her chores to keep her company—or maybe out of trouble—in the mornings. There was no reason for that. She would be glad to learn more about the bison and other critters the three of them managed. Glad to spend more time with Anders, too.

"The bison don't need much tending," Anders explained. "We make sure they're all accounted for and that none of the animals have gotten sick or injured, but mostly they take care of themselves. One of us rides out each morning just to check. Want to come along?"

"On a horse?" She wasn't sure about that.

"Don't you ride?"

"Not since I was eight." She'd taken lessons for two years, then gotten involved in swim club at the local pool, before softball and track had taken over her life.

"It's like riding a bike. You won't have forgotten."

"I can't ride in this." She plucked at her gown.

Anders's face fell. "No, I suppose not." He glanced at the sun. "Time's passing. I'd better get to it. Why don't you wear pants tomorrow and we'll try it then."

"You can help me with the goats and chickens in the meantime," Avery told her.

Eve glanced at Walker, who had just lifted a saddle down. Evidently, he'd ride with Anders this morning, and no one would get any time alone with the person they were lusting after. Avery didn't seem to expect anything else, and Eve remembered their prior conversation.

"Walker, what's up with you and Avery?" she asked.

She didn't think she'd ever seen the big man stumble before, either in person or on the show. He set the saddle down awkwardly on a sawhorse as the camera crew swiveled to get his reaction and considered her for a long moment before nodding at Avery. "Ask her."

Avery threw her arms up in the air and stalked out of the barn.

Eve quickly followed her. "Sorry," she said when she caught up. "I shouldn't have pried into your affairs."

"I'm not sorry. Did you see him? He nearly tripped over his own feet. That was worth it if nothing else."

"So… what is up with you two?"

"Oh, my God, stop it!" Avery stalked on toward another outbuilding. "Walker's got some stupid obligation he needs to sort out. He won't tell me anything more than that. When I get pissed off, he asks me to wait. That's what he says. 'Wait.' It's driving me crazy."

"But you're waiting," Eve pointed out.

"What else can I do? That… man… I don't know. He's got me. Right here." She put a hand over her heart. "If I don't end up with him, I think I'll just die. I'm not even the melodramatic type, but—okay, fine. I am the melodramatic type. But still, can you blame me?"

"No." Anyone could see Avery's desire for Walker. Given her own budding, impractical, impossible infatuation with Anders, she couldn't blame Avery for anything. At least Avery had a chance of a happy ending. Although—

Eve stumbled herself, seeing the future with sudden clarity. She was going to bring a nightmare down on all these people if she tried to expose Hansen Oil on air. If she pulled it off and showed the whole world the way Hansen Oil was poisoning North Run's water supply, the company would surely retaliate against Base Camp, and these people were already struggling to pursue their dream. They were low on food stores, and every forty days someone had to marry. Then there was the requirement for babies.

Heat washed through her. Why on earth was she thinking about the requirement for babies?

She'd never thought of it before.

Another lie, she admitted to herself. In her most private fantasies about meeting and marrying Anders, she had thought of it.

Someday she wanted a family.

"Eve? You okay?"

"No." Heck, she hadn't meant to say that out loud. "I mean—"

Avery nodded sympathetically. "You had no idea what you were getting into when you landed here, did you?"

She was so wrong—and so right. "I don't think this is going to work," she admitted. "And... I want it to."

"Why can't it work?"

Eve wasn't sure how to talk about it without exposing herself. "Have you ever had to choose between your own happiness—and what's right?"

Avery nodded slowly. "Sort of. Coming here was a big risk. Riley, Nora, Savannah and I had no idea what would happen when we decided to sell everything and take six months to give our dream careers a whirl. We could have ended up broke, homeless, jobless—but it worked out." She waved a hand to encompass Base Camp and the manor. "In ways I never could have dreamed of. Maybe you have to have a little faith."

"Maybe."

Avery studied her. "When you're ready to talk about it—whatever it is—I'm here. And I'm willing to help."

Eve felt a rush of gratitude. "You're a really good friend." She had a feeling Avery would want to help her take down Hansen Oil if they'd met anywhere else, which made her feel even worse about keeping the information from her.

"I hope so." Avery smiled a little wryly. "It seems to be my job around here: befriending single women who get swept up into Base Camp's insanity. Then they marry, and I have to start all over again."

"Whether or not I marry, you and I will stay friends," Eve said. Impulsively, she reached out and hugged Avery. "It's all going to work out in the end with you and Walker."

"God, I hope so. Here are the goats." She led the way to a little pen.

Eve allowed Avery to change the subject and helped her tend the funny animals. They checked their enclosure to make sure it hadn't been compromised, made sure they had enough food. Avery told her they were all female, most of them pregnant. "We keep the billy goat separate. He's a troublemaker."

They tended the billy goat, too. Moved on to the chickens, where they gathered eggs in a basket and fed them scraps from the kitchen.

"They eat anything," Avery said. "They'd eat us if they could figure out how to do it. They look innocent, but they're not."

Eve knew what she meant; she'd already been pecked. Twice.

"Have you decided to stay? At least until New Year's?" Avery asked as they made their way back to the barn.

It looked like Anders and Walker were back, too,

just dismounting near the stables.

Eve found her footsteps speeding up to meet them.

"Yes. At least until New Year's." Which meant she needed to contact Kevin and extend her vacation—without tipping him off to what she planned to do.

CHAPTER EIGHT

"**G**ET HER A ring," Greg said later that morning. "Time's passing, man. Get on with the main event."

"It's way too soon to propose," Anders told him. They were in the bunkhouse waiting for lunch. Anders wasn't sure where Eve was. She'd said something about meeting up with Renata.

"Maybe, but Christmas is coming fast. How can you not propose on Christmas?"

Anders knew what he meant; it would certainly be a romantic gesture, but it was far too soon. He needed to handle this right or he'd lose her in an instant, which meant he needed to come up with something else to give her as a Christmas present. Something that didn't presume too much but said enough about what he felt for her.

"Give her a bit of this," Clem said from behind the cameramen who were capturing this conversation. He clutched his groin with one hand and thrust his hips suggestively. "It's what she came here for," he taunted

Anders. "She wants some celebrity ass. Your ass."

Anders ignored him, although as far as he was concerned, Eve could have his ass—and the rest of him—any time she wanted.

"I don't know. Some other kind of jewelry?" Greg suggested. "Clothing? Books?"

"Books," Clem jeered.

"What's wrong with books?" Riley said, passing by them. "I like books."

"Eve doesn't want books. She wants your co—"

"Watch your mouth," Anders snapped at Clem.

"Ask Renata what to give her," Greg suggested. "Those two spend a lot of time together. Maybe she'll know."

"Better ask quick, while she's still here." Clem smirked.

Anders stilled. Was Clem supposed to replace Renata altogether? He met Greg's gaze. The other man shook his head.

"Is Renata leaving soon?" Anders asked, keeping his voice even.

"If she doesn't get her act together. Fulsom wants spectacular. Renata hasn't been delivering." Clem spotted Curtis and Hope entering the bunkhouse. "Let's go torture the newlyweds," he said to the cameramen.

"Be back in a minute," Anders told Greg.

He slipped out of the bunkhouse and spotted Renata with Eve trudging toward him from the direction of the manor. Anders hurried to meet them. "Renata? Can I talk to you a minute? See you in the bunkhouse," he added to Eve.

Eve nodded and kept going. He'd been afraid she'd be curious, but she seemed lost in her own thoughts. He wondered what those thoughts were.

"What's up?" Renata asked sharply. "I'm hungry, so make it fast."

Anders waited until Eve was too far away to overhear them. "I need to get something for Eve for Christmas. Thought you might have an idea."

"You're not getting her a ring?"

"I don't think we're quite there yet. I want to be ready when we are, so I'll get a ring soon, but I don't want to blow it by proposing too early."

Renata opened her mouth to deliver what looked to be a snappy answer, then closed it again. Thought a moment.

"I actually do have an idea," she said wryly. She pulled out her phone and tapped on it a moment. "She'd be interested in one of these." She held up the phone, and Anders moved to see the screen more clearly.

"A video camera? Why doesn't she use her phone if she wants to get footage of something?"

"Now that she's had a taste for a real video camera, a cell phone isn't going to cut it. This will do the trick. For now." Renata pocketed her phone again and started walking.

Anders came after her. "If I order one, it won't get here on time."

"I can get you one—today. We keep extra equipment on hand. You pay me for the replacement, and you can have it. I'll order a new one for us."

He stopped in his tracks, then sped up to catch her. "You'd do that?"

"Why not?"

Because she'd never done anything for him before. He didn't say that, though. Instead, he found himself telling her about what Clem had said in the bunkhouse.

"I'd watch your back if I were you," he finished. "And figure out how you can get better footage than he's getting. Sounds like Fulsom is looking for a reason to can you."

He didn't think he'd ever seen Renata truly upset before. Angry, yes, but not... shaken. She stood rigid, her mouth set in a thin line.

"I guess he is. I knew that, but there's knowing and... knowing."

Anders watched her worriedly. "None of us wants Clem to replace you. How can we help?"

She lifted her hands helplessly. "Get me better footage, I guess."

"I'll see what I can do." Meanwhile, it was time to get that ring. He wasn't under any illusions that Eve was ready to commit to him, but they'd definitely made progress.

An hour later, he opened the door to Thayer's Jewelers and made his way inside. The small store boasted a variety of glassed-in cases. In one corner was an office, where Mia Matheson ran her event-planning service.

Rose Johnson, wife of Cab, the sheriff, presided

over the rest of the store. He knew she was the artist who'd created the beautiful landscape paintings that hung gallery-style over one wall. Anders stopped to look at them, his gaze arrested by one that depicted a ranch at sunrise, the silhouette of a bison far in the distance.

"That's Alice." Rose smiled. "Hannah Matheson rescued her a few years back. Now she and her husband raise a herd of them."

"Is she named after Alice Reed?"

"I don't think so." Rose's smile grew. "Alice is special." She recounted the story of the way the bison had saved several people's lives. "I figured she needed to star in a painting."

"I'll take it." He'd hang it in his tiny house.

"Really?" Rose beamed at him. "Sales have been a little slow," she admitted. "I sell a lot more engagement rings than paintings these days."

"I'm here for one of those, too."

"I thought so. I watch *Base Camp*," she explained as she lifted the painting down off the wall and carried it to the counter. "Why don't you take a look at these while I wrap this up?" She set the painting down, pulled a key ring from her pocket and unlocked a glass case. Taking out several trays of rings, she set them on the counter. "Are you proposing to someone? I haven't seen any women on the episodes—except the usual ones."

"It's a bit of a surprise," he told her. "Can't go into it."

"Intriguing. Don't worry," she added. "I can keep a secret."

He bent over the tray, taking his time. He wanted to find a special ring for Eve, one that suited her. Something elegant that fit an active, outdoorsy woman like her.

Did that exist?

One ring drew his gaze, the way the painting had. It held a single diamond but a rather spectacular one.

"That's an emerald-cut diamond. It really makes a statement, doesn't it?" Rose said.

"I like it."

"I always say, go with your gut." Rose smiled a little. "Serves me well."

"Okay. Sold."

Rose came back over, popped the ring out of the tray and handed it to him. Anders took a closer look and nodded. "That's the one."

Rose took it back, held it in the palm of her hand—

And frowned.

"There's an obstacle," she said. "Something you need to take care of first."

Anders cocked his head. Obstacle? His father? But—

No, not his father, Anders realized.

His own lies. If he wanted to marry Eve, he needed to come clean to her. He wished he didn't have to, though. Eve had stated more than once she was an environmentalist. Just picturing her expression when she learned what his father did for a living—

He wasn't looking forward to that.

"Sorry," Rose said. "I… just get hunches about

couples' futures when I hold their engagement ring."

Oh yeah. He'd heard about that. "But I'll be able to take care of it? The obstacle?" he pressed her.

"That I can't say."

"I NEED TO get Anders something good," Eve said. She was at the manor with the other women, cleaning the ballroom, both for Christmas Eve festivities and for the guests expected a few days later. Eve had offered to pitch in. She wanted a more thorough look at the manor than she'd gotten last time they'd come here. Armed with a dustcloth, she was getting up close and personal with every windowsill, fireplace mantel and decorative item in the large room.

Anders was in town for the moment, and they'd agreed to meet up later. She knew she needed to let the camera crews get more footage of them together, but if she spent much more time with Anders, Clem might get some footage that wasn't safe for prime-time television.

He'd probably like that just fine.

"Wrap yourself in some pretty lingerie and get Anders alone. I'm sure he'd appreciate that," Avery suggested.

Eve's pulse sped up at the thought of it. She'd appreciate that, too, and it was exactly the kind of thing Clem would like to film…

"I don't know."

"Men are impossible," Riley said. "How about a shovel?"

"A shovel?" Eve and Avery said in unison.

"He takes care of the horses, right?"

"There's got to be something between a shovel and sex," Avery said.

"One would hope," Savannah said dryly. Hugely pregnant, she was supervising their cleaning efforts from one of the ornate sofas.

"A saddle? Boots? A good pair of work gloves? God, men things are so boring," Avery said.

"Ask Boone," Riley suggested.

That was a good idea, Eve decided as her phone buzzed.

It was a text from Kevin, who was probably racing to clean his inbox before the holiday. An answer to the message she'd sent to him earlier: *Would like to extend my stay in Maine through New Year's. Is that okay?*

Fine.

That was it? Fine? Kevin wasn't particularly talkative, but that seemed terse even for him.

Maybe it wasn't fine at all. Maybe he'd guessed what she was planning—

Eve snorted. Guessed that she planned to crash Base Camp and expose Hansen Oil on a reality television show? She doubted he had that much imagination.

"Everything all right?" Savannah asked her from the couch.

"Yes. Just work." Eve pocketed the phone and kept cleaning.

She cornered Boone later, before dinner, near the door to his tiny house. Worn out from her afternoon's labors, her breath puffing white plumes in the frigid air, she was more than ready for one of Kai's hearty dinners. It was amazing how quickly she was coming to feel at home here.

"Boone, can I talk to you a minute?" she asked.

"Sure thing. Come on in."

Inside, Eve stopped and stared. She'd seen the tiny houses on the show, of course, but hadn't been in one yet.

This one was wonderful.

Riley and Boone kept a tidy home, with everything in its place. The wooden walls and furniture gleamed with care, and a tiny woodstove kept it toasty warm. The south-facing wall was all windows, and the view of the hillside and the manor perching atop the opposite rise of ground was beautiful.

Boone waved her to a seat at a built-in table to one side of the kitchen. "What can I do for you?" He shucked off his coat.

"I want to give Anders something for Christmas, but I don't know what."

"Aside from an 'I do'?" Boone quipped and winced. "Hell. Sorry. Not really funny, huh?"

"It's a little early for that, wouldn't you say?" Eve joked back quickly, but his answer had unnerved her. It was far from fair to take up so much of Anders's time when she knew she didn't mean to stay. It wasn't like she was unaware of the deadline he was facing. For the first time she realized the forbearance he was showing, taking things with her a step at a time when he must be desperate to find a wife.

"It's definitely too early. Forget I said anything. As far as a present for Anders goes, he'd be happy with anything that has to do with bison."

She wanted to forget about Anders's impending marriage, she really did, but alone in this tiny house, away from the cameras for a moment, the situation was hard to ignore. "Do you have a backup bride lined up?"

After a moment, Boone nodded once.

"Can I... see her?"

She didn't think he'd go for it, and the silence between them stretched out uncomfortably until Boone pulled out his phone, tapped at it and turned it to face her.

Eve took it from him and forced herself to look at the photograph featured on its screen. The woman was a pretty blonde. She looked serene, intelligent and forthright—a country girl who'd fit in a place like this.

"What's her name?"

"Jane."

"Jane," Eve echoed. Jane looked like a good match for Anders. And for Base Camp. Eve swallowed the ache that bloomed in her throat and tried to think sensibly. Even if she did think she could care for Anders deeply, maybe that was caused only by their circumstances. They were thrown together all the time, and she'd been lonely for so long—

Eve let that sink in. She had been lonely. And afraid she'd never get another chance at love. Even her own mother thought she was unlikely to settle down with anyone. Anders wouldn't want her when he realized how she was using him, anyway.

"Anders likes you," Boone said as if he'd heard her thoughts.

"Anders doesn't know me."

Boone considered her. "Is there something in particular he should know?"

Uh-oh. Eve searched for an answer. "My family is in Virginia."

"And family is important to you?"

"Of course."

He nodded. "Anything else?"

"I spent years overseas working for NGOs." Eve wasn't sure why she'd said that when she'd kept it from Anders, but she wanted Boone to know she had environmental chops, too. She could have belonged here at Base Camp if not for the circumstances she found herself in. For one moment, she wished she could simply explain everything to him. Maybe he'd take this problem off her hands and confront Hansen Oil himself. Americans would listen to Boone. He appeared in their living rooms every week—a known quantity. Unlike her.

"Which ones?" he asked.

She gave him a rundown of some of her projects.

"Sounds like you'd fit right in around here. Is there anything we're involved in you find interesting?"

"Renewable energy," she said without hesitation. "Not the nuts and bolts of it. I'm not that practical, I'm afraid. The policy. I really think the United States should be doing everything it can to switch over its grid to renewables. It's a huge task, and I don't know why we're not treating it like a moon shot."

"I hear you." Boone folded his arms over his chest. "So you want to get the word out rather than build the grid yourself."

"Right. I'm like Renata—I enjoy working with film."

"Like Avery."

"Yes."

Boone was quiet a minute, and Eve fidgeted, worried he'd somehow seen through her.

"I wish it wasn't all up to people like us," he said quietly. "I wish…" He shook his head. "If the oil companies could just see their way to making the change—they have so much money. So much infrastructure. If they invested in renewables—in a real way—we'd get it done so much faster, and the whole world would benefit."

"Hansen Oil." Eve wanted to clap a hand over her mouth. She couldn't believe she'd said that out loud.

"You're right. A company like Hansen Oil could lead the way to a new America."

Boone had clearly thought about this before, and Eve wished there were more men like him around. Men who cared about the future so deeply they'd reroute their entire lives to fight for what was right.

"You never call out companies like Hansen on the show," she said tentatively. "You have a big platform, but you don't use it." She held her breath, hoping maybe he'd say he was ready to start and solve all her problems.

"We can't," Boone said matter-of-factly. "At the end of the day this is a TV show, and the stations that run it rely on advertising profit. Companies like Hansen Oil aren't going to run ads during *Base Camp*, of course, but they run ads during other shows the station carries. We have to walk a line between being informative and not being too controversial. We're trying to encourage people to live like we do; we won't get anywhere by bashing individual companies."

Eve deflated. He couldn't get any clearer than that. She was on her own when it came to exposing Hansen Oil. Her only hope was that if she made her revelation exciting—and sexy—Clem would air it, no matter what it did to *Base Camp*'s brand as a whole.

But when she took down Hansen Oil, she'd destroy her connection with Boone—and Anders.

"I think you can get as much done by setting a good example as you can by calling out the bad guys," Boone said.

"I guess."

"I think you have a lot to offer Base Camp," he went on. "Try to keep an open mind about staying, okay?"

"Okay." But Eve wondered if keeping an open mind was going to do anything other than break her heart.

She found Avery in the kitchen a few minutes later and remembered she still needed to find that present. Boone had said Anders would like anything related to bison. How could she find something when she had no way to even get to a store?

"I need help," she said to Avery. "I want to get Anders something for Christmas, and I know of a book that would be perfect for him. Problem is, if I order it, it'll never get here on time."

"I'm running errands in town later. Want me to see if I can find it there?"

"Would you? You're a lifesaver!" Eve gave her an impulsive hug.

"No problem. Text me the title and author so I'll have it with me."

Eve did so and hugged her again.

"I'm so glad you two are getting along so well," Avery said, hugging her back. "You fit right in here."

And Eve remembered with a sinking heart how unlikely it was she'd get to stay.

"HOW ABOUT WE take that ride today?" Anders asked the following morning. He was growing impatient with the way things were going. He liked spending time with Eve, but everywhere they went, someone else tagged along—usually a cameraperson. Boone had filled him in about his conversation with her the previous day. "I think she's a bit more radical about her activism than we are. We might be boring her," he'd summed up. Anders wanted to know more, and he was especially curious why she hadn't told him about her overseas adventures earlier. He was sure he'd asked her what she'd done before she joined AltaVista.

Eve was an enigma. He knew she'd gone along with

Clem's demand only in order to have a place to lie low over Christmas, so he couldn't fault her for making the most of her time. If she was as interested in film and editing as she appeared to be, of course she'd want to hang out with Avery and Renata. It stung a little, though.

On the other hand, when they were together, he would swear she was as attracted to him as he was to her. He couldn't help remembering what Rose had said when he bought the engagement ring. There was some impediment to them moving forward. Was it her hurry to learn as much as she could from the other women before it was time to leave?

Hadn't he made it clear enough he didn't want her to leave?

Maybe not. There was always something getting in the way of them spending time together. It was as if everyone had forgotten he had to convince her to marry him in short order.

"Okay," Eve said, glancing outside. It was a sunny morning, but Anders already knew it was cold, with a sharp wind that got in between the layers of your winter clothes.

"You need to wear pants, and dress as warm as you possibly can. I'm sure Avery can help."

"Already on it," Avery announced, passing by.

Forty-five minutes later, they were walking their horses through Westfield's far pastures. Despite her protestations, Eve remembered the basics, and while she was tentative with her mount, she was doing better than Anders had expected. Better yet, they'd shaken the camera crews. Clem had been pissed, but none of the cameramen rode well, and they claimed the cold was bad for their equipment. Despite all of Clem's threats, he hadn't been able to make them budge.

Anders took a deep breath and let out some of the tension that dogged him these days.

"Freedom," he said.

Eve grinned. "I've been here only a few days, and I know exactly what you mean. It must get old being filmed all the time."

"It's for a good cause."

"Westfield Ranch is beautiful. No wonder you guys built Base Camp here." She surveyed the terrain.

He knew what she meant. The fields were covered with snow, and the sky was leaden, but the mountains in the distance were mysterious and beautiful, and the bison were always interesting to watch. Sometimes Anders wondered if the creatures were humoring them, allowing them to fence them in and dictate where to feed or roam. That when they decided they'd have enough, they'd simply take off.

"I don't think Boone and the others had a lot of choice when it came to location, but they were happy to build here where they grew up. I like it just fine, too."

"I can see why."

"Eve." Anders hesitated, but he knew he needed to press on. "What do you really think of Base Camp? Could you ever see it as your home?"

Her horse sidestepped, and she concentrated on

steadying him. "I… think so," she said carefully. "I guess I figured if I settled down, it would be in Virginia. I have a good job there, and my family all lives there."

"But…" he prompted her when she stopped.

"But this is pretty interesting, I have to admit."

"What grabs you the most about Base Camp?" He wanted to understand how she saw things.

"The community. Your dedication to finding local answers to global problems. The fact that all of you are even willing to try."

He nodded. "I like that, too."

"It's more than that, though. It's… purpose. Everyone here has a purpose. I think that's both a positive and a negative for me."

Anders urged his horse forward a few paces, moving closer to Eve. Now they were getting somewhere. "Negative in what way?"

"In that I don't have a purpose here."

Hell. If there was one thing Anders knew, it was that people needed reasons to do the things they did. He had to find her a reason to stay here—fast. Given what Boone said, she might be afraid she wouldn't have a platform for her causes if she stayed here. If she'd worked for NGOs in the past, she probably wanted to get things done. Work on policy, like she'd told Boone, rather than simply be an example that other people could follow.

"How about we keep going?"

"Sure." As they rode on, Anders turned the problem over in his mind. Where would Eve fit in here if she stayed? She liked details. Images. Video. It seemed to him her budding friendships with Avery and Renata said a lot. Both women liked working with film, too. Could they put those skills to a purpose together? Make documentaries of specific skills used at Base Camp to teach other people about sustainable living or something to that effect?

Before he could ask if she'd like that, his phone buzzed in his pocket. It was Johannes. Anders considered not answering it, but his father hadn't seemed himself the other day.

"I've got to take this." He accepted the call and urged his horse a little ways away. Eve got the hint and kept going forward at a slow pace.

"Someone called this morning. Asking questions about the Terrence field," his father said without preamble.

Someone was researching Hansen's fracking operation? That didn't bode well. When Anders left Texas, fracking wasn't a major part of the family business. It had grown exponentially in the last decade, though.

"Has nothing to do with me," he managed to say with a glance toward Eve. She was looking over the fields to where the bison were grazing.

"I doubt that very much. You're on that show. Doesn't matter how much money I've spent over the years; I can't stop people from talking about who you are. Someone puts the puzzle pieces together. Figures they can cause a big scandal, send Hansen stock prices tumbling—"

"Is that what this is about? Stock prices?"

"Has it ever occurred to you not everyone has the legacy you have waiting for you? There are people—lots of people—who want a piece of Hansen Oil. And they'll get it any way they can. I can't protect you forever. Whoever you've got over there sniffing around the Terrence field, call them off, because if Hansen Oil stock plummets, I'm not the only one with a problem on his hands. And get your ass back here. Now. I need you." Johannes hung up.

"Problems?" Eve asked when Anders pocketed his phone.

"Family." Johannes was losing his cool, and Anders wondered what was happening with the fracking operation to make him so jittery. His father's last sentence had unnerved him. Johannes *needed* him? Johannes never needed anyone.

"Thought you didn't talk to your father."

"I don't. Usually. It's the show," he added. "Clem's people, probably. Digging for dirt, trying to get a story on me. My dad's not too happy about it." Johannes's comment about protecting him seemed rich. Anders didn't own any Hansen Oil stock, and he'd long ago turned his back on the idea of coming home to take over the company. Johannes was protecting himself.

Eve stilled. "Does your family have a lot of dirt?"

She was smiling, but Anders knew he needed to tread carefully, especially after that strange question she'd asked about his name the other day. He still wasn't sure why she'd brought that up. His gut told him she didn't know he was a Hansen, but something had to have prompted it.

Maybe he should fess up to everything right now. Anders wished he could, but some part of him was still hoping he'd make it through this year with his secret intact. He liked being his own man. Anders Olsen, Navy SEAL. Anders Hansen was dead as far as he was concerned. He wanted him to stay dead.

"I haven't seen eye to eye with my father in years. I don't want to be held accountable for him, and he doesn't want to be held accountable for me." True, as far as it went, but there was a lot more to it than that. His father wanted Anders to be an oil man, too. That was never going to happen.

"You miss him," Eve said softly.

Anders wanted to deny it, but it was true. "There was a time when we were close. When my mom was alive and it was the three of us. I was proud of him. We hadn't started fighting yet." He gazed at the bison grazing in the distance and thought about his early years in Texas. "We used to fish a lot, my dad and I. Until— well, until things went downhill. I loved those days at the river."

Eve looked as if she'd ask another question but then shook her head and kept quiet.

"When my mom died, everything changed. He changed. He became a harder man."

"You can't blame yourself for anything your father's done."

"Can't I? What if I'd stuck around? Talked to him—

made him see the error of his ways?"

"You were a child."

"I grew up," he pointed out. "That's all the past, though," he added, realizing they were treading on dangerous ground. He was worried Eve would press further, but she glanced down, shifted her reins into one hand, pulled her own phone out of her pocket and tapped it.

"Sorry," she mouthed to Anders. "Hello?" she said into the phone. "Oh, hi, Mary. What's up?"

She listened for a moment and rolled her eyes. "I meant just what I texted you. I won't be home until after New Year's."

Anders wanted to correct her. Until after New Year's *at the earliest.*

"I already told you I wasn't coming for Christmas. Because I had to work on the twenty-seventh, remember?" Another pause. "I know I just said I'm staying here until New Year's. My plans changed. You're going to be with Phillip's family. You don't need me there." Pause. "I want to do something new this year." A hesitation. "I don't want to always be the extra person, okay? Can't you see it from my perspective?"

She turned to Anders and made a face. "Yes," she went on. "Everything's fine. I'm having a good time, and I'll tell you all about it when I get home." Eve sighed. "Yes, I'll take pictures. I've got to go. Hug the kids, all right? Talk soon. Bye."

She ended the call and put her phone away. "Nothing like a nosy sister to make you feel ten years old again."

"I'm glad you're staying through the holidays," Anders said.

"Me, too." She perked up a little. "Beats being irresponsible Aunt Eve."

"Is that the way your family sees you?" He couldn't imagine it.

"Irresponsible, hopeless, ridiculously bad at planning for the future."

"Boone said you told him you worked for a bunch of NGOs."

Eve's horse sidestepped again, and Anders wondered if she'd flinched. Why didn't she want him to know about that? "You're right. I did."

"And that didn't take planning and responsibility?"

"Of course it did, and I was good at my work, but Mary and the others are right about one thing. I didn't show much staying power. I liked to take on a project, get it done, get out and move onto the next thing. Then I got hurt…"

She fidgeted with the reins, and Anders waited, his gut telling him this next bit would be important if he wanted to understand what made Eve tick.

"I had to be medevaced out of my last assignment. Broken leg. It was so expensive my parents had to loan me the money to pay for all my medical bills. I'm still paying them back. As far as saving the world goes, I've been sidelined." She shrugged her shoulders, but Anders heard what she didn't say. She'd been living her dream, and then she'd lost it. She'd had the world at her fingertips and then found herself back in Virginia.

"Sounds to me like you probably touched a lot of people's lives, and you'll do so again when you've paid back your folks." He urged his horse nearer.

The gratitude in her expression hardened his resolve to have a word with her sister—and the rest of her family—if he ever met them. If she married him, he'd help her pay her debts. He had no doubt she'd be an asset to Base Camp.

More than that, he wanted her to be happy.

"I'm going to kiss you," he warned her.

"I'd like that," Eve admitted.

ANDERS DISMOUNTED AND held Eve's horse steady so she could get down. He held the reins of both animals in one hand, gathered her close and kissed her thoroughly.

Eve loved the way it felt when he did that. Was coming to crave it in between times. She and Anders simply worked together in a way she couldn't remember feeling before. He understood her in a way she wasn't sure anyone else but Melissa ever had.

"I like you, Eve Wright," he murmured when he pulled away.

"I like you, too."

"I've got to marry someone in just a few weeks. You know that, right?"

She nodded, a breathless, unsteady feeling twisting inside her.

"I'm going to ask you. Not now. Not for a little

while. We need to get to know each other a lot better. But I am going to ask you. You need to know that."

She could only nod again. Despite her attempts not to think about it, she did know it, and her heart ached because she knew he might not feel the same way if he knew what she intended to do. For one rash moment she wanted to give up trying to beat Hansen Oil and simply say yes to Anders. Why was it her responsibility to take on a behemoth no one else had managed to rein in?

If only she was the kind of person who could walk away from injustice.

She wasn't, though. This was her best chance to make a difference to a lot of people's lives, and she had to take it. Martin Fulsom would make sure Base Camp survived, she was sure of it, but Anders, Boone, Avery and the rest of them would know she'd balanced her need to stop Hansen Oil with the safety of Base Camp's future and had chosen to go ahead with her plans. How could they trust her to be one of them when she hadn't prioritized their needs?

"I think we could be happy together. I know I'd work hard at it," Anders went on.

A fine tremor ran through her body. How unfair to finally meet the man of her dreams and know that being with him was impossible.

Anders slid a hand behind the nape of her neck and moved closer to kiss her again. The brush of his mouth over hers had her standing on tiptoe, leaning into him, wanting so much more.

"I know you want a purpose here," he said. "I'll do anything I can to help you find it. Maybe it will take a while to discover what you want to do, but you're smart and creative, and there's a lot of people here to support you along the way. What if you looked at it as a challenge? What would you do if you could do anything?"

Right now, the only thing she could think of doing was him.

Could he feel her longing?

He pressed another lingering kiss to her mouth, held her close a moment, and she could feel the evidence of his desire.

"I'm going to ask about that, too," he said huskily. "Soon. I want you to want it as much as I do, but I don't want to blow forever with you by pushing you for more right now."

Eve wanted to say she didn't want to wait another minute—that she'd be glad to do it right here. Standing up. Lying down. Whatever he wanted. But he wasn't talking about a fling. He was talking about marrying her.

If she slept with him, he'd think she wanted to marry him.

Maybe she did want that, more than she'd ever dreamed possible. But first she had to take down Hansen Oil.

Was there any way to get everything she wanted? Stop Hansen Oil without losing her chance with Anders?

Eve made a promise to herself she'd try her best.

"Soon?" Anders asked softly.

Eve nodded. "Soon," she said. Another promise.

One she meant to keep.

CHAPTER NINE

"I HAVEN'T SEEN her all afternoon," Anders told Walker as they entered the bunkhouse near to dinnertime. He was frustrated. Aching to be with Eve, if he was honest. Half-hard and horny after their talk that morning, with no outlet for his desire.

Walker grunted.

"I mean it. She's been gone for ages."

"Ages?" Walker repeated.

"Well, hours. When we got back from riding this morning, she disappeared with Avery. They missed lunch. Something's up."

"Holidays," Walker said.

"You mean… like gifts and things like that? You think she's trying to surprise me with something?" It was a comforting thought, but it didn't soothe his frustration. Why hadn't he kept riding with Eve all the way to some motel where they could have been alone together? He didn't know what he'd expected to happen after they spoke, but it wasn't that she'd head off for the whole day with Avery.

Boone cleared his throat. He was seated at his desk in the corner, paperwork spread before him, but he half turned to face them. "I hope I'm not the problem."

"Why would you be?" Anders asked him.

"I've been meaning to tell you I might have made a mistake when I talked to her."

"What'd you do?" Anders moved closer.

"I showed her a photo of your backup bride."

Anders was nonplussed. "Hell, Boone—what were you thinking?"

"She asked me point-blank. I froze."

"You're lucky she didn't leave right then!" He couldn't believe it. Eve knew the identity of the woman he'd have to marry if she left Base Camp? Did she think he was happy about the situation?

"Well, she didn't. And you two seem to be getting on okay."

Anders thought about their ride—and their conversation—again. Had he made a mistake being so gentlemanly? There they'd been—away from the cameras. Alone. And he'd let the moment slip away.

"Maybe knowing she has competition has made her want you more," Boone suggested.

"Maybe." He wasn't convinced.

"She likes you. Try harder."

"I'm trying."

Anders got out of there and took a walk down to Pittance Creek, which had frozen over weeks ago. Once there, he changed his mind and decided to try to find Eve. When he did so, he was surprised to find her alone, hunched over Avery's laptop, which she shut quickly when he walked in.

He remembered what Walker had said. Maybe she was working on some kind of surprise for him. He pretended not to notice.

"Where's Renata and Avery?"

"They're—out. I'm just finishing up—something."

"It's getting close to dinnertime. Can I walk you to the bunkhouse?"

"Sure." Eve quickly gathered her things, taking a moment to open the laptop and close a few documents. Anders made a big show of looking elsewhere, then helped her on with her coat when she stood up.

She passed the laptop back to Avery when they reached the bunkhouse, and soon the two of them were seated with everyone else enjoying the dinner Kai and Samantha had created.

It was Christmas Eve, so after dinner they all piled into the Base Camp trucks to attend a candlelight service at Chance Creek Reformed Church, the camera crews following them as usual and taking their places in the back. Anders made sure to be seated next to Eve in their pew, with Boone on her other side. Boone seemed to notice his maneuvering and had helped corral Eve into position between them before anyone else could sit next to her.

Good old Boone.

As the choir sang and Reverend Halpern took his place at the lectern, Anders took Eve's hand and held it firmly. He wanted her to know he was serious in his pursuit of her. The last thirty-six hours had proved to him his heart was already thoroughly engaged in the idea of getting to know her.

He understood what it meant that she would consider staying in Chance Creek, even though as she said, her job and her family were in Virginia. Could he possibly ask her to give all that up for someone she'd just met? Things worked fast here at Base Camp. He'd grown used to it. She hadn't.

Eve didn't pull her hand away, and they stayed like that throughout the service, even though it meant juggling the hymnal a bit when it came time to find the songs. Like Anders, Eve knew the first verse of most of them, but then they both got lost and had to bend close over the book to get through the rest of them.

Anders liked that. Eve smelled good, and when she leaned into him to read the small text, he wanted to put an arm around her.

He didn't want to get into a scuffle at church, though, should she not be ready for a public display of affection like that. He stuck to holding her hand.

When it came time for candles to be brought around, he waited patiently for an usher to light his, then turned to carefully light Eve's.

"Merry Christmas," he told her and kissed her cheek. "Glad I'm getting to spend it with you."

Her lips parted, and he thought she might kiss him back, but she glanced at Boone, found him waiting for her to light his candle and busied herself doing so. By the time she was done, the moment was lost.

They sang the final hymns and listened to Halpern's last words before extinguishing their candles and filing out of the church quietly. Peace filled Anders's heart, alongside the now-familiar desire to get Eve alone.

Outside, snow had started falling.

"Eve," Anders began and stopped. He didn't know how to say to her everything that was in his heart. He wanted to beg her to give them a chance, but he wasn't a man to beg. She had to want it, too.

She went up on tiptoe and kissed the bottom of his jaw—the only thing within reach to her. "Merry Christmas," she told him softly.

Somehow Anders knew he needed to leave it at that. He did manage to steal another kiss in the kitchen later when they helped to put out a midnight spread of snacks and eggnog. Settled down in his sleeping bag afterward, he was far too aware of Eve sleeping across the room to drift off easily. He must have eventually, for when he woke up again it was Christmas morning, and judging by the sound of it, a snowball fight was raging outside.

After breakfast, everyone trooped up to the manor for the gift exchange. Husbands and wives were allowed to give each other presents. A round-robin affair had been set up for everyone else, each of them giving one gift and receiving one from their "secret Santa."

Eve hadn't been around long enough to be part of that, so Anders felt justified in giving her something, even though they weren't married.

He wasn't entirely surprised to receive not one secret Santa package but two in return.

Jericho gave him a tooled leather saddlebag that was a work of art. "Thanks," Anders said and meant it. It was the kind of thing that could stay in a family for generations, and he'd get a lot of use out of it. He took up the second package curiously. Looked at the tag.

It was from Eve.

She smiled at him from where she sat between Avery and Riley near the huge Christmas tree that stood in the ballroom.

He looked back down at the gift; it had to be a book by the heft of it. He remembered Clem's derisive comment about books. Riley's defense of them as gifts.

What kind of book had Eve gotten for him?

When he tore open the paper, satisfaction filled him.

The kind of book that showed she'd been listening and understood where his interests lay.

"*The Wilson Guide to Regenerative Grazing*?" Boone said, reading over his shoulder. "Hey, let me see that. I've heard about this guy."

He reached for the book just as Curtis leaned in from the other side. "Doesn't he have a podcast about restoring native ecology through managed grazing? He's got this idea that you can use cattle to restore ranch land the way we're using bison—" He reached out, too.

Anders had to tug the book away from both of them. "Mine," he declared loudly. "Thank you," he mouthed to Eve. She grinned back as Boone and Curtis both craned their necks to get a better look as he opened it.

"Books," Clem said derisively behind them.

"I like books," Riley declared loudly. "Look, I got one, too!" she cried as she finished opening one of her gifts from Boone.

"What'd I tell you?" Boone said to Anders.

Huh. Maybe he should have gotten Eve a book, too, Anders thought as she began to unwrap her gift from him.

But when she held up the video camera with shining eyes, he knew he'd done right.

"I love it," she told him. "Anders, how did you know that's what I wanted?"

He shrugged, but when he met Renata's gaze across the room where she was lingering behind the camera crews, he nodded in acknowledgement of her help.

At the same time, he noticed how Renata was holding back while Clem was front and center, running the show, and it occurred to him she'd been doing that a lot lately. His chest tightened with worry. If Fulsom booted Renata and left Clem in charge, things would go to hell in a handbasket around here quickly.

Renata had helped him. He needed to do something to help her in return. He'd start by getting word out to everyone else that they needed to give Renata something extra to work with.

"I DON'T UNDERSTAND why you all don't live in the manor," Eve said to Savannah later that morning as they sat at breakfast. Jericho's wife was getting close to her due date and moved clumsily but glowed with happiness. Jericho was a doting father-to-be, touching Savannah often, especially her belly. Eve envied them their clear satisfaction with their situation. Would she ever get a chance to be a couple like that? Or would she spend her life alone in her parents' backyard?

She'd gotten a text from Melissa earlier. She was still looking into Anders's mysterious lack of a past and doing her best to gather more information about Hansen Oil that might come in handy when Eve exposed it on air. She'd asked Eve if it was all right to spend Christmas with Harry Enright, her cowboy beau.

Eve was glad she wasn't spending the holiday alone.

She couldn't believe Anders had given her a professional-style video camera, one that would make creating a presentation for New Year's Eve that much easier. She still needed footage to create her tell-all film, and now she wouldn't have to borrow Avery's equipment to get it.

She'd decided the best way to get her point across at the New Year's bash was to make the world's shortest documentary film. An exposé about Hansen Oil that featured the images she'd stolen from AltaVista but also included interesting footage from Base Camp to put things in perspective. She'd told Avery and Renata she was working on a practice video to explain why she wanted footage of the solar panels and energy grid running the community. "I'm making an introduction to Base Camp video," she'd said. "We can put it up on the website when I'm done."

Renata and Avery had bought her cover story.

How would they feel when they learned they were wrong?

Thank goodness Anders hadn't pried when he caught her at it yesterday. Eve had a feeling going home after New Year's was going to be worse than coming home from Africa on a stretcher had been. There was nothing else for it, though.

"We can't live in the manor. It's part of the deal we made with Fulsom when he set up the show," Savannah said. "At first he wanted to shut down the manor altogether. The compromise is that we live down here and use it only for business purposes as long as the television show is running."

Eve glanced at Anders and found him watching her. He raised his glass to her, and Savannah remarked, lowering her voice, "Everyone's curious. Are you into Anders or not?"

Eve looked down at the plate of goodies she held. Kai had served up a buffet of yummy Christmas food he'd somehow produced from his limited resources. The man was a god in the kitchen.

"I'm into him, but…" she hedged.

"But you know he's got to marry in less than a month, and you're not sure you're down for that."

"Exactly. I mean, it's tempting, but…" She let the end of the sentence hang since she couldn't say what was really on her mind. One way or another, this time next week she'd have done her part to expose Hansen Oil and would know what Anders—and everyone else—thought of that.

"It's hard having a deadline." Savannah eyed her husband, and Eve remembered that the two of them had gone through some rough moments before they decided to throw in their lots together. "But all of us have been through it in one way or another. You don't need to be embarrassed or try to pretend it isn't happening."

Eve hadn't thought about it like that. "Thanks. That helps."

"It isn't fair to rush you, but you need to make up your mind pretty soon. If you aren't staying, Anders needs time to prepare himself to be with someone else."

She meant the backup bride. Eve bristled just thinking about Jane. The thought of Anders marrying her. Sleeping with her—

Eve shut her eyes. She wanted to be the one sharing his bed.

She glanced his way.

Saw him watching her.

Her pulse kicked up. She knew he wanted her, too.

Could they slip away?

THERE WAS NO way he could know Eve was thinking about making love to him, but somehow Anders did know it.

She stood there calmly chatting to Savannah, glancing his way now and then, but he knew in the privacy of her own mind, she was weighing her options. Deciding whether or not to be with him.

Which was playing havoc with his libido. God knew

he wanted to be with her. No question about it, as far as he was concerned. If they were on the same page, it was up to him to make it happen.

Anders set his plate and drink down on a side table and began to make his way around the clusters of people.

"Hey, Anders. Merry Christmas." Clay stepped into his path and shook his hand. "Good luck with the marriage thing. You making any progress?"

He would be if Clay would get out of his way.

Anders forced himself to shake his friend's hand. "Working on it."

He stepped past Clay to be confronted by Jericho. "Way to go, man. I've seen the way Eve's looking at you. There'll be another wedding soon, huh?"

"Maybe." Anders pushed past him, too.

"Why are you over here? You should be with Eve," Sam chided him when he nearly bumped into her.

"Trying," he managed to say and kept going.

By the time he reached Eve, she'd gone back to the buffet with Savannah, and he was beginning to think he'd read far too much into the few glances she'd sent his way. Maybe he had an overactive imagination. Maybe she'd turn him down if he made his desires known.

"Hey," he said, grabbing a new plate and filling it, although he had already eaten enough.

"Hey, yourself. Thanks again for the video camera." She smiled up at him.

"Thanks for the book."

"You don't think it's boring?"

"Not at all. Look, do you want to get out of here? Go somewhere we can talk?" He wanted to do far more than talk, but—

"Sounds good." She set her plate down on the table with a thump.

Anders grabbed her hand and led her quickly into the kitchen, where they could slip out the back door. As soon as they were on the manor's generous back porch, Anders wrapped an arm around her, backed her against the outside wall of the manor and claimed the kiss he'd been wanting all day.

"Let's go," he said. "To my house." He didn't want to stop kissing her long enough to walk there, but there was nothing for it. He kept an arm around her waist as they stumbled down the path to Base Camp, laughing like teenagers, veering across to his tiny house, which looked completed on the outside but inside still had a ways to go.

When they made it through the door, Anders picked Eve up, sat her down on the wooden kitchen counter-top Curtis had installed only days ago, cupped her face and kissed her again. Her gown hiked up around her knees as she kicked off her boots and wrapped her legs around his waist. The pressure of her against his groin nearly undid him right then.

He unbuttoned her jacket with fingers that felt far too big, shucked it off her, did the same with his own and wrapped his arms around her, needing her to be as close as possible.

"Eve," he growled against her neck. He fumbled at the back of her gown. How could he get her out of it?

"That'll take too long," she told him. She took his hands in hers, slid them into the bodice of her gown and let out a ragged breath when he palmed her breasts.

Anders knew exactly how she felt. They were soft but heavy in his hands. He wanted to see them—kiss them.

Eve wriggled against him, and he dropped one hand to the waistband of his jeans, freeing the button and unzipping them. This was going fast, and he wasn't sure if she'd regret it later, but for now Eve seemed as eager as he was to get as close as they possibly could. In another minute he'd be inside her—

"There you are!" Clem exclaimed, sticking his head in the doorway of the tiny house. "We've got a mock-up of the current episode ready to play—"

"Out!" Anders threw one of Eve's boots at him. It bounced off the door as Clem quickly shut it.

Clem called from outside. "You've got three minutes to get to the bunkhouse, or I'm coming in with cameras!"

"Shit."

Anders pulled back, tugged his pants up, zipped his fly and ran a hand through his hair as Eve jumped down from the counter, reached inside her bodice to set her breasts back to rights inside her corset and smoothed down her gown.

"Eve—"

"He's going to come in again," she hissed. "This

isn't going to happen."

He tangled a hand in her hair, tilted her head back and claimed her mouth with his. "I want it to happen," he said when they broke apart again.

"I want that, too."

"You do?"

"Wasn't I making that clear?" She sent him a lopsided grin.

"I guess I need to be told explicitly," he joked and held out his hand. She took it.

"If we're ever alone, I'll make things very explicit."

When they reached the door, he tugged her close again. He hated to let Clem ruin this.

"I'll make sure we get the chance. Soon."

"I'll hold you to that."

Outside, Clem trailed them back to the manor, speculating loudly on what they might have been doing when he interrupted them. Anders simmered as his descriptions got more and more lewd.

Until a well-aimed snowball thrown by Eve shut Clem up again.

"BRACE YOURSELF," NORA said to Eve as they all settled down to watch the latest *Base Camp* episode. "This is never pleasant."

"She's right," Avery said ruefully. "They manage to film the worst things."

"You learn not to let it get to you," Anders told her. He'd pulled two chairs together and kept an arm around her as Boone and Clem fiddled with equipment at the head of the room and the show appeared on a large screen hung against one wall.

The episode opened with the familiar theme song and introduction but soon changed to footage showing a number of the Base Camp men wrestling the huge Christmas tree up the hill and into the manor. Interspersed with the footage of the women decorating the manor for the holiday, there were lots of snippets showing people finding gifts for their secret Santa victims—and trying to guess who had drawn whom for the gift exchange.

There was footage of Clem arriving at Base Camp, looking around, being introduced to its inhabitants. A line or two from a speech he'd given and reactions from all the men and women Eve had come to know over the last few days. It looked like Clem had been a thorn in everyone's side since the moment he arrived.

"You need to marry—spectacularly," he announced onscreen to Anders. Beside Eve, Anders shifted in his seat, and she had to concentrate not to do the same.

The scene changed to footage of Riley and Samantha interacting with guests at the manor.

"One more night, and we're off until after New Year's," Riley said onscreen.

"I'm ready for a break," Samantha agreed.

The scene shifted again, this time to Clem approaching the bunkhouse on a snowy night and shouldering open the door. A woman's yelp split the air—her yelp, Eve realized—that had been the night she arrived and pretended to faint in Anders's arms. The show cut to a break—just dead space in the mock-up that would be filled by commercials when the episode aired.

"You okay so far?" Anders asked.

"Yeah." But from here on in she'd be part of the story, and she wished she could leave now, before she had to see the rest of it.

"It gets easier," Anders said grimly.

"Are you sure?"

When the show came back on, she braced herself, and it was even worse than she'd thought. She'd been a mess when she'd reached Base Camp—dirty, disheveled, soaked and shivering. It was amazing Anders had looked twice at her. She looked silly in the gown she'd borrowed from Avery that first night, which was far too short, and more than once the camera caught her looking furtively around. Looking guilty, she thought.

Her story about her ex-boyfriend seemed lame, and she realized that the slightest bit of fact-checking on the part of the crew would have exposed it as fake. But just when Eve was in despair at the way she was coming off, things changed. The focus shifted to Anders, and Anders seemed... smitten with her. Almost from the start.

Eve wasn't sure if that was worse or better, given what was to come. Even more disturbing was the fact that Clem seemed to have caught footage of several situations when she hadn't been aware he was near. One time he'd filmed her helping Avery with the animals. Another time she'd been working with Renata editing video at the manor when she'd been sure they were alone.

She wasn't the only one murmuring about what was onscreen. Interspersed with the footage of her and Anders was plenty more of the rest of the inhabitants. "How'd you get that?" Riley burst out at one point after a scene that showed her singing as she painted. Clearly, she'd thought she was alone.

Clem shrugged, his smug grin firmly in place.

Worry twisted in Eve's gut. He was obviously intent on making trouble. It wouldn't be hard to mess things up for her.

Her worst fears were realized when the scene changed and showed the Night Sky Bonfire. She was fine with footage of her looking through the telescopes and skating with Anders. She was even fine when hoots and whistles broke out when she and Anders kissed onscreen.

Please, please, please don't show it, she implored the screen, and of course there was no footage of Clem confronting her at the bonfire, making all his insinuations about Anders, but there was footage of her sitting on a log talking to Melissa.

Thank goodness there wasn't any audio of her conversation with Melissa. At least not at first. As the scene progressed, however, the cameraman seemed to get closer and closer, and Eve's breath caught. What had Clem overheard? She'd have to warn Melissa to stay away from now on.

"Have a good time," Melissa said onscreen, got up and moved away.

"Who's that?" Anders asked.

"Just someone I met there," Eve lied and sighed with relief when Anders seemed to accept that. Onscreen, Anders sat down beside her on the log, handed her a cup of hot chocolate, and she remembered how their conversation had gone that night. Surely Clem hadn't recorded that.

"Thanks. What a night, huh?" she said on the show. A young man walked by in a down jacket and shorts.

"I've been people watching," Anders said. "There are definitely some characters out."

"You got that right. Anders Olsen is your real name, right?"

Oh no, Eve thought. Of all the things for Clem to put in the show. The question seemed to come out of left field, and onscreen Anders choked on his drink, coughed and spluttered. "What kind of question is that? Is Eve Wright *your* real name?"

Eve cringed as everyone in the room turned to look at her and Anders. Now they'd all be searching for information about her on the internet. Beside her, Anders stared straight ahead.

"Eve Olsen," she said onscreen. "Has a ring to it, doesn't it?"

Eve cringed all over again as more than one person chuckled. Some of the tension in the room evaporated. Her quick response had saved the day again.

"Now we're getting somewhere," Angus yelled in the overblown Scottish accent he used when he was joking around. Eve relaxed a little.

"Eve Olsen," Anders repeated onscreen. "Yeah. It does have a ring. But—"

"I didn't mean you have to marry me. Shit. Shit, shit, shit," Eve said. "Now you think I'm some desperate celebrity chaser, and I'm not. I swear. I just—it just popped into my head—"

She sounded deranged, Eve thought, sinking lower in her chair, but to her surprise Anders took her hand and squeezed it.

Onscreen he said, "I didn't think you were proposing. You just caught me off guard. I always thought I would be the one to pop the question."

"Stop quibbling, you blethering idiot, and marry the girl," Angus shouted. The room erupted in laughter.

"You will be! I mean, I want it to be you. I mean, I don't want—" Eve said onscreen. She covered her face with her hands. "I'm just going to curl up on the ground and die," she said on the show. "Me and my big mouth."

"When it's time to propose—if it's time to propose—I'll do the honors." Anders nudged her with his shoulder. "Does this mean you're considering it?"

"For God's sake, talk, talk, talk," Angus shouted from the audience. "Are you waiting for the pope himself to jump out and put the ring on her finger for you?"

Even Eve had to laugh at that. She risked a look at Anders and found a smile tugging at his lips.

"Marrying you? I don't expect you to want to marry me," she said onscreen, "but with Clem practically dictating that you do, it's hard for me not to at least think about it—abstractly."

"And what do you think about marrying me and living at Base Camp for good—abstractly?"

"I don't know. I didn't come here looking for this, you know?"

"Say yes!" Avery yelled at the screen. "Put the poor guy out of his misery!"

"I do know. You had a boyfriend," Anders said onscreen.

"Oh, for the love of—have you lost your mind, man?" Angus turned around in his chair to point a finger at him. "You brought up her ex-boyfriend during your proposal?"

"I… like it here," Eve said onscreen. "I like… you."

Avery cheered and clapped. A few other people joined in.

"That's a good start," Anders said onscreen.

"That is a good start," Boone said loudly, standing up from his chair as the show's credits rolled. "I look forward to hearing better news soon."

"No pressure," Angus called out.

Eve was thankful for the man's comic relief. The situation would be unbearable otherwise. Clem, standing to one side with his arms folded, looked more than pleased with himself for creeping them all out with his sneaky tactics. Renata's mouth was pinched into a thin line. As everyone stood up and stretched, her phone buzzed, and she slipped off gratefully to the bathroom to read the text in private.

Merry Christmas, Melissa wrote.

You, too. How's it going?

I've got some news.

Eve decided she could use the distraction. *Good news or bad news?*

Both. Brace yourself.

Eve sighed. She wasn't sure how much more she could take today. *Tell me.*

The good news is Jana called. She asked around about Clem Bailey. Turns out he got canned from Tracking the Stars *for harassing one of the camerawomen. Got drunk at a party and wouldn't take no for an answer. She got some of it on film, got away and turned him in. He took a payout in exchange for keeping quiet and left the show. She took an even bigger payoff to do the same.*

Ugh. I'll warn the women here, Eve texted.

Jana is working on getting the footage.

Great. That was good news. Leverage she might very well need before all was said and done. *What's the bad news?*

It's really bad, Eve.

Tell me!

First tell me—are you falling for Anders for real now that you've met him?

What does that have to do with anything? She felt exposed enough after viewing the *Base Camp* episode.

Answer the question.

Eve thought about what she'd said onscreen. *I like him.*

I was afraid of that. Okay, here goes. Clem was right. An-

ders Olsen only appears when he's 18. Before that he was someone else.

Someone else. Who? The muscles in her neck tightened. Melissa didn't exaggerate. If she said it was bad, then it was bad.

Anders Hansen.

Eve lowered the phone. Hansen?

No.

Her phone buzzed again. *He's Johannes Hansen's son, Eve.*

No. There was no way Anders could be connected to that man.

I'm sorry.

Eve stared at the screen, unable to take in Melissa's words. Anders was an environmentalist. He was a good man—

How? Eve texted, her heart sinking. *Did he infiltrate the show? Is he going to sabotage it?*

I don't know. Maybe not. He changed his name years ago. Maybe he turned his back on his family.

He said he has differences with his father. Eve thought about it. *I'll have to ask him.*

NO!

A knock sounded at the bathroom door.

I have to go.

You can't let Anders know you know. He'll get you kicked off the show. You have to stay until New Year's. Otherwise Hansen Oil wins!

Melissa was right, but Eve couldn't gather her thoughts fast enough to answer her. It was as if the ground had tilted beneath her feet and everything was beginning to slide.

How could Anders be Johannes's son?

What was he doing here? Trying to make amends for his family's business—or trying to ruin everything?

The knock came again. "Eve? Everything okay?" Avery called.

"Just a minute!"

Can you hold it together for one more week? Melissa texted.

I think so. She was far from sure. How could she look at Anders without giving everything away? How could she let him kiss her—touch her—if he was part of the company she'd come here to expose?

I'll email you all the details as soon as I find them, Melissa texted. *Go, but say nothing.*

OK.

What else could she do?

Eve pocketed her phone, faced her reflection in the mirror and stared into her own eyes. She hadn't just been falling for Anders; she'd been falling in love with him. With the son of her enemy.

She'd been acting ever since she came here, Eve reminded herself sternly. Now she'd have to up her game. How could she keep away from Anders without tipping him off?

She wasn't sure, but she was about to find out.

CHAPTER TEN

ANDERS RELAXED A little when the bathroom door opened and Eve rejoined Avery and the others. She looked pale, but she didn't look like she'd been crying. He'd been afraid the show had put her off Base Camp—and him—for good. All around him people talked in small groups. Everyone was unnerved about the stealth footage, as Jericho had termed it. Clem had been sneaky about filming—and recording—people. Everyone wondered how far he meant to go. Meanwhile, Clem had opened a can of beer and was bragging about his inaugural episode to a knot of crew members.

"Come on, people. It's Christmas," Boone called out. "Forget the episode. Let's get some music going. Help yourselves to more food. Let's try to enjoy ourselves."

Savannah went to the old upright piano and began to play some Christmas carols, and several people went to refill their plates, but the mood in the room was flat. When his phone buzzed in his pocket, and he saw it was his father, Anders crossed the room, grabbed his coat and stepped outside, more paranoid than usual about Clem recording him.

"It happened again," Johannes said, his voice husky on the other end of the phone. "Someone's been asking questions about our operations—especially the Terrence field. It's because you're on that damn show. I know it is."

"No one here knows who I am."

"You sure about that?"

Anders wasn't. He knew Renata must have investigated him early in the show, and he was positive Clem would be trying hard to dig up dirt, too. "What if someone does figure out who I am?" he asked.

"We don't need the extra scrutiny right now. It's not a good thing for either of us—you or me."

Anders's scalp prickled. Even as Johannes blustered on about stockholders and investments, he knew his father. He had just inadvertently let something important slip.

"Why don't you need the extra scrutiny? Did something happen?"

Johannes hesitated a moment too long, confirming Anders's suspicions. "We've always got someone on our back, slowing us down," he blustered. "We meet the current regulations, and those bleeding heart liberals come up with new ones. It's all a scam. And profits—"

"The rules are meant to protect people," Anders contradicted him. "Especially the people whose backyards you're drilling in."

"We're not drilling in anyone's backyards."

"The Terrence field isn't very far from North Run."

"We do our best. This is a business—things happen—the money—it just isn't—"

This was serious, Anders realized, awareness zinging along the back of his neck, as if someone was spying on him even now, hearing this conversation. His normally suave father was almost stuttering. If Clem got wind of any problems at Hansen Oil and put two and two together to figure out who he really was, he was in trouble.

"You've come under fire plenty of times before. Why is it different this time?" As much as he hated to admit it, problems with Hansen Oil could all too easily become his problems.

Another too-long pause. "There's proof. And the wrong person has seen it. And this is a very delicate time."

"Proof? Who saw it?" That was different all right. Hansen Oil was generally good at covering its tracks.

"Some underling at a satellite imaging company. Eve... something. I've got people on it, but so far we can't get a line on her. She's supposed to be on vacation in Maine, but we can't track her down. God knows where she really is."

Satellite imaging? Eve? Anders's grip tightened on his phone until he was surprised it didn't shatter. His chest tightened, too, until he could hardly breathe.

He nearly said her name out loud but just as quickly realized he couldn't. Not until he knew what this was all about. If Eve knew something about Hansen Oil, why was she at Base Camp? Had she figured out who he was? Did she plan to... what? Come after him? Blackmail him?

"I gotta go," he told his father.

"You've got to come home. It's time to circle the wagons. Make some changes around here. For that, I need you."

"I'll get back to you." Anders hung up.

Hell.

Usually his father handled interference in his company with an iron fist. Johannes was a powerful adversary. Today he'd sounded... shaken. As for Eve, he couldn't believe for a minute she'd come here to ruin him, but—

Why else would she be here?

He'd have to figure that out fast—without letting her know he was onto her.

That episode they'd all just previewed would go live in a few days. His father would know Eve was here. Would know he'd covered for her.

Would come after her.

He didn't have long to think about the implications. A sound behind him made him whirl around. He was relieved to find Renata exiting the bunkhouse behind him rather than Clem, given the circumstances.

"Everything all right?"

He searched for a way to answer that. "That episode was pretty intense. How is Clem getting all that footage?"

She shrugged. "You're the Navy SEAL. Aren't you

supposed to know about being sneaky?"

Something about her tone put him on alert. "I thought so. Maybe I was wrong." He'd obviously been fooled by Eve. Or had he? Could it possibly be coincidence that brought her here?

Doubtful.

But how would a woman in Virginia piece together his past when he—and Johannes—had been so careful to hide it?

"It's not going to be easy to convince Fulsom I should stay on as director when Clem is getting all the scoops."

"Guess not." He'd forgotten to tell the others to come up with exclusives to give her. Was she fishing for one right now? How much did Renata know about him?

"Thought you were going to get me something big. Something to upstage Clem."

"Working on it." Of course, he wasn't. He didn't know what scoop he could give her that would work that kind of magic. He certainly couldn't tell her about Hansen Oil. Or about Eve.

"Well, that's what I want for Christmas, and there's still a few hours left in the day," she joked, but she headed toward the vehicles parked nearby. "Figure I might as well go back to town. Nothing for me to do here now that Clem's got it all under control."

Anders watched her go. He'd always thought of Renata as the adversary, standing between him and his friends and their goal of preserving Base Camp. Now he realized she was a powerful ally. One he'd miss if she left.

He couldn't think about that now, though. He needed to figure out the situation with Eve. If she had an image that proved Hansen Oil was doing something wrong, why hadn't she exposed it already? She could have uploaded it to the internet. Gotten it to go viral on social media. Heck, she'd worked with NGOs for years. She must have a web of contacts ready to spread her information all around.

So why end up here?

He watched Renata get in one of the SUVs and drive off, considering the problem.

Because *Base Camp* was a nationally acclaimed television show, and if she could spill the beans about Hansen Oil during an episode, news about it would spread like wildfire all over North America.

She hadn't been dumped by her boyfriend on the side of the road. She hadn't come to marry him, either. Eve had come here to take down Hansen Oil once and for all.

Should he stop her?

Or help her?

The door opened behind him again. Eve slipped out, Avery close behind her.

"Eve's sick," Avery announced as she hustled Eve along the path. "I'm taking her up to the manor, where she can get away from the crowd."

"I just need to lie down for a while," Eve said, not meeting his eyes.

"Anything I can do?" Anders made himself ask as if

he hadn't just had the rug pulled out from under him.

Eve shook her head, and the women kept going. Anders was relieved not to have to pretend he didn't know what he knew, but he couldn't help tracing their path with his gaze. He found himself wishing he could talk over this conundrum with her. If it hadn't concerned her, she would have been his first choice as an advisor.

It did concern her, though. Eve was here on false pretenses, and now he needed to reevaluate everything. He needed a plan.

In the end he slipped away to his tiny house, shut the door behind him and wandered through the small space, trying to take stock. The wood finishes and custom touches couldn't soothe his racing thoughts. Neither could the painting of Alice the bison that he'd hung on one of the walls.

He needed to keep his identity secret.

He needed a wife.

Now what was he going to do?

"I DON'T THINK you should be alone," Avery said. "What if you get worse?"

"I won't. It's just a headache." Eve climbed into one of the manor's sumptuous guest beds and pulled the covers around her shoulders, grateful for the quiet in the large, empty house.

"Back at the bunkhouse you said it was a stomach-ache."

"It's both," Eve groaned. A headache and stomach-ache brought on by finding out the man she was falling for—hard—was the heir to the Hansen Oil fortune.

"Did something happen between you and Anders? He looked a little strange back there."

Eve had no idea why Anders would look strange. She was the one who'd just had her world rocked. "I just need to sleep."

"Okay. I'll check on you in an hour or so. Meanwhile I'll bring you a cup of tea."

Eve's thoughts were whirling so fast she barely heard Avery leave or come back again with a cup she set on the bedside table. Avery must have thought she was asleep because she crept out of the room again quietly, and then the house was silent again.

Over and over, Eve came back to the same questions. Why was a Hansen here at Base Camp? Why had Anders changed his name when he was eighteen? He'd said his relationship with his father was strained. Was that because he was an environmentalist and his father was an oil man, or had something else gone wrong between them?

And even if he was estranged from Johannes, would he rally to his father if he learned Hansen Oil was under attack? Blood ties ran deep.

Eve had never felt so alone.

She didn't have to be, though. Sitting up, she pulled out her phone.

You there? she texted Melissa.

Of course. You okay?

Not sure. I don't know what to do.

Maybe it's time to admit defeat.

No. The answer came so swiftly, Eve knew it was right. *I don't want to give up. I have the perfect information and the perfect venue to force Hansen Oil to do the right thing for once.*

Agreed. Much as I want you to be safe and happy.

Eve thought a moment. *I'm calling you.* She was alone, after all. It would be far easier to do this on the phone.

"I wish I was there with you," Melissa said when she picked up. "Harry's gone to spend a couple of hours with family. He'll be back later."

"I wish you were, too. I don't know what I'd do without you," Eve admitted.

"That's what friends are for," Melissa said. "Now it's time to make a plan."

Eve settled back against the headboard. She and Melissa had hashed out their problems like this more times than she could count, and she was confident they would figure something out, but that didn't dull the pain that came from knowing her relationship with Anders, such as it was, was over.

"I have one chance to expose Hansen Oil," Eve said. "Doing it in front of everyone at the New Year's bash will certainly make it more likely for Clem to keep it in the episode—and for local news to cover it. Hopefully from there, national media will pick it up. It's risky, though. Maybe I should give my material to Renata and let her run with it."

"You could do that, but isn't Clem the one in charge right now?"

"I think so."

"From the sound of it, he won't do anything with footage like that if it doesn't forward the show. I think we should keep to the original plan, if you think you can keep from blowing your cover before then."

"I think you're right." It wouldn't be easy. She'd have to get through six more days.

"I'll prep posts for social media and press releases for local and national news outlets. I'll get Jana involved, too," Melissa said. "We'll do all the legwork for that kind of thing, and I'll case out the New Year's bash venue to see how we can get your presentation live. Harry and I have our tickets."

"You'll have to be ready to whisk me out of there and get me on a plane as soon as it's over," Eve said. "I'm going to be like Cinderella at the ball, ready to run for it at midnight."

"I'll have a car ready to go," Melissa promised. "But Eve—would you be mad if I didn't go back to Virginia with you? I thought I might stay in Chance Creek a little longer."

Eve's heart sank, but she forced herself to answer cheerfully. "Of course I won't be mad. You and Harry are becoming a thing, aren't you?"

"Eve." Melissa sounded breathless. "I think… I think he could be the one."

"I'm so happy for you." Eve closed her eyes and dug the fingernails of her free hand into her covers, sudden tears stinging her eyes. She thought maybe she'd found the one, too. Wishful thinking all along.

"I'm really sorry," Melissa said. "My timing sucks."

"It's not like you planned it," Eve said. "Anyway, if I'm going to destroy Anders by taking down his father's company, someone should be happy."

A crash behind her made Eve scramble to her knees on the bed. Avery stood in the doorway, a shattered teapot on the floor by her feet.

"Oh, shit," Eve said into the phone. "I've got to go."

"EVERYTHING ALL RIGHT?" Curtis asked when Anders opened the door of his tiny house. "I assumed you went up to the manor with Eve, but Hope said she saw you head this way. Did you and Eve have a fight?"

Anders shook his head and let him inside. "Not a fight," he said. Normally he trusted Curtis to give him good advice, but this time he was on his own. They stood near the tall windows that looked out over a hillside. "I don't think we're going to make it, though."

"This morning you two looked fine. What changed?"

Anders chose his words carefully. "I think Eve came here for a specific purpose."

Curtis nodded. "Tell me."

"Washing up here, on the run—that's a cover story. I think she plans to use the show to advance a personal cause."

"That sounds pretty specific. How do you know all this? Did she tell you?"

"No, and keep this between us, will you?" Anders

said quickly.

"Sure thing. What's her cause? Is she against what we're doing here?"

Anders shook his head. "Far as I can tell, she was truthful about being an environmentalist. A passionate one. But—she might be in too deep. She's taking on an enemy who won't hesitate to retaliate."

"Against her—or us?"

Straight to the point. Anders appreciated that. "Both."

Curtis moved closer to the windows and gazed outside, too. The tiny houses were dug into the hillside at various locations. Across the way, on another rise of ground, sat the manor—where Eve was.

"She could have the best intentions in the world," Curtis said slowly, "and still wind up being the end of us."

"That's right." And he'd be the weapon she'd point at the community he loved. Anders scraped a hand over his jaw. What a mess.

Curtis turned. "Is there something else I should know?"

Anders held his gaze. "There's a lot you should know, but I have to take this step by step. See if I can salvage things somehow and not blow everything up while trying." He thought Curtis saw through his deflection, but the man didn't push him.

"Tell me one thing. This cause of hers—if everything else was equal, would you back it or thwart it?" he asked.

"I'd back it," Anders said without hesitation. "She's in the right. She's also going to lose."

"And take us down with her. Got it." Curtis studied him. "You like her."

"I love her." Anders didn't realize the words were true until he said them. "And I've got no idea what I'm going to do."

Curtis clapped a hand on his shoulder. "You're going to work a miracle," he said. "And I know who can help."

"Who?"

"Renata."

"ANDERS LOVES YOU."

Eve's heart was pounding so hard she didn't think she'd heard Avery right. She was on her knees mopping up the spilled tea and teapot shards with a towel she'd fetched from the bathroom. Avery still stood in the doorway, watching her as if she'd never laid eyes on Eve before.

"He *likes* me," Eve corrected. She had no idea how she was going to fix this. Avery would tell everyone else what she'd heard. An hour from now she'd probably find herself at the airport flying back to Virginia—without Melissa.

"He loves you. And you're going to ruin him? Is that why you came here? What did Anders ever do to you?"

"I was being dramatic." Eve left the towel in a sodden heap on the floor and got to her feet. She had to salvage this somehow. "And no, I didn't come here to ruin Anders. That's the last thing I'd want to do." She rubbed the back of her neck and ushered Avery into the bedroom. There was nothing for it but to take her into her confidence. She'd have to let Avery decide what happened next.

"You're right; I came here on false pretenses." She waved Avery to sit on the bed and climbed back to her position near the headboard. "I came here because I need to blow the whistle on Hansen Oil. It's letting chemicals get into the water supply of a town near its fracking operation." Short and sweet. Either Avery would get it, or she wouldn't.

"Hansen Oil? Jesus, Eve."

Eve was heartened by Avery's exclamation and the way she sat there thinking things over. She hadn't laughed off Eve's assertion. That was something.

"I know Hansen's track record," Avery said a minute later. "What kind of information do you have? Wait—" She shook her head. "Satellite images."

"That's right. It's plain as day what's happening. When the images crossed my desk, I took them to my boss. I expected him to help, but..." She shrugged.

"Let me guess. He told you to keep your mouth shut."

Eve nodded. "I can't blame him. Hansen goes after its adversaries—hard."

"So you came here to what—show the images on the show? You thought Fulsom would allow you to do that?"

"Wouldn't he? The whole point of Base Camp is to change the world." Eve gathered her thoughts. "Fulsom is rich enough to be Johannes Hansen's equal. I don't know anyone else who could possibly stand up to him."

"I guess that makes sense." Avery pleated the comforter between her fingers. "What about us, though? Stands to reason if you cross Hansen on our show, he'll come after Base Camp."

"You're right," Eve admitted. "The longer I stay here, the harder that is to contemplate."

"And then there's Anders."

Eve stilled. Did Avery know who Anders really was?

"He loves you. How will he react if your actions damage this community?"

Maybe she didn't know, and Eve wasn't ready to expose Anders. "He'll hate me," she said succinctly. Even if he theoretically agreed that what Hansen Oil was doing was wrong, he would hate her for attacking his father. She would in his place.

"They're really poisoning people's drinking water?"

"Looks like it."

Avery hugged herself, and Eve would have done anything to take away her misery. "If I ask you not to do it, I'm as bad as Hansen," Avery said.

"I'm sorry. I really am." Tears welled in Eve's eyes again, and she realized she'd come to know the inhabitants of Base Camp too well. She couldn't stand up on New Year's and make the announcement that might destroy everything they'd built. Who knew what Johannes Hansen was capable of? Eve came to a decision.

"Forget it—I won't do it. I'll leave—tonight. I'll find another way—"

"There isn't another way," Avery said slowly. "Not like this. Coming here, getting Anders to love you—getting the audience to care for you—that's brilliant. When everyone sees your first episode in a few days, they'll want you and Anders to get together. They'll be invested in your story. I don't know when you planned to spill the beans—"

"New Year's Eve," Eve said.

"Of course. Clem will be all over that," Avery added. "I bet you're lining up news coverage, too."

Eve nodded.

"You're a natural at this—drawing attention to a cause."

"I've done it before." Eve explained her work overseas. "I participated in all kinds of campaigns to get the word out about environmental and social justice problems."

"What do you plan to do on New Year's?"

"I'm going to interrupt the dancing and show a short movie," Eve said. She went through the steps she and Melissa had outlined, without mentioning she had a friend in town.

"Brilliant," Avery said again. "I'll help. I've got lots of footage you can use."

"Help? Why would you do that?"

"Because it's the right thing to do." Avery tilted her head. "Eve, we're all here because we care, you know that, right?"

"What about Base Camp?"

"Do you love Anders?" Avery countered. "The truth," she added. "No more bullshit."

"No more bullshit," Eve agreed. "Of course I love Anders."

"Then let's figure out how to expose Hansen Oil without exposing us, too."

"How are we going to do that?" Eve's pulse quickened. If she could expose Hansen without losing Anders—

But Anders was a Hansen.

"I don't know. But I know who's going to help."

"Who?" Eve asked suspiciously. She didn't want anyone else to know about this.

"Renata, of course."

CHAPTER ELEVEN

IF ANDERS DIDN'T know better, he'd have thought Eve was avoiding him as much as he was her. They still sat together at meals and exchanged small talk when they bumped into each other. He'd even managed a joke once and made her laugh. For one second, it had been like old times, and he'd fought the urge to pull her close.

The awkwardness between them most of the time was unmistakable, though. A day passed, and then another, and Anders realized everyone at Base Camp had noticed the distance between them. He'd made no progress figuring out what to do about her, either. Renata had taken to staying in town, and when Clem got in his face, peppering him with questions about his obvious failure to *bag* Eve, as he put it, Anders knew something had to change.

The next morning he asked Eve to join him for morning chores. She agreed after a moment's hesitation.

"Ready to ride? Are you wearing pants under there?" He gestured to her gown.

"Yes."

She was quiet on the way to the stable. Was she wondering why he'd been so cool to her the last few days?

Outside, the wind was blowing. Most of the snow was skimmed off the pastures and caught against fences, buildings and other protuberances in the landscape. It was cold, but it was safe to ride.

He helped her up into her saddle, wishing he knew what to say or do to put her at ease again. She perched there a little uncertainly. "This still feels a lot higher up than I remember from being a kid," she said, patting her horse's neck.

"We'll go slow again."

He mounted his favourite horse, a roan mare named Wishful. It felt good to be in the saddle, something he'd enjoyed all his life and hadn't gotten to do enough during his time in the service. Coming to this ranch in Montana had in some ways been like coming home, Anders thought, not for the first time. He'd missed his uncle's ranch while he'd been in the Navy.

Back when he was a kid, it had never occurred to him to make a way of life out of ranching, but now it made sense, and if he was honest, spending his days tending the bison, as little as they needed tending, brought him a profound joy. There was something so right about seeing the animals move across the pastures. A connection between bison and prairie that was ancient and that he felt he was helping to restore. Eve's book had given him plenty to think about in that respect, however. He realized now they'd done only the most rudimentary steps to put things to rights. They had to think like the animals. Allow them to move in their ancient ways. Only then would balance truly be restored.

At first, Eve's horse, a black gelding named Bart, was a little balky under her rusty movements, but soon horse and rider settled down to each other, and Eve began to be able to look around her.

Anders liked the way she scanned the horizon, glanced at the herd and scanned the horizon again. She was being aware of her surroundings, and that was important out here. Whether or not somebody might be chasing you.

"You look like you've ridden all your life," he said.

Eve laughed. "Hardly. But it's coming back to me a lot faster than I thought it would."

He set the pace, leading the way out along the closest pasture, where the herd was currently grazing, using their powerful hooves to kick away the scrim of snow and get at the grasses below it.

"It's beautiful out here," Eve said.

Anders's heart swelled in his chest before he remembered why she had come here. It took a special kind of person to see the beauty in a December landscape in Montana, on a day when the clouds had lowered so far down that he felt he could touch them if he reached up his hand. If Eve could connect to the landscape on a day like this, she would have made him a good partner. She hadn't come here to be his partner, though.

"More snow coming," he said.

"We could build ourselves an igloo out here," she said.

"That would be cozy." He pictured crawling into a little structure like that with Eve. A structure with no windows for Clem to look through and film them.

Never going to happen now.

"I looked up Montana's climate, and it seems you have more snow than usual this year."

She'd looked up Montana's climate? Anders's heart swelled again before he could stifle his feelings. She was digging in, in her own way. Learning about Base Camp, Chance Creek and Montana at large. If it wasn't for Hansen Oil, he had a feeling she'd want to stay.

For the last couple of days, he'd steered clear of conversations that touched on Eve staying or going, or anything else to do with their relationship, including whether or not they were having one. What else could he do? He had no idea how to stop her—or help her, for that matter. Meanwhile, Curtis was on him all the time to sit down with Renata and tell her everything.

"I think you're right." He, too, still had a lot to learn about his new home. It struck him that he should have been doing a lot more studying. A lot more reading. He'd gotten enamored of the *doing* part of the job, but there was still a lot more to know. They weren't the only ones working on sustainability issues. Why reinvent the wheel twice?

"According to the book I gave you, ranchers are experimenting with smaller enclosures and revolving the cattle through them more quickly," Eve said. "I wish it had more to say about bison."

"Bison are a whole different animal," Anders said and smiled. He hadn't meant to make the joke, but there it was.

"Do you think—" Eve broke off. "Look. Someone else has been out here."

Anders steered his mare over to where Eve was pointing. She was right; there were tracks over here. Snowshoe tracks. Someone had walked through.

He wondered who.

The tracks came from the opposite direction, and he guessed that somebody had come in off the country road that led to Base Camp, parked somewhere along it and walked onto the property. They had gotten this far and stopped. Milled around a little bit. Checked out the bison, probably. Then turned and gone back the way they'd come.

Odd.

"Do you often get people snowshoeing on the ranch?" Eve asked.

"Never," Anders said grimly. And they'd been patrolling lately, ever since their food supply had been broken into and much of it stolen. Anders knew beyond a shadow of a doubt that there would be other tracks out here. Footprints and vehicle tracks from where he and the other men patrolled each night. These tracks had to have been made during the span of time that started after the last patrol went through, which had been shortly after midnight, and before he and Eve arrived. Who would snowshoe onto the property in the middle of the night? And why had they stopped here? The fences hadn't been tampered with, so it hadn't been someone after the bison. Instead, it looked like somebody had simply come to check things out. To get the lay of the land, so to speak.

Recently, they'd learned Fulsom himself had instigated the theft of their food—to make the show more compelling. Now he'd sent Clem. Anders thought about Greg's early misgivings about Eve.

Could Fulsom somehow be behind Eve's arrival, too? Was Fulsom upping the ante again, sending a new director who employed sneaky observation tactics and a woman determined to take on one of the biggest oil companies around—a company conveniently owned by his father?

This was all getting way too complicated.

He couldn't see Eve working with Clem on anything, Anders decided, let alone planning this whole series of events together. He could see her working with Fulsom if she thought he'd help her take on Hansen Oil.

Still, something didn't sit right with him as far as that line of thinking went. Fulsom liked to storm in and throw them curveballs, but they were direct, hard-hitting curveballs, not tricky convoluted ones.

He'd bet his life Eve wasn't working with Clem or Fulsom. She was running her own mission, letting nothing stand in her way of achieving it. Not even him.

That left him two choices. Stop her or help her. Like Curtis said, it was time to work a miracle. Time to make

Eve understand that he was on her side—without letting her know what he knew about her plans.

Talk about complicated.

Anders knew one of the best ways to establish rapport with someone who didn't trust you was to offer them information.

He urged his horse closer to Eve's, looked around to establish they truly were alone and said, "Fulsom's the one who robbed the food stores."

Eve's head snapped up. "You're kidding!"

"No. Don't know who he hired to do it. Maybe someone on the crew. But it was him. He did it for ratings. We were meeting our goals too easily."

She indicated the snowshoe prints. "One of Fulsom's people again?"

"Maybe. Maybe not. Maybe Nora isn't the only one who has enemies from before. We've all led interesting lives."

She took that in. Time to make his point.

"The thing that Fulsom doesn't understand is that we stand by each other. We're a family. We're not going to sacrifice anyone to save ourselves. We learned something when Nora was attacked. When she started seeing things that weren't right, we didn't believe her because the signs were so subtle. Nora nearly paid for that with her life. We won't make that mistake twice. We're watching all the time. We're looking for signs of trouble. Noticing them when they happen. Making plans to fight them. But when someone here attracts trouble, we don't kick them out. We help them."

Eve had gone very still. He didn't know how else to warn her—or convince her to trust him. "Clem's not the only one who knows more than he lets on," he added. Could he be clearer without coming out and telling her he knew who she was?

"No, he's not," she said.

Anders swallowed and resisted the urge to swing his mount away from Eve. What the hell did that mean? Had he been wrong in thinking she didn't know who he really was?

Anders's neck and shoulders prickled, and he turned Wishful all the way around, scanning the horizon in every direction. Suddenly, he felt far too exposed. Was someone watching them?

"Time to head back," he said shortly. He expected Eve to protest. After all, they'd barely started their ride, and they hadn't discussed the grazing of the bison at all.

Instead she urged her horse around back the way they'd come.

"I think you're right. I've watched *Base Camp* since the beginning," Eve went on, "but I forgot Nora's stalker was watching her from right here on the ranch. I've been in the manor a dozen times and never thought about the fact he was in there, too." She shivered. "There are so many ways someone can get on this land."

"That's why we patrol it now. I'll be out here tonight."

"So many people think this world is safe."

That was an odd thing to say. Was Eve thinking

about Nora's stalker, what she herself had seen over-seas, or was she thinking about Hansen Oil?

It occurred to Anders for the first time Eve might actually have the measure of his father and what he was capable of if he felt threatened. Had she looked up past cases against the company? Had she seen what had happened to whistleblowers and activist groups who'd gone against him? Had she read about the various ways his father had conspired to ruin his adversaries' lives?

If so, she'd feel as vulnerable as he did.

Eve was brave, Anders realized. One woman taking on Hansen Oil alone. He was afraid of losing Base Camp. She had to be afraid of losing everything.

This was the kind of woman he'd always hoped he'd meet. The kind of woman he wanted to marry. How ironic she'd be the one person guaranteed not to love him when she found out who he was—

His phone buzzed. Anders pulled it out as they ap-proached the stable.

"Anders here."

"Hey, it's Mason Hall. The charity hockey fundraiser is coming up. Just reminding you to be at the high school a half hour before game time."

It took Anders a minute to remember what Mason was talking about.

The charity hockey fundraiser. He'd promised months ago to join Mason's team. Had gone around town collecting pledges. "I'll be there," he said reluc-tantly. How the hell was he supposed to play hockey when his world was falling down around his ears?

"Good. See you then." Mason hung up, presumably to call the next man on his list.

"Who was that?" Eve asked as they rode toward the stable.

"The charity hockey fundraiser game is coming up. I'm playing on one of the teams. I think Curtis and some of the guys are coming to watch." Of course, who knew what would happen between now and then.

"Everyone's going to watch," she said. "Avery told me about it yesterday."

Anders looked up at the steel-gray sky. "Better dress warm if you're going to sit in the stands for a few hours. It'll be cold."

"It's always cold."

"I thought you thought Montana was beautiful, even in winter."

"I spoke too soon."

THE DAYS PASSED swiftly, with Eve slipping away every chance she could to work on her film. Avery had agreed to work with her and to put off talking to Renata until the film was done.

Avery proved to be a pro at losing Clem's cameramen and seemed to know every method of traversing Base Camp and the manor without being seen. She had forwarded Eve a number of files that highlighted different aspects of green energy use at Base Camp. Eve had been reaching out to various activist groups asking for video clips and images of the damage Hansen Oil had done to the environment over the years. It was painstaking work to put the footage together in an interesting way, and she was all too aware she didn't have much time left to finish it.

It helped that Renata had suddenly changed her tactics. After retreating to the crew's headquarters at a local hotel for a few days to lick her wounds, she'd come back with a vengeance, apparently having decided she wasn't going to give up and let Clem win without a fight. She'd taken to trailing him around all day, offering unsolicited critiques of his methods until he lost his cool. Eve thought Clem was used to being top bully in any given situation. Renata was driving him crazy.

Anders had been preoccupied, too, as were some of the other men. The tracks near the bison pasture had set them all on alert. Kai had confessed to her he was really on edge. "If they come for our food supply again, it'll be nothing but bison for the rest of the year. If they come for our bison, we'll really be in trouble."

On the second night she found it hard to concentrate at dinnertime. Seated with Anders, she could hardly make herself come up with conversation. She still wasn't done with her film, and Avery was growing more adamant by the minute that they enlist Renata in their cause. After lots of soul-searching, Eve had told Avery about Melissa and put the two of them in contact with each other. It felt good to know she wasn't in this alone, but tonight the first episode of *Base Camp* in which she was featured would air nationwide.

When Anders asked if she was okay, and she confessed her discomfort, he only shrugged. "Best thing is to ignore it. Definitely don't check out the *Base Camp* website. Just keep living your life."

She wished it was that simple.

Two nights later, the charity hockey fundraiser was held at the same outdoor rink the Night Sky Bonfire had been held at, and Eve had a strong sense of déjà vu as they parked in the high school parking lot and made their way to the ice rink. She was grateful for all the layers she'd added to her Regency ensemble, including two pairs of long underwear underneath her gown and several sweaters under her coat.

She followed the rest of the Base Camp crowd to the bleachers that had been set up around the outdoor rink. Anders peeled off to join Mason Hall and the other men on their team while they took their seats.

While everyone around her chatted, Eve sat lost in her thoughts until a whistle blew and the men on the ice began to play. She hadn't even noticed them entering the rink.

She took more notice after that. Anders hadn't been joking; he was good, and soon she was cheering and yelling along with everyone else. It felt good to put down her troubles for a minute.

"Go, Mason—go, Anders!" Avery screamed as the combination of men nearly scored a goal early on. Anders missed, but the next time he scored.

Eve leaped to her feet. "Go, Anders!" All around her, others were doing the same.

This was fun, Eve decided as she settled down again. Just for an hour or two she would enjoy herself.

She could worry about the future later.

WHY HAD HE ever stopped playing hockey?

Anders raced after the puck, passed it to Colt Hall, who passed it to Mason, who scored again. They were up two to zero, and the rush of winning felt great.

All his worries faded away as he concentrated on the game, losing himself in it like he had in high school. Back then, it had made a welcome escape from the rigors of grades and the constant need to prove himself to everyone, including his father. He was good at hockey, always had been. He knew instinctively where the puck would go, how the goalie would react, where to put the shot.

Out here there was just the ice and the puck. The other team blocking his way. His own team helping him. There were boundaries to the game, walls to keep the puck in.

Why couldn't more of life be like this?

Mason Hall took the face-off, got control of the puck again but quickly lost it to a man on the other team who threaded his way through the players and scored before anyone could react.

Two to one.

The next time Mason got the puck, he passed it to Anders, who turned, saw a clear path to the goal and took a shot.

A player from the other side came out of nowhere. Body blocked it, corralled the puck with his stick when it bounced off the ice and shot it down the rink to score another goal.

Hell.

The game was all tied up, and they'd only been play-ing ten minutes.

All thoughts of Eve and his father forgotten, Anders bent to the game—

And went after the puck again.

IN BETWEEN PERIODS, Eve and Avery went with Boone and the rest of the women to grab some hot chocolate. As bundled up as she was, it was chilly sitting in the bleachers; the hot chocolate was the only thing saving her. Clustered together, the women drew a lot of attention as people commented on their old-fashioned clothes, called questions about the show or simply greeted them. It was slow going, but they finally made it to the concession stand and got in line.

"Anders better score some more goals," Avery said as they waited.

"I wish I was playing," Boone said.

"Next year you men should form a team. The tour-nament goes all week," Riley said.

"Maybe we will," Boone said. "If we're here next year."

Riley elbowed him, and Boone hurried to add, "Sor-ry—just superstitious. Don't want to assume anything."

"We'll be here," Avery said. "Right, Eve?"

Eve could only shrug. Who knew what would hap-pen next?

After an uncomfortable pause, Riley turned the

conversation, and soon they were back in the bleachers clutching their drinks. A breeze had picked up, and Eve huddled among the others. This time she sat between Riley and Avery, with Boone on Riley's other side.

Eve settled in to watch the next period and, as soon as the game started, forgot the cold and everything else.

As usual, Mason took the face-off, but Anders exploded from behind him, caught Mason's pass and streaked down the ice to score a quick goal.

Eve leaped to her feet with everyone else and cheered. The risers reverberated with the din of their feet as they jumped and stomped in appreciation.

"Go, Anders!" Eve screamed. She nearly spilled her hot chocolate but caught it in time and took another gulp, burning her tongue.

"He's really good," Avery said.

"He is!"

"Someday this reality TV show will be over and life will get back to normal," Avery said wistfully. "We'll be able to do more things like this when Base Camp is established and everything isn't so pressured. The men can join hockey teams. We can do things, too."

"It's been hard, hasn't it?" Eve asked as they sat down again. "You all have been under such a microscope. Sometimes you must want to take off and be on your own for a while."

"It has. Always cameras. Except now," Avery joked. She pointed to where the crews had lined up along the rink. "I think the cameramen really like hockey."

"I think you're right." Eve had to laugh when all the

video cameras turned as one to follow the puck. "Where are Renata and Clem? They're going to be mad later that none of those cameras were trained on us. They should be showing our reactions to the shots. Things like that."

"There they are." Avery pointed, and Eve groaned.

"They're fighting!"

"Sure looks that way."

Renata was pointing a finger in Clem's face. Clem had his hands on his hips.

Avery pulled her phone out of a pocket in her coat. "Guess we'll have to document ourselves. Show some team spirit!"

Eve jumped up and shouted, making everyone around them look, since currently the two teams were milling around on the ice, waiting for the ref to make a call. Avery filmed her.

She sat down again. "How was that?"

"Perfect. Now you do me."

Eve did so, but both of them settled down and turned their attention back to the game when it started up again.

At the second intermission, the score was four to three—in favor of the other team.

"Hot chocolate refill!" Riley called out, and they all stood up, their mood somewhat dampened in comparison to their earlier trip to the concession stand.

When they reached the ground and were walking toward the stand, Eve realized the first cup had caught up to her. "Bathroom break," she shouted, and the women veered off together like a school of fish. "Boone, hold our place in line," Riley ordered.

Boone saluted and kept going.

Eve couldn't remember the last time she'd traveled in a group like this. In high school maybe? It was fun. It was easy to let her worries slide amid the laughter and chatter.

Washing her hands afterward, she was still trying to come up with an equivalent experience when Avery nudged her. "Hurry, the game's going to start again." Riley did a head count, and when everyone was accounted for, they caught up with Boone, who was nearly at the head of the line waiting to order their hot chocolate.

Ten minutes later, steaming cups in hand, they were nearing the risers again when the announcer came back on the air. Boone and Riley led the way to where Walker and the rest of the men were saving their seats. Avery, Nora, Samantha, Addison and Hope followed.

Savannah had a hard time negotiating the steps up onto the riser. Eve hung back behind her, giving her time, not envying the other woman climbing stairs this many months into her pregnancy.

"Mmph!" Eve exclaimed when a hand clamped over her mouth.

"You move, you talk, you do anything and you'll regret it," a man hissed in her ear. "Duck." Before she could react, he shoved her under the bleachers and pushed her forward, wending a path between the metal struts holding them up. Eve struggled against his grip, but he was far too big for her to escape. His fingers dug into her face. She screamed, but hardly any sound escaped.

All her friends were directly overhead. In a moment someone would come after her, she thought wildly. He wouldn't get away with this, whoever he was.

When the crowd overhead roared, her heart leaped in relief. Someone had seen what had happened. Now they'd come and save her.

Then she realized they were reacting to the game, now back in full swing.

Horror mounted within her, and Eve tried to dig in her heels. She grabbed a support strut and hung on.

The man shoved her forward, and she had no choice but to let go or break her wrist. Her breath was coming in short gasps, her long skirts tangling around her legs. Chills ran through her veins as he half shoved, half carried her through the maze of the support struts and out the far side.

This couldn't be happening. It couldn't—

But it was.

Kevin must have seen the *Base Camp* episode that featured her. He must have spilled his suspicions to Johannes Hansen, and Hansen must have sent one of his henchmen after her. What would he do with her? Intimidate her? Make her disappear?

Did he have a weapon?

Manhandled along, Eve struggled to make their progress as difficult as possible. The man swore when she caused him to stumble, lifted her bodily off the ground and kept going, bursting into a dead run when they reached the parking lot.

No one came to stop him.

She was on her own.

CHAPTER TWELVE

WHEN ANDERS SCORED his third goal of the night, he grabbed Mason, slapped him on the back and bumped fists with Colt. They were unstoppable as a team.

He turned to the bleachers to see if Eve had caught his shot but found the section where the inhabitants of Base Camp were sitting in an uproar.

There was Boone—and Riley, who was gesturing wildly.

There was Avery, calling up to Boone from the base of the risers. Harris was with her, Greg close by.

"What's going on?" Mason asked.

"I don't know."

He scanned the women again, hard to do when everyone was moving. There was Sam, Addison. Hope.

"Anders!"

That was Curtis calling from beside the ice rink. Anders kept scanning the crowd. There was Nora. Savannah was still seated, cradling her belly.

Where was Eve?

"Anders—we can't find Eve!" Curtis called out.

Hell.

Anders dropped his stick, skated for the edge of the rink and vaulted over the wall. "Where is she? What happened?" he yelled, making awkward progress through the snow in his skates.

Avery reached him just as Curtis did.

"She's gone!" Avery cried. "I don't know where— she's just gone!"

"Avery thinks she's in trouble—I don't know why," Curtis said.

Half-hysterical, Avery grabbed Anders's arm and shook it. "She was behind me. Behind Savannah. One second she was there, then she was gone. She didn't just run off, I swear it, Anders. She was determined to stay until she—" Avery broke off. "We checked the washrooms, the concession stand—she's nowhere!"

Anders's stomach tightened. Eve was in Chance Creek for a reason. She'd risked a lot to get on the show and was risking even more going up against his father. Avery was right, Eve wouldn't just cut and run. He didn't want to think his father capable of taking her, but Johannes had a way of making problems disappear. He'd sounded so paranoid on the phone. So angry. So... dangerous. Eve had really gotten under his skin.

The crackle of the loudspeaker caught Anders's attention. Another face-off was underway.

This was a nightmare. People all around them. Crowds moving this way and that. Eve could be anywhere.

"Nobody saw anything?" he demanded.

"No."

Had his father come for Eve? Or, more likely, sent someone to shut her up?

"We've got to spread out."

Curtis was fumbling with his phone. "I'll do a group text and tell everyone to keep searching."

"Anders? What's going on?" Mason called from the rink.

"Gotta go!"

He raced to the bench where he'd stowed his boots, stripped his skates off as fast as he could and caught up to Curtis and Avery again, scanning his surroundings.

"Harris and Greg are heading for the parking lot," Curtis told him.

"Good idea." He took off running. Steps behind him told him Curtis was following. His lungs were burning by the time he reached the parking lot, Curtis pounding on his heels.

"Over there," Curtis hollered, racing past him as they reached the outskirts of the parking lot.

Anders saw what he meant. A truck was screeching toward the exit. Another one—one of theirs—had its lights on, engine gunning. It took off before they could reach it, Harris and Greg inside.

"This way!" Anders grabbed Curtis's arm and dragged him toward the truck they'd come in. A minute later, he was flooring the gas as he raced for the exit. "Damn it!" Anders pounded the steering wheel. "I should have been with her!"

"Focus!" Curtis grabbed the wheel and yanked it before Anders went off the road. Anders yanked it back. He focused on driving and gunned the truck until the speedometer needle went off the register.

"Watch it—watch it," Curtis yelled as they skidded again.

"We're not going to catch them."

"The others will."

"We don't know that. Those guys had a head start!" Anders kept driving, kept trying to catch up, but the road ahead of them was empty.

He was going to be too late.

"KEEP QUIET IF you don't want to get hurt," the man growled as he tossed Eve into the back seat of the extended cab of his truck. He slammed the door closed, leaving her sprawled across the tattered bench seat, and got behind the wheel. He'd zip-tied her wrists together, but he hadn't bothered with her feet, and Eve fought to turn over and face forward as he revved the engine and burst out of his parking spot. She nearly slid onto the floor when he took a corner at full speed.

As the truck hurtled through the darkness, getting farther from Base Camp with each passing moment, she managed to scoot up on her seat until she was half-sitting.

Eve knew whatever she did now would determine her fate. She had no doubt Anders and the others would do their best to help her, but they'd have no idea where to even look for her.

A phone trilled—her abductor's phone. He pulled it out and tapped it, one hand still on the wheel, his movements jerky. Eve could just see the screen around the back of the seat. A man's face filled it. Someone she didn't recognize.

"You got her?"

Was he trying to see into the interior of the truck? Eve ducked down behind the seat.

"I got her," the driver said. "Coming your way now."

"Good. Don't fuck this up."

It wasn't Johannes Hansen. The man was younger— in his early forties, maybe. His face was round, his eyes blue. A far cry from the dark eyes and hawk-like visage of the oil man.

Eve didn't know if that was a bad thing or a good thing. She'd thought she'd known who her enemy was. Now she wasn't so sure.

"Where the hell is she at, Terry?" the man on the screen said, craning his neck. "I can't see anyone in the back seat."

Terry glanced over his shoulder. "Settle down back there."

"Fuck you."

On the screen the other man chuckled. "Now I see her. Feisty. I like that."

"Won't be feisty for long," Terry said. "Be there in a minute." He cut the call and tossed the phone on the passenger seat.

Eve realized she was holding her breath. *Won't be*

feisty for long. What did they plan to do with her?

Nothing good, she decided, which meant she had to act fast.

Eve held still for another minute, thinking through her options. With her wrists tied, she didn't have many. She'd get one chance at this, so whatever she did next needed to count.

Slowly she edged down in her seat again.

"What are you doing back there?" Terry asked, but he was having trouble seeing her, and the truck swerved as he half turned in his seat.

Eve didn't answer. She moved into a position that would give her more power, wriggling down until she was almost on her back, her bottom nearly hanging off the seat, but not quite. When Terry swore and focused on the road again, she quickly pulled her knees up tight to her chest and kicked out high with all her strength.

Her feet hit the back of his headrest just as he craned his neck again to see what she was doing. His head snapped forward, and he lost hold of the wheel. The truck hit a patch of ice, and Eve shrieked as it spun in a circle, throwing her down into the space between the seats. Terry regained control, swore, gunned the engine and drove another quarter mile before he veered sharply off the road onto a track that led into an evergreen forest. The truck bucked and struggled over what must have been a dirt track before coming to a stop among some trees.

Eve struggled to get upright again, but before she made it off the floor, the driver's door flung open, then her door, and Terry yanked her out of the truck and threw her to the ground.

"You… bitch! Nearly got me killed." He stood over her, hands on his hips.

Eve held her breath. Was this the way it would all end? Lying on her back in the snow, the dark shapes of the trees swaying in a cold wind overhead against the even darker sky? Would he strangle her? Pull out a gun and do her in with a single bullet?

Would anyone ever find her body? Or—

"Back off, Terry." Another man stepped into view. The one from the phone. "There you are," he said to Eve. "Get her on her feet," he ordered. "Time for us to have a little talk."

"HARRIS AND GREG are stopping!" Curtis pointed at the red taillights of the truck ahead of them.

"Where's the other truck?" Anders demanded. Peering forward through the darkness, he couldn't see a sign of it anywhere.

The door of the vehicle in front of them swung open, and Greg jogged back to meet them.

"They got too far ahead of us. One minute we could see their taillights, then we rounded a turn and they were gone. I thought they sped up, but they must have ducked off the road back there somewhere."

"We passed them?"

"I don't see any other explanation."

"What if you're wrong?" Time was passing. With every minute they were losing Eve.

"Tell you what—we'll keep going, you turn back and scan the side of the road. Look for tracks turning off."

"Good idea." Anders was already revving the engine. "Call if you see anything."

"Will do."

As soon as Greg had loped back to the other truck, Anders executed a three-point turn and drove back the way they'd come.

"Slow down," Curtis cautioned him. "We don't want to miss something."

Anders did so, but it was killing him. He needed to know what was happening to Eve.

"Why the hell would someone kidnap her?" Curtis asked him. "Do you think it's her ex-boyfriend?"

"Don't know." Anders gripped the wheel and kept scanning the ground to either side of the road. The snowbanks made an unbreaking obstacle to either side. It would be clear if anyone had tried to drive over them.

"There!" Curtis pointed suddenly, and Anders hit the brakes. He was right; there was a break in the snow to their left where a track branched off from the main road and wound into the woods.

Anders pulled to the side of the road and killed the headlights. Curtis pulled out his pistol. The men of Base Camp tended to be armed after the trouble that had gone down with Nora. Anders passed him the key to the glove compartment, and Curtis passed him back another firearm a moment later. Anders hadn't wanted to bring it to the hockey game, but he was glad to have it now. Outside, he scanned the woods and motioned for Curtis to follow him.

It seemed to take forever to follow the track silently until it curved around and led deeper into the trees. There, Anders stopped and waved Curtis up to his position. A truck was parked, its motor running, its lights on. Another vehicle was farther on. In between them stood three people. Eve, her wrists bound behind her back. A burly man with his hands on his hips.

And someone else Anders recognized. His father's right-hand man. Steve Bollard, Hansen Oil's CEO.

CHAPTER THIRTEEN

"**Y**OU REALLY SHOULD have listened to your boss and kept your nose out of my business," the stranger said. "Now you've created all kinds of trouble for yourself."

"I don't know what you're talking about," Eve managed.

"I'm talking about Hansen Oil."

"Then it's not your business. You're not Johannes Hansen."

"You're right; I'm not. I'm someone who actually gives a damn about the company."

Eve wished he'd stop talking in riddles. She'd been sure Terry worked for Johannes. Why else would he kidnap her and drag her to the middle of nowhere?

"I'm not Johannes Hansen," the man said, stepping closer, "but I own a hell of a lot of shares in Hansen Oil. That means when you mess with its reputation, you mess with mine."

Shares. Reputation. This man, whoever he was, worked for Hansen Oil. That made him as bad as

Johannes in her books.

"Someone has to stop you. All of you," Eve said.

The man laughed. "Is that what you think you're doing? Stopping me?" He waved a hand as if to say he wasn't the one who'd been dragged by a stranger into a lonely forest.

"Trying to." She refused to let him see how frightened she was.

"You realize I have to shut you up now," the man said.

"That's right. Mr. Bollard's going to shut you up good," Terry snarled at her.

"By killing me? Don't you think that will shine a spotlight bright and clear on your company? I doubt your practices will hold up to any scrutiny."

"No one has any idea I'm here," Bollard said. "You're just a deluded little girl who went chasing after a reality television star. Then something happened. Maybe you had a fight. Who knows? You ran away. Went missing." The man's eyes narrowed. "No one's going to think to pin the blame on me. Much more likely Anders will take the fall, don't you think?"

Eve nearly screamed when another man stepped out from behind a tree and put a handgun to Bollard's temple. "Not if I can help it," Johannes Hansen said. He nodded to Terry. "Drop it, or Mr. Bollard dies, and then you won't get paid."

It was the first time Eve had seen Terry look uncertain.

"Do it," Bollard snapped.

"But—"

"Do it!"

"Toss it over here," Johannes said. When Terry did so, he kicked it farther away among the trees.

Eve couldn't believe Johannes Hansen was really here—or that he'd come to her rescue.

"I assume you've got more of those zip-ties handy?" Johannes asked Terry, indicating Eve's hands trussed behind her back. "Tie your boss's hands. Tight."

"You're going to regret this, Johannes," Bollard hissed as Terry followed his orders.

Johannes ignored him. "As for you," he said to Eve. "What are we going to do with you, hmm?"

"Let me go so I can get on with my work!"

"Exposing my company's mistakes? That doesn't seem prudent, does it?"

"I wouldn't even have to be here if you'd just clean up the messes you make!"

"Easy for you to say," Johannes snapped. "Cleaning something up means admitting you made a mistake in the first place. Admitting a mistake means paying fines. Paying fines means coming up short as far as your shareholders are concerned, and God forbid you ever do that. Look—there's one of my biggest shareholders now. Willing to murder to keep the valuation of his stock high. My own CEO—" He caught himself. Took a breath. "I would have cleaned up the tailing ponds if you hadn't interfered, you know. I needed time."

"What for?" Eve demanded.

Johannes waved over Terry, who'd finished tying

Bollard's hands, and quickly secured his hands behind his back. "Sit down," he ordered both the men, then turned back to Eve with a withering look. "To do it without anyone noticing I'd done it. You have no idea what we deal with every day trying to get that oil out of the ground. Rules for everything. Fines for everything. It's always wait, wait, wait to do what you need to do and then pay, pay, pay to be allowed to do it."

"Then why do it at all?" Eve cried.

Johannes laughed again. "Someone has to do it. God, you kids. Am I right, Bollard?" His CEO didn't answer, but it was clear he was furious. "You act like you know it all while forgetting everything that came before. People like me built this country. Without oil we'd have gotten nowhere. Now you want to invent new power sources and say everything that came before is evil. You wouldn't have the technology you have today without the work we did. The work we're doing now."

"I have no idea what you're talking about." Or what it had to do with her. Did Hansen think he could persuade her to feel sorry for him?

"You… environmentalists. Do you think solar panels and wind turbines sprout fully formed? What does it take to manufacture them? Oil. What did it take to invent them? Oil! Now you want to pretend you've got nothing to do with us. None of you are spotless!"

"Not even your son?"

That stopped him—for a moment. He nodded. "I wondered if that's why you chose Base Camp—"

"It wasn't, actually," Eve interrupted him. "I didn't have any idea who Anders was until a few days ago."

"Won't marry him now, though, will you? He's an evil Hansen. He probably should be taken out back and executed!" Johannes blazed.

Did he... want her to marry Anders?

Eve couldn't tell which side Johannes was on at all. Maybe that was it, she thought. Maybe he wasn't on a side. Maybe he was stuck in the middle.

"He won't marry me, in any case." The absurdity of their conversation struck her. They were out in the middle of a forest, in the middle of winter, in the middle of the night. A man had dragged her here like a sack of potatoes. Another man had threatened to kill her. And now here she was, discussing the sorry state of her love life with the oil baron she'd set out to bring down.

"Then we have something in common. He turned his back on me, too. Won't even let me finish a sentence when we talk."

Eve tried to corral her scattered thoughts. She'd figured if they ever met, Johannes would do whatever it took to end her attack against his company. Instead he was lingering as if he wanted something else altogether.

What did he want?

"I want him to come home," Johannes said as if she'd asked the question out loud. "I want him to take his place in my company. I built it for him."

"I don't think that's true. If you had, Hansen Oil would be a very different entity."

"I made it profitable. One of the most profitable

companies—"

"Who cares?" Eve stared him down. "Really—who cares? Anders doesn't. I don't. Profit doesn't matter if fires are raging across California and Australia, droughts are draining the water tables in the southeast and Midwest, and Malaria and Lyme disease are surging with the spread of insects. Profit isn't the same as happiness, or safety, or health."

"Spoken like a—"

"Realist?" Eve broke in. "Like someone who's seen hundreds of satellite images that show cropland degradation, increased instances of coastal flooding and forest fires?"

"That's not the word I was going to use."

"No, I'm sure it wasn't." She was shivering. The cold had seeped under the layers of old-fashioned clothing she wore, and her feet were freezing in their boots.

"You and Anders make a perfect couple." He didn't mean it as a compliment, but she decided to take it as one.

"You're right. We do. I respect Anders, and you should, too. Anders wants to preserve the health of the world. To do that, he wants to help get the word out about green energy, regenerative ranching, healthy food production. You have a company with massive resources. Can't you see your way to help him? He doesn't know what I planned to do, by the way. He isn't involved at all."

"Oh, he knows, all right." Johannes shook his head.

Eve tried to process his words. Anders… knew who she was?

"That's right," Johannes said. "Didn't tell you, did he? I wonder why not? As for helping him, if he would just be patient for another year or so, I could have this whole mess cleaned up, and we could make the shift he—"

"For God's sake, Johannes, shut the fuck up," Bollard roared suddenly from where he was sitting in the snow. "You actually think I'm going to let you take Hansen Oil and give it to that radical environmentalist son of yours? You think I'm going to let you take a billion-dollar company and tear it to pieces trying to get into solar farms and windmills? Are you out of your ever-loving mind?"

"You know what's coming as well as I do," Johannes spat. "Everyone's changing course. We have to change, too."

"Fuck that! I'm not changing until every last ounce of oil is out of the ground. You're a sucker, and you don't deserve to run anything, least of all Hansen Oil."

"Shut your mouth!" Johannes kept his pistol pointed at him and Terry, but Bollard got to his feet.

"No. It's time to end this once and for all. Your time at the head of Hansen Oil is over. Time for some new blood." Bollard turned and hollered, "Come and get him, boys—he's all yours!" Six more men stepped out of the woods—all of them armed.

WHEN CURTIS HAD laid a hand on Anders's shoulder

and silently pointed to one tree and then another, it had taken Anders a moment to see what he meant, but when he did, he cursed himself for a fool. He'd nearly walked right into the trap Bollard had set. Bollard had to have known someone from Base Camp would follow them. He was making sure whoever did met the same fate Eve was about to. His men had taken up positions in the woods surrounding the clearing farther back among the trees than Anders would have set his guard.

He and Curtis withdrew, Curtis moving far enough back that he could call the others and apprise them of the situation without being overheard. That left Anders to wait and watch, his heart thumping strong and steady in his chest the way it always did when trouble went down. He'd bet anything the two men he could see weren't the only men waiting for Bollard's orders. In time he spotted two more, and then another. And another. Based on their spacing, he estimated at least two more of them would be situated across the clearing where he couldn't see them.

Anders crept forward again, keeping low to the ground, moving so slowly he almost wasn't moving at all, wanting a better sightline into the clearing. He found a place between two of Bollard's men without tipping them off to his presence—

Then nearly had a heart attack when his own father stepped into the light. For a moment, Anders thought he was working with Bollard, until Johannes put a pistol to Bollard's temple. Anders tensed, paralyzed by shock and dread, sure all hell would break lose.

Bollard's men were professionals, though. He hadn't given them a signal, and they hadn't budged. Their attention was squarely on the situation in the clearing.

Good.

That gave him a little wiggle room.

EVE'S STOMACH SANK as the clearing crowded with men. The look on Johannes's face said it all. There was no way either of them were getting out of this alive.

"You kill me, and Anders will inherit the company," Johannes said to Bollard as a man relieved him of his pistol, cuffed his hands behind his back and shoved him to the ground. "You know what he'll do with it without me to smooth the way."

"You're going to hand it over to him anyway." Bollard rubbed his wrists after another man set him free. "I've worked with you for over thirty years, Hansen. I know you better than you know yourself. I realized a long time ago you don't want to die without reconciling with your son. You'll roll over and let him do whatever he wants with Hansen Oil. No, when we're through here with you, we'll take care of Anders."

"Why don't you take care of me right now?"

"Anders!" Eve's voice cracked on his name. Her heart stopped as Bollard's men turned as one and pointed their weapons at Anders as he stalked into the clearing.

"Anders, get out of here!" Johannes shouted, but Eve could see it was far too late for him to turn and run. Why had he done such a foolhardy thing?

"Killing me isn't going to stop progress," Anders said to Bollard. "I get it; you own a lot of shares in Hansen Oil. If Dad tries to change the course it's on, those shares will take a beating."

"So you've got some sense in you, after all—"

"And then they'll rise again. I guarantee it. What do you think is going to happen when more and more people lose their homes and livelihoods to climate change—when insurance companies can't or won't pay their claims? Who do you think people will blame? Who are they going to go after?"

"They won't win. They can't win—"

"Yes, they can," Johannes said to his CEO. "They can and they will."

Anders watched his father curiously. Eve wondered if this was the first time he'd heard his father speak this way. He gestured as if to invite some silent audience to come closer and hear the unusual conversation.

"No. You're wrong. You're always wrong—"

Eve shrieked again as more men stepped out of the woods all around them, swarming around each of Bollard's men. When she recognized Boone, Clay, Kai, Greg and all the other Base Camp men, she bit her lip and sent a silent thank-you to the heavens.

"You're the one who's wrong," Anders said. "What's more; you're surrounded. Let's wrap this up without anyone getting hurt."

Eve thought Bollard would refuse, but sirens sliced the air close by.

Bollard's face was knotted with rage as he gestured

to his men. In a matter of moments, the eight were disarmed, their hands tied and members of the local sheriff's department had stormed into the clearing.

Anders cut the ties binding Eve's wrists and pulled her into a tight embrace. Eve clung to him, unable to speak as relief left her limp. She hadn't realized how scared she was until the danger was gone.

"It's okay," Anders murmured into her hair. "You're safe now. I'll never let anything happen to you again."

When he stiffened, Eve looked up, bracing herself for another turn of fortune, but it was only Johannes standing uncertainly a few feet away. Anders let go of Eve and gestured for her and Johannes to follow him away from the others. "No one knows who I am," he said to Johannes.

"Except me," Eve pointed out. "I've known since Christmas."

Anders shook his head. "No one else knows. They may have some suspicions after tonight, but none of them were positioned close enough to hear what Bollard said, and I want the chance to tell them my way."

Johannes nodded. "That was close," he said, his voice uneven. Eve noticed his hands trembling.

"Too close." The men surveyed each other. "You almost sounded like an environmentalist back there," Anders added wryly.

Johannes snorted. "Not quite."

Anders sighed. "Seems like you've had a bit of a change of heart, though."

"Maybe." His father made a face. "Forced to have a

change of heart, more like."

"It doesn't matter. However it happened, I'm glad. My friends and I—and Eve—are fighting against something that's coming at all of us so fast we don't know if we're going to win, and we could use your help."

An expression crossed Johannes's face Eve couldn't quite decipher. Something almost like… longing. Then it was gone again.

"But let me guess; first you expect me to condemn my life's work," Johannes said. "To tell the world I was wrong to supply energy to my country the best way I know how. Right?"

Anders moved closer to him, bringing Eve along with him, his arm still around her waist. "Is that what you're afraid of?"

"I'm not afraid of anything—" He trailed off when he took in Anders's expression. "What?"

Anders searched his father's face for so long, Eve thought he wasn't going to answer. When he finally did, his words were unexpected.

"I'm… sorry."

Eve wasn't sure which of the men was most surprised. Johannes, to hear Anders's words, or Anders to say them.

"I'm sorry if you thought I was asking you to do that, because you're right—you did give our country what it needed," Anders went on. "I'm not asking you to be ashamed of the past. I'm asking you to help make a shift toward the future. When cars came along, no one expected carriage-makers to be ashamed of their lives' work. It went better for the ones who got into the auto industry, though. Right?" he added. "Look, I'm not naive. I know Hansen Oil can keep running for years but not forever. Solar and wind and other renewable energy sources aren't just coming—they're here. Don't you want to make the transition ahead of the pack rather than be the last carriage-maker in town?"

"Your girl looks like she'd be more comfortable with a carriage-maker as a father-in-law," Johannes quipped feebly, waving a hand at Eve's old-fashioned outfit, but Eve could see Anders's words had touched him.

"Are you looking forward to being a father-in-law?" Anders asked. Eve thought he was surprised all over again.

"A man wants his legacy in order," Johannes said stiffly.

"What forced your change of heart?"

Johannes lifted his hands. "The writing is on the wall. Everyone's getting into renewables. My friends, my enemies—everyone. I'm already practically the last carriage-maker in town. My competitors aren't just building Model Ts, though—they're working on self-driving cars. I'm just an oil man. I can't keep up."

Eve would bet the man had never told the truth about himself so baldly in his life. *Say something*, she willed at Anders. His father had put himself in a vulnerable position. Anders needed to meet him halfway.

"I could help with that," Anders said slowly, "if we

could agree on a plan. I'd want to take Hansen Energy to the start of the pack, though." He emphasized *Energy*. Eve understood he meant he wasn't going to run an oil company.

Johannes nodded. "That's where we used to be. Guess I wouldn't mind being there again."

"Then I'd be honored to work with you." Anders held out his hand. After a moment, Johannes took it and shook.

He turned to Eve. "I suppose you still expect to publish those images for the whole world to see? Doing that will bring down the company before we have a chance to take it in a new direction."

Eve thought quickly. "I had a plan, you know. I made a movie and included the images of the tailing pond leaks in it. I planned to show it at the New Year's bash in town and invite the press to be present."

"You did?" Anders asked.

Eve held up her phone. "Shall I play it?" she asked Johannes.

After a moment, he nodded. She tapped the screen a few times and held out the phone so both Anders and Johannes could see. The latest version of her little film was far from done, but it hung together well enough for them to get the general gist of it. The short movie contrasted beautiful footage Avery had taken months ago of Base Camp, its inhabitants, its homes and green energy sources with the satellite images and other footage Eve had gotten from her contacts of all the ways in which Hansen Oil's operations had left the environment degraded. She'd thrown statistics in about climate change, too, highlighting the bigger problem continued use of oil and gas would bring about.

When she was done, she didn't wait for Johannes's comment. The sour look on his face told her all she needed to know.

"I made another film," she said hurriedly. "I think you might like it better."

She'd made it on a whim, piecing it together at the same time she'd made the first one, hoping to find a way to both expose Hansen Oil and somehow maintain her relationship with Anders. She meant for it to demonstrate how Hansen Oil could salvage its reputation by doing the right thing. More than once she'd thought herself foolish for spending the time on it, believing she'd never get the opportunity to show it after she exposed what she knew. As she tapped on her screen again, she was grateful she'd followed through on her whim.

This film was set in Texas, and she'd had to scramble to find all the footage she'd needed. She'd done the voiceover, meaning to get a professional narrator to redo it before it New Year's.

"Hansen Oil has a long history in Texas," the film began, with a flyover footage from a drone of one of the company's oil fields. "We've been a name you can trust for all your energy needs, but times are changing, and so are we." The film went on to detail the forms of green energy that Eve had wanted Johannes to think about investing in, with images of solar arrays and wind farms surrounded by pristine natural settings. Her voiceover quoted more statistics about the benefits of making the switch. "We're moving forward," the voiceover ended, "so that Texas keeps its status as one of the greatest states around."

She'd lucked out with the final shot. Melissa had found footage of a father and son fishing in a Texas river and had secured permission to use it in the film.

Both Anders and Johannes focused on that footage, and the surprise evident on their faces made Eve bite back a smile. Direct hit.

She let the movie end and put her phone back in her pocket. "Considering I've never made a movie before, I'm pretty proud of these, but I think we'll need a third one now."

"What third one?" Johannes demanded.

"The one you make. The one where you introduce your son—and his mission to transform Hansen Oil to a green energy company—to the world."

Johannes and Anders considered this. "What do you say, Dad? You ready to get into the movie-making business?"

Johannes sighed gustily. "Hell, I guess so. You realize how much money we're going to leave on the table being the good guys, though?"

"You realize how much money we're going to make by being early adopters?" Anders countered.

"Are you… going to leave Base Camp?" Eve asked him, suddenly stricken by the possibility.

"No." Anders turned to his father. "No, I'm not

leaving Base Camp. We'll have to find a way to make that work. In fact—" He hesitated. "I can't do anything until the show ends."

"I don't want you doing anything until we've cleaned up the tailing pond fiasco. That's my mess, not yours. We'll bring you in when it's time to start fresh." Johannes turned to Eve. "You going to marry my son?"

"Y-yes," Eve said and swallowed hard.

"Good." As the sheriff approached them, Johannes went to meet him.

Anders pulled Eve into another embrace, held her for a long moment. "I thought I'd lost you," he said huskily. "I thought I'd be too late. Are you sure you're all right?"

She nodded. She was.

"I love you. I want to spend my life with you." He pulled back and chuckled. "Guess my dad already sorted that out. Look at us, engaged and all."

Eve humphed. "I thought you said you'd be the one to propose."

"How are you going to get Clem off the ranch?" Anders asked Renata in the bunkhouse kitchen the next morning. They'd headed off Clem's and Renata's initial curiosity about Eve's disappearance by saying it had all been a misunderstanding. That Eve had gotten sick again, and Greg and Harris had driven her home, and then everyone else had gone off half-cocked when they couldn't find her. Clem and Renata had been so busy sniping at each other, they'd missed the action, although more than a few crew members looked like they might know more than they were letting on.

Clem hadn't been too pleased, and Renata had looked downright suspicious, but Anders had managed to get her alone long enough to set the record straight and tell her his plan for this morning.

He needed to come clean to everyone at Base Camp about his identity and what would happen next. He didn't want Clem in charge of the narrative of that encounter, however. This was the scoop he could give Renata. She'd agreed to get Clem off *Base Camp* if he provided her with footage of his confession.

"Just leave it to me," Renata said. "Watch and learn." She strode into the main room, and Anders followed, curious to see what she'd do. "Byron, Ed, Craig, come with me," she said loudly. "Dress warm, get some coffee for the road. This will take a while."

"Where do you think you're going?" Clem, who'd been flopped in a folding chair, listlessly marking up a sheaf of notes while waiting for breakfast to end and something exciting to happen, got to his feet.

"Nothing to do with you. Move it, Byron." Renata urged him on. "Just background material," she said to Clem. "Totally dull. Ed, come on. Let's go."

"What's the hurry then?" Clem demanded.

"The sun's up, breakfast is over, it's time to get to work. I've got an assignment. I'm going to get it done."

"Assignment." Clem crossed the room to where Renata was pulling on her outer gear. "Assignment from who?"

"Who do you think? My boss."

"Fulsom? He gave you an assignment? He didn't tell me."

"Why would he tell you? Car's leaving in one minute," she called to the crew members. "We've got a deadline. Let's get going!"

"I'm coming, too."

"Like hell you are." Renata strode out the door. Byron hurried after her, only half in his winter duds. Ed and Craig followed more slowly.

"What's this about?" Clem asked them.

Craig shrugged. "Who knows, but when Renata says move, I move. That's the job."

"See you later," Ed said.

Anders wanted to shove Clem out the door along with them when they left, but he forced himself to stay seated, thumbing through a newsfeed on his phone as if he had nothing better to do.

"Hell," Clem said a minute later after crossing to one of the windows and watching Renata's SUV begin to pull down the lane. "William, Dan," he called to a couple of the cameramen, "grab your gear. Come on. Hurry!" He returned to the door, pulled on a jacket and kept going. William and Dan followed as fast as they could.

When the door slammed behind them, Boone stood up. "Okay, folks. Meeting time. Is everyone accounted for?" The few remaining cameramen hurried to capture the action, exchanging startled looks. Boone waited for Kai and Addison to join them from the kitchen and take their seats. "So what's this all about?" he asked Anders. "We've all got bits and pieces of the story last night, but I've got to say, it doesn't add up."

Anders stood at the front of the room, like Fulsom always did when he came to harangue them, and suddenly he felt as exposed as if he'd stepped out onto a Broadway stage naked. He was dead tired. He hadn't got a wink of sleep last night, knowing this was coming. According to Eve, Avery knew everything, but she was the only one. It was time to come clean to everyone else.

All eyes in the room were on him. His friends stood or sat spread around the room in the way they always did at these meetings. Boone was close to the front, leaning against the desk Clay had built for him months ago. Riley was perched on a chair close by him. Savannah and Jericho sat side by side on folding chairs, holding hands, Savannah's prominently pregnant belly hard to miss.

Clay and Nora sat a little farther toward the back. They were a quiet couple but a physically demonstrative one. Clay often had his arm around Nora, almost as if he were still shielding her from the man who'd once tried to attack her—and was now dead. Nora didn't need shielding, though. She was a strong woman in her own right. She rested a hand on her slightly rounded belly with a serene smile.

Harris and Samantha were front and center, as if ready to take on whatever was coming next. Close to them sat Kai and Addison. Samantha and Addison had become nearly inseparable.

Curtis and Hope were snuggled together like new-lyweds near the back of the room. Of course, they were newlyweds, Anders supposed.

Greg sat near the window, still carving. Angus sat a little apart from everyone else. He'd been growing more and more morose as the year dwindled. Soon it would be his time to marry, and Anders figured he was still pining for Win Lisle, who'd left Base Camp to return home.

Walker and Avery were sitting right in the center of the room—close, but not too close. Chatting quietly. Their relationship status a mystery to Anders.

Then there was Eve.

The woman he wanted to spend his life with.

Together, these people were his family. He counted on them, and they counted on him. They'd shared so much since he'd arrived here in June. He wished he'd never lied to them. He should have trusted them to understand his circumstances.

Would his good news about Hansen Oil make up for the deception he'd practiced on them?

"Thank you all for the chance to explain," he said to the room at large. "Boone's right—you need to hear the story from the beginning if you want to understand what happened last night, but first let me say how much I appreciate that you helped Eve and me last night before you even knew what was happening. I couldn't ask for better friends."

He took a moment to collect his thoughts. "There's

something I need to tell you all. Something that might come as a bit of a shock." Anders had decided earlier the only way to do this was rip the bandage off all at once. Get it over with and keep moving, even if that meant moving right out the door if the rest of them decided they didn't want him to stay. "Eve came here for one purpose only: to expose Hansen Oil's wrongdoing. She has proof that there's been a breach in its tailing ponds and that toxic chemicals are leaching into the water supply of North Run. That's why Hansen's CEO, Steve Bollard, kidnapped her last night. Again, thanks to all of you for ensuring I didn't lose the woman I love."

He paused again. Decided to get it over with. "Here's the kicker, though. I wasn't always Anders Olsen. I changed my name—legally—when I was eighteen, before I joined the military. Everything else you know about me is true. I served for a little over a decade as a Navy SEAL. I love ranching. I love everything about living here, and I'm willing to dedicate my life to this community. I'm willing to do whatever it takes to win this thing," he added to Boone.

"I changed my name because I wanted to turn my back on the values that name stood for—values I didn't share. I thought a lot about it, and when I made the change, I left all of that behind, despite my father's attempts to draw me back into the fold. It's important to me that you all know that who my father is doesn't change who I am."

The room was silent, and Anders's shoulders lowered a fraction of an inch. Despite everything that had happened, he was terrified he was going to lose this place—lose these friends. He looked to Eve. Would she stick by him if everyone else decided to give him the boot?

"I think you'd better spit it out." Angus's voice was devoid of the accent he usually played up to the hilt.

Anders sighed. "Guess you're right. Like I said, I wasn't always Anders Olsen. I was born... Anders Hansen."

Boone straightened. His features transformed. A low murmur swept around the room.

"Did you come here to spy on us?" Jericho asked slowly. "You talked to Johannes Hansen a long time last night."

"That's because he's my father, and he'd had a pistol held to his head for trying to save Eve. He caught wind of Bollard's plans to kidnap her. Followed him out here to do what he could. It wasn't enough, though. If not for all of you, I'm afraid Eve, my father and I would all be dead now."

He let that sink in. "You have to remember, I was eighteen when I changed my name. I didn't do it to spy on anyone. I changed it to distance myself from Hansen Oil. I've been an environmentalist since I was a teenager, and when my father refused to change Hansen Oil's practices, I decided I had to walk away from him."

"What did he think about you joining Base Camp?" Clay asked.

"He hated it," Anders said honestly. "He knew it

was a matter of time before I was exposed—and he was exposed, too. He's dreaded being the laughingstock of the cable news channels, and now he's in a race against time to clean up his tailing pond fiasco before that gets reported on."

"Your old man must be worth a fortune," Jericho said. "You really walked away from all that?"

Anders nodded.

"So, Eve was trying to expose Hansen Oil?" Riley said. "I thought her boyfriend dumped her."

Eve stood up. "Recently an image came across my desk at AltaVista Imaging showing one of Hansen Oil's tailing ponds was leaking chemicals into a watershed that feeds the water supply of a nearby town. I came here because I wanted to expose Hansen Oil to the world, and I thought I could use the show to do that."

"In other words… no ex-boyfriend?" Kai asked.

"No. I'm sorry for the subterfuge," Eve said. "I needed a reason to wind up here on the show."

"How did you know Anders was a Hansen?" Nora asked.

"I didn't. Not until a couple of days ago," Eve said. "I watch the show every week. I saw he needed a bride. I thought maybe I could stick around here long enough to get my images on the show and expose Hansen Oil to national scrutiny. I needed to make it hard for Clem and Renata to cut me out of the footage."

"So you got involved in everything." Savannah nodded. "You pretended to like Anders."

"Oh, I like Anders," Eve protested. "I like all of

you. I came here with a mission, but I never realized what being here—being a part of this—would mean to me. I know I haven't been here long, but Base Camp already feels like home. It kills me to think my actions could endanger anything about this place and what you're trying to do here. I just… I didn't know what else to do. Hansen Oil had to be stopped." She met Anders's gaze.

Anders's heart warmed.

"What happens now?" Clay asked.

"That's up to all of you," Anders said. "This is my home, and I would love to stay, but I won't endanger Base Camp or any of you. I'm going to step outside. I think the rest of you need to talk things over and take a vote. Decide if you want me to stick around after the television show is over. I'll make sure I do my part so that we win, but I'll get the hell out the minute the show ends if that's what you all want."

He strode to the door and exited through it without giving anyone a chance to answer.

There. It was done. Now he'd let the others decide his fate.

EVE SAT BACK in her chair. Would the other members of Base Camp kick Anders out for what he'd done?

He'd lied to them.

He hadn't told them about his father's change of heart, either. Getting Hansen Oil to turn green was huge.

Should she say something?

Before she could, Avery turned to face the others. "I say he stays no matter what. Anders is a good guy, he supports our cause and he was only trying to distance himself from his father."

"He put us all in jeopardy," Boone pointed out. "I think he's right; we should vote."

"Then I vote he stays," Clay said. "I can't think of a stronger message to send to our audience than someone sticking to their principles like he is."

"I vote he stays, too," Nora said. "Your past can follow you no matter how you try to shake it, and it shouldn't be allowed to swallow you whole."

"I vote he stays," Riley piped up. "Anders has been here since day one helping with this place. He's never done anything to make me feel he wasn't on our side."

"I agree," Samantha said. "I haven't been here since day one, but he always made me feel like one of you."

"I vote he stays," Harris said. "I know who he is and who he isn't."

"I vote he stays," Angus said. "We need him."

"Me, too," Savannah said. "Anyone who can walk away from billions is really on our side."

"Yep," Jericho said and seemed to be content to leave it at that.

As one by one the others voted to keep Anders on, Eve felt something in her chest loosen, just a little. Anders had been right; these people stood by each other. It reminded her of the type of camaraderie she'd experienced in her early years working for NGOs.

These were far more than coworkers. More than

friends, even.

These people had bonded in a way most people would never experience. Was this what it once had felt like to be human? Thousands of years ago when little bands of people worked together for their very survival—depending on each other and loving each other in equal measure?

Eve wanted that.

Badly.

She'd never felt so simultaneously blessed to be in a place—and so irrevocably outside of it. The inhabitants of Base Camp were voting to keep Anders.

What would they do with her?

"It's unanimous so far," Boone said quietly. "And I vote Anders stays, too. Which leaves one vote uncounted. Eve? What do you say?"

Eve blinked. "Me? But—"

"You're going to stay, right?"

"At Base Camp? I want to—but—I lied to you—I endangered you just as much as Anders did, if not more—" Her throat was thick, and she struggled to form the words. She wanted so badly to be one of them.

"You were willing to do what you had to in order to save an entire town full of people Hansen Oil's tailing ponds were threatening. I think that's reasoning we can all understand." He waved a hand to indicate those assembled in the room. "And just so you know, marrying Anders isn't a requirement," he added gently. "It's your choice whether to join us or not. We'd love to have you here."

All around the room, people were nodding their heads.

Her choice? She could simply say—yes? Eve found she couldn't speak. Her eyes filled, and she swallowed.

Avery crossed the room to crouch by her. "Please stay," she said. "Boone can find you a backup husband if you don't want Anders. If you want a husband, that is."

Eve laughed, which almost sent her tears spilling. Almost.

She struggled to control them.

"Please?" Avery asked.

"Yes," Eve said. She nodded vigorously. "Yes, I want to stay."

"What about Anders?"

"Yes, I want him, too. I mean—" She broke off in confusion.

"I think we know what you mean," Angus said in his thickest accent yet.

Jericho crossed to the door, flung it open, grabbed Anders's arm and yanked him inside the bunkhouse. "We voted to keep you," he said, shoving him to the center of the room. "It was unanimous, so you won't have to watch your back."

"Unanimous?" Anders broke into a grin, and Eve's insides melted all over again. Anders was going to stay, and so was she—

"Now propose to your girlfriend so we can get on with it!"

Eve thought Anders would say they'd already discussed marriage, but Anders just grinned. "Good idea!" He crossed the room to stand before her, fished around in his pocket, drew out a little velvet box and dropped to one knee.

Avery whooped. Eve couldn't find her breath. She wasn't sure she could stand on her feet. She hadn't even realized she'd risen from her chair, but here she was, looking down at Anders, who was looking up at her. She'd already told him yes—no, she'd told his father yes, Eve realized. This was a real proposal, and it was getting hard to keep her tears in check.

"I don't know what kind of environmentalist would marry the son of an oilman, but—"

"Me. I'm that kind of environmentalist," Eve said, then bit her lip as the room erupted in laughter. She wondered when Anders would tell the others about his agreement with his father.

"I swear to you I will work every day to make your home the most wonderful place on earth," Anders went on. "I will work to build this community and to make this whole world a better place. I will love you all my life, and—"

"Yes," Eve said.

"He hasn't asked—" Avery said.

"EveWrightwouldyoumarryme?" Anders blurted out.

"Yes!"

Anders surged up, wrapped his arms around her, swung her off her feet in a circle, plunked her down again and kissed her.

"Are you sure?" he asked when they came up for air amid applause and congratulations.

"I'm sure," she said.

He opened the little box, showed her its contents and slid the ring on her finger.

"It's beautiful," she said, her heart so full she thought it would burst.

"I love you," Anders murmured into her hair, drawing her close again, as if he never wanted to let her go.

"I love you, too."

"I'm going to need your help to be the man I want to be. My dad's going to fight us tooth and nail all the way as we change from Hansen Oil to Hansen Energy," he said quietly.

"I know."

"You're willing to take on the challenge?"

"Yes, absolutely."

"Then you really are the woman for me."

CHAPTER FOURTEEN

Life hadn't been this good in a long time. There were plenty of problems still to solve, Anders knew, but the most important one had been solved.

Eve had said yes.

Now he needed to get out of this crowd and spend some time alone with her.

"Go ahead," Boone told Anders as if reading his mind. "Go spend some time with your fiancée. We'll cover your chores and deflect Clem as long as we can when he gets back."

"Owe you one," Anders said.

"What was that about?" Eve asked when he took her hand and led her to the door.

"That was about you and me getting to be alone for once." When they made it outside, he added, "You don't mind keeping the news about Hansen Energy a secret until New Year's, do you? Kind of afraid to say it out loud until we see if the old man comes through."

"I don't mind at all."

They floundered through the snow to Anders's tiny

house, which was nearing completion.

"Kitchen or loft?" Anders asked when they got inside, wishing his loft contained a bed rather than the hard floor. A day or two ago, he'd snagged a sleeping bag from the bunkhouse and left it here just in case, but that wasn't going to help much.

"Kitchen, then loft. Hurry."

"You got it." Once more Anders set her up on the kitchen counter. Once more her dress hitched up as she wrapped her legs around his waist.

Once more he kissed her and fumbled at his pants.

This time he got them open. He kicked off his boots, still kissing Eve, then danced around until he'd gotten his jeans off, too.

"That's pretty impressive," Eve said, breaking away from him for a moment to speak the words.

"You ain't seen nothing yet." Anders lifted her a couple of inches, dragged her gown up and over her head—and promptly got it stuck there. "What the hell?"

"You have to undo the back." Eve wriggled around until she could poke her head out of her skirts again and showed him what to do.

"This is way too complicated."

"You haven't seen nothing yet," she echoed. After he'd finally lifted her gown over her head, she presented him with the ties of her stays.

"Can't I just cut that thing off you?"

"Don't you dare!"

He got to work on the ties and, after a struggle, managed to get the old-fashioned corset off.

"There's more," he said.

She still wore her shift, and Eve laughed as he gathered folds of it into his hands and yanked it up and over her head, too.

"Finally," he said when presented with her bare torso. Unlike her Regency predecessors, Eve wore modern-day stockings under her gown. Anders glanced at them pointedly. "I'll deal with those in a minute. But first…" He slid both hands up her waist to her breasts, cupped them and groaned.

Eve groaned, too, as he palmed them, rubbing her sensitive nipples with his thumbs and lifting first one breast, then the other to take into his mouth and play with.

She'd waited for this for so long. Daydreamed about it for hours at night when she couldn't sleep in the bunkhouse. Finally, she was here with him.

Alone.

Anders had decided to take his time, and Eve gripped the counter, steadying herself against the pressure of his hands and tongue. Her skin heated under his touch, her desire for him sparking into a blaze inside her. When she couldn't take it any longer, she said, "Anders… please."

He lifted her again, tugged at the waistband of her stockings and inched them down, his fingers exploring her as he went. He cupped her bottom, playfully stroking the core of her, then tugging down even more, until she could get them the rest of the way off with her feet and kick them away.

This time when she linked her legs around his waist, only the soft fabric of his boxer-briefs came between them, and his hardness pushed against her in a delightful way. She couldn't wait to take him inside, but first she'd allow him to explore all of her.

He did, first with his hands, then he crouched down between her legs to explore her with his mouth. Eve clung to the counter, holding on—barely—while he stoked her desire even higher. Each pass of his tongue along the innermost part of her made her want to give in—to give him everything. When he stood up again, shucked off his boxer-briefs and positioned himself between her legs, she wriggled forward until he nudged against her and tried to take him in.

"Protection," he breathed against her neck.

"I don't want protection."

Anders pulled back. "Are you sure?"

"Only Nora and Savannah are pregnant so far, and time is running out. We need to do our part, don't you think?"

Desire flooded him, hot and urgent. This was what true joy felt like. His heart had to be swelling in his chest. Making a baby with Eve sounded perfect. When he nodded, Eve smiled.

Anders couldn't hold back another second. With a strong, slow stroke, he pushed inside her, sure he'd finally found exactly where he belonged.

AS HE LIFTED her, cupped her bottom with his hands and established a rhythm, all Eve could do was hold on.

She had never started an encounter like this so turned on she was clinging to every shred of self-control. The desire to start a family with Anders was one she'd barely admitted to herself before she'd voiced it out loud. His unequivocal endorsement of the idea had washed any lingering reservations away.

This was the man she'd spend her life with, and together they'd help build Base Camp into a community that was here to stay. Then they'd take on Hansen Oil and turn it into a company they could be proud of. That was real progress—the kind she'd always wanted to be a part of.

"I love you," Anders said, his voice a rugged rasp in her ear. "I will always love you." He increased his pace, filling her until she couldn't hold back.

Eve came with a cry he echoed, and as her release pulsed through her, she felt him go over the edge, too. Bucking against her, pulsing within her, Anders took her all the way until a second orgasm overtook her, leaving her crying out into his shoulder, shuddering with her release again and again until she thought it would last forever.

When it was over, she clung to him, breathing hard. "That was worth waiting for."

Anders chuckled, a rumbling sound she heard through her own body. "Hell, yeah. How about we take this upstairs and try it again?"

"Lead the way."

The second time around they took things much slower, even though the floor of the loft was hard, and the sleeping bag Anders had brought did little to ameliorate matters. Anders took the brunt of it, rolling over on his back and bringing Eve up to straddle him when it was time for him to push inside her again.

"I like the view," he said as she bent over him.

She liked this position, too, especially since it gave Anders free rein to run his hands all over her. She'd thought it would take them longer to be ready again, but they were like teenagers getting naked for the first time, and neither of them could get enough.

This time when he pushed inside her, she was able to control the rhythm. She moved slowly, easing him in and out of her, building up her hunger for him until the ache inside her grew too strong to ignore. The rocking of her hips brought her breasts into reach of his mouth, and as he nuzzled and teased them, she bit her lip, straining to hold on for a little longer.

When he gripped her hips and thrust into her again, she lost that last vestige of control. Throwing her head back, crying out and riding him, she let him bring her over the edge, into an orgasm that pulsed through her until she was spent.

Anders bucked against her several more times before collapsing back against the floor. Eve joined him, disengaging and cuddling into the crook of his arm. He tugged the sleeping bag up around them, and when Eve woke, daylight was coming through the windows. She vaguely registered that she'd have to do a walk of shame in her gown to the bunkhouse to get clothes to change into.

Maybe she could send Anders to get them.

"Morning," Anders said, and she realized he was awake.

"Morning. Did you sleep?"

"Right through the night. Guess we'd better get going, though. Let's get you over to the bunkhouse before the whole camp is there. All we need is to bump into Clem before we're dressed."

Eve groaned but allowed him to unzip the sleeping bag, and she followed him to the ladder. He helped her down, touching and caressing her body far more than necessary to accomplish the maneuver until both of them were laughing and tangled together by the time they made it to the first floor.

"We could skip breakfast and go right back up there," he offered.

"I need a toothbrush and a trip to the bathroom first," she said.

"Fine," he growled.

He helped her back into her shift and gown, skipping the corset since she'd need to shower and change anyway. She tucked it under her arm and hurried after him. By the time they reached the bunkhouse, a fair number of Base Camp inhabitants were already there. The minute Anders pushed open the door, Eve darted for the bathroom and slammed the door shut, then realized she didn't have any clothes to change into. She didn't want to do another walk of shame after her shower. Luckily, Avery knocked on the door a moment later.

"Let me in," she said and brought Eve everything she needed. While Eve showered, Avery perched on the bathroom counter and kept up a running commentary on the events of the previous evening. "But enough about that. Fill me in on you and Anders."

"Nothing to tell," Eve said, stepping out of the shower and wrapping up in a towel. She dried her hair as best she could with another towel and pulled her shift over her head.

"There must be something to tell," Avery said, helping her into her corset.

"It was good. And that's all I'm saying."

"You're no fun. You should still come to the manor after breakfast, though. There'll be a surprise for you."

"A surprise? Sounds intriguing."

When she reached the manor some time later, she found a fitting in progress for seemingly every woman at Base Camp at once.

"What's going on?" she asked the room at large.

"It's our dresses for the New Year's bash. Alice brought them over," Avery said happily.

Eve stepped farther into the room and gasped at the beautiful gowns the women were wearing. All together like this, they made up a bouquet of the most stunning colors. "Those are gorgeous," she told Alice. "Every one is a work of art."

"Here's yours." Alice lifted up a midnight-blue gown.

"For me?" She thought it was even more beautiful than the rest.

"Of course. You're not Cinderella," Avery said. "You're going to the ball, aren't you?" In a lower voice, she added, "If you're going to help unveil Hansen Oil's rebranding in front of the whole town—and the whole world—you have to look good."

Eve had filled her in on Anders's decision to help his father, figuring she owed Avery that much. Avery was being instrumental in setting things up for the New Year's bash.

Alice helped Eve change, and Eve stared at her reflection in the large mirror propped in one corner of the room for the occasion. Behind her, all the other women were talking, laughing, helping each other with their gowns. Once again, emotions overwhelmed her. She'd have to call her parents soon and tell them everything that had happened. She wondered what they'd think about the new adventure she meant to take.

"What about school?" she could hear her mother say. Eve bit back a smile. Maybe she'd still go one day, although who needed film school when she had Renata to teach her all she needed to know.

"Just a few nips and tucks," Alice said, looking her over. "Otherwise, it's perfect, if I do say so myself."

"Anders is going to love you in that," Avery said.

"You'll be the belle of the ball," Savannah said. She patted her large stomach ruefully. "I'm happy to be pregnant, don't get me wrong, but I wish I looked like you do in that dress."

"You're more beautiful than any of us," Riley told her. "Jericho will look at you all night. Everyone else will be staring at you, Eve. It should be a party to remember."

That afternoon, while Clem stormed around the bunkhouse ranting about the twenty-four-hour goose chase Renata had led him on, Renata tugged Eve into the kitchen.

"You think Hansen's actually going to show up tomorrow?"

"I sure hope so. Are you ready to film it?"

"Sure am. Got a plan to get rid of Clem again."

"He's already pretty mad." From what Eve had heard, Renata had spent most of the previous day staking out the entrance to the public library, filming everyone who came in and out. Then, when it closed, she switched to one of the local bars. There'd been an incident with several of the patrons before she bought a round of drinks for everyone there. "Background material for two possible new series," she'd apparently told Clem when he finally confronted her. "*Small Town Scholars* and *Who's Getting Drunk Today*. What do you think? Do I have a hit on my hands?"

Clem hadn't been amused.

"He's furious." Renata grinned. "Most fun I've had in ages."

"I can't wait until this is over," Eve confessed to her. "I'm terrified that Johannes won't show or that he'll backtrack from his promises and do nothing but embarrass Anders."

"If he does, he'll embarrass himself, too. You two will get through this, no matter what happens."

Eve hoped she was right.

Late that night she got an email from Kevin with a subject line that made her blink: Severance Package.

Eve,

Johannes Hansen has asked me to apologize on both of our behalfs for not including you in the decision-making process for how to handle the tailing pond spill you discovered. As I'm sure you understand by now, the spill had already been brought to Mr. Hansen's attention, and procedures to contain it were in the works. I was overzealous in protecting a valued client, and my secrecy—our secrecy—forced you into a difficult choice. Let it go and think you'd betrayed a community in danger, or listen to your conscience and face losing your job.

Mr. Hansen informs me you'll be taking on a new position with his company, along with his son, once his operations are in order, and that you'll help to supervise Hansen Oil's transition to a clean energy company. I couldn't be more proud of you.

I hope in time you'll be able to forgive me for what I did. I wish I had your moral clarity and courage. Good luck in your marriage and in your future life. Please find enclosed a severance package I hope does a little to bridge the gap to your new career.

Kevin

"Everything okay?" Avery asked, coming to sit near her. Most of the inhabitants of Base Camp had already dispersed to their tiny houses. Those who were left were getting ready for bed. Anders was on patrol tonight;

he'd be back early in the morning.

Eve handed her phone to Avery. "Kevin is my boss at AltaVista. I thought he'd be furious."

"Sounds like he understands," Avery said when she'd finished reading. "You did the right thing."

Eve nodded, finding it hard to speak. "I was so scared I was making a big mistake."

"You don't feel that way now, do you?"

"No. Not at all. I feel like I've found my home."

Avery hugged her. "Damn right you have!"

EVE WAS QUIET as they drove to the New Year's bash, and Anders wondered if she was nervous about what was to come. Once they reached the party, however, she brightened up again, and Anders understood why. The hall had been decorated with boughs of greenery and sparkly fairy lights, and a live orchestra played at the head of the room. The place was packed with people.

They gave their coats and wraps to the coat clerk and made their way into the main room, pausing to watch the couples already swirling around the dance floor. People were dressed in a variety of clothes, from full-on evening wear to much more casual outfits. The Base Camp group definitely stuck out, and Eve especially in her low-cut, deep-blue gown. All eyes were on them as they circulated through the hall.

Anders was surprised when she suddenly gave a little bounce and hurried to enfold a woman he didn't recognize in her arms. She waved him over.

"Anders, this is Melissa, my best friend. She's the

one who dropped me on the road near Base Camp that first night we met. Melissa, this is—"

"Anders Olsen. Navy SEAL, bison wrangler, environmentalist," Melissa finished for her. "Nice to finally meet you."

"Nice to meet you, too." Anders didn't know what else to say. Eve was full of surprises.

"I'm Harry Enright," the man standing next to Melissa said. "I've got a ranch about ten miles from here. The Lazy L."

"I've heard of it."

"Harry is my... fiancé," Melissa said shyly. She lifted her left hand.

Eve pounced on it and shrieked. "You're getting married? Why didn't you say?"

"It's just happened."

Harry beamed. "Proposed at dinnertime. Melissa said yes. Fastest courtship I've ever heard about, but I didn't want to lose her."

"I told him I'd have to go home soon," Melissa said. "Guess I'm not going anywhere now."

Eve hugged her again.

"Looks like you're engaged, too." Harry pointed to Eve's hand.

It was Melissa's turn to shriek. As the women fell into a third hug, the tension in Anders's shoulders eased a bit. Until someone tapped him on the back and he turned to find Clem behind him.

"What's all this?" he demanded.

"Nothing for you to worry about," Anders said.

"Go bug someone else."

"More secrets?" Clem sneered at him. "You're not the only one. Enjoy yourself while you can."

When he left, Anders found Harry considering him. "That sounded ominous."

"He's not up to anything I don't know about," Anders assured him. He noticed Melissa and Eve listening now. "I think he's been poking around my hometown, asking questions."

"That was me," Melissa said a little ruefully. "Sorry."

Anders considered this. "Maybe it was both of you."

"I've told Melissa what to expect tonight," Eve said.

"And I told Harry," Melissa said. "If he's going to be my husband—"

"That's all right. We'd better keep circulating, though." Anders took Eve's arm in his. "Sooner or later my dad's going to show up, and I want to be ready for him."

"See you later," Eve told Melissa. "I'm so happy for you."

"I'm happy, too." Melissa grew serious. "You did it, Eve."

"We did it," Eve corrected her. "Are you really going to marry Harry and stay here?"

Melissa nodded. "We'll be neighbors," she said.

"I can't wait."

"HAVING FUN YET?" Curtis asked when Anders met up with him later at the bar.

"I'd be having a lot more fun if this was over."

Where was his father? He hadn't heard from Johannes since their meeting in the woods. He hoped like hell his father hadn't chickened out. Eve and all the men of Base Camp had been called back for questioning by Cab Johnson, but when Anders asked Cab about his father, Cab told him he couldn't divulge anything about their dealings. "We're in touch," he said. "Johannes has agreed to testify against his CEO. Sounds like Bollard intends to testify against him in return. Something about tailing ponds?"

Anders had nodded. "Won't be the first time Hansen Oil is in hot water," he'd told Cab. He was thankful he wasn't the one who had to sort out that mess.

Curtis clapped him on the shoulder. "Relax. I'm sure your dad will come."

"Easy for you to say." Anders had filled Curtis in on more of the details of his deal with Johannes than he'd told anyone else except Eve. Curtis had been gratifyingly impressed. "Changing Hansen Oil's trajectory is huge," he'd said. "You're the man for the job.

"Yep," Curtis said now. "You're right; it is easy for me to say. Go dance with your fiancée. Have a little fun. Worrying about your dad won't make the time pass more quickly."

"Guess you're right."

A minute later, he threaded his way through the bevy of women surrounding Eve and tugged her aside. "Want to dance?"

"Definitely. Thought you were getting us some drinks."

"Changed my mind. I wanted to be with you." He led her out onto the dance floor and took her in his arms just as the music switched to a slow song. As he pulled her close, a sigh escaped him. This was a good idea.

"I love this," Eve confessed. "Moving with you. Feeling your arms around me."

"You don't feel like I rushed you into anything?"

She tilted her head to look at him. "No, I don't. In fact, to my way of thinking it took you much too long."

She wasn't talking about marriage, Anders thought. She was talking about this—the two of them touching. Swaying together. Sharing a moment that was just theirs.

"Your dad won't arrive until later." She glanced at a large clock on the auditorium's wall. "He'll want to be sure everyone is here. We've got time to enjoy ourselves."

Eve was right; Johannes would want to make an entrance late in the evening. Meanwhile he would soak up every moment he could with the woman who was going to be his bride.

Eve laced her arms around his neck and snuggled even closer as Anders's hands slid down to rest on her hips. Lust stirred low inside him. If only this night was over and they were alone—

"We could slip away," Eve murmured. "Work on that baby thing again."

Anders wasn't sure he'd heard her right. "Where?"

"There has to be someplace."

He leaned back. "You mean—?

Eve nodded, eyes shining. "Clem's not around."

Anders scanned the room. She was right. He had no idea where the director had gotten to, but he remembered what Renata had said. She was running interference for them tonight. He took Eve's hand. "Let's go."

It took them fifteen minutes to locate a small room with a door that could be locked. It took a moment for Anders to spin Eve around, flip up her gown and flick her panties down.

"This okay?" he asked as she braced her hands on the shelf of the metal rack that covered one wall.

"It's perfect. Hurry."

Normally, Anders would take his time and enjoy the experience. He could spend hours with Eve, but she was right; they didn't have a lot of time. Who knew when someone might need a mop or bucket, and come with a key?

He unbuttoned his fly, tugged his pants down and snugged himself up behind Eve. Just the brush of her skin against his hardness was enough to make him ache. He'd been afraid she wouldn't be ready, but he was wrong. She was warm and wet, and when he positioned himself behind her and nudged forward, he slid right in on one long stroke.

They both let go of a breath. Anders chuckled, but it took everything he had to hold back. Instead, he eased out and pushed back in again, eliciting another sigh from Eve. He wished he could get her out of these clothes, but in a way they added to the experience.

Her bottom was nicely framed by the dark-blue gown. His view of their joining only heightened the need clawing at him from the inside. He did his best to keep his pace slow and smooth, but he found himself speeding up in spite of himself.

"That's good," Eve breathed. "Keep going." Anders sped up more. With each thrust, Eve pressed back against him, encouraging him.

Making him lose control.

Anders kept one hand on her hip, grabbed the metal pole holding up the shelves with the other high over Eve's head. He bucked against her until she melted around him, her soft cries tugging him straight over the edge of his own release. Nothing could have stopped him then, and when at last he was done, panting and shuddering, Eve leaned against him, as spent as he was.

She tipped her head back and twisted to kiss his neck. "You're amazing."

"No, you're the one who's amazing. I could do this all night."

"I'm all for that." She threw a glance at the locked door. "But we'd better get back. Another time."

"I'll hold you to it."

EVE DOUBTED SHE'D ever forget the last fifteen minutes. She wished she could run away with Anders and spend the next week reenacting this bout of love-making, but they still had work to do.

"Someday it will be just us, alone, every night," Anders promised her with a lingering kiss under her ear.

"I know."

They set themselves to rights, but before they left, Anders backed Eve against the door. "I just need another minute."

Eve wrapped her arms around his neck and enjoyed the sensation of Anders's kisses. Five minutes later, they finally shut the door behind them and followed the sound of music back to the auditorium.

"I've been looking all over for you two," Curtis hissed when he met them just inside the door. His gaze flicked to Eve's flushed face and Anders's disheveled clothes. "Guess you figured out how to relax."

Anders elbowed him. "Focus. Why were you looking for us?"

"There's a limo in the parking lot. I figure you know the occupant. Renata has done her part; Clem's long gone on another wild goose chase."

Anders left Eve with him and went to find his father.

"I don't know about this," Johannes said as he unfolded himself from the back seat of the limousine. "Seems silly to announce Hansen Oil's succession plan at a country shindig."

"You're announcing Hansen Energy's new direction on a television show that's all about taking a new direction. A show with a huge national audience," Anders corrected him. "Come on, Dad. Let's go bring Hansen Energy into the twenty-first century."

Johannes grumbled but allowed himself to be led inside the modest community center. He gave a sniff when they entered into the outer hall, but the crowd inside the auditorium cheered him up a little.

True to her word, Melissa had rigged an audiovisual system and had somehow squared it with the dance's organizers to let them make their presentation. She'd mentioned telling the committee they'd play up Chance Creek's charms on upcoming episodes to encourage tourism. She and Avery met them inside the doors with Eve and led them all up onstage at the front of the large room.

The music died down, and a spotlight illuminated a lectern and laptop on the stage and a large screen behind and to one side of them.

"Where's your film?" Avery asked Johannes.

He passed her a memory stick, and Avery went to fiddle with the laptop.

Renata met her there, leaned toward the microphone, cleared her throat and waited until the dull roar of conversation in the room died down. Eve spotted several members of the crew filming but didn't see Clem. She wondered how Renata had gotten rid of him.

"Hello," Renata said to the crowd. "I'm Renata Ludlow, and I'm the director—one of the directors—of *Base Camp*, the television show that's being filmed outside town at Westfield Ranch. First, I'd like to thank you all for your continuing hospitality to us. I know it can be strange to have a television production being filmed in your backyard." She paused until the applause died down. "Second, I'd like to thank you for allowing us to interrupt your evening for a special announcement that has to do with one of our cast members. Anders, would you like to introduce our special guest?"

Anders took the podium, still holding Eve's hand. "Hi, folks. I'm Anders Olsen, and this is Eve Wright. If you watched our last episode, you'll know who she is. What you don't know is that in the last few days Eve helped me repair a relationship with someone close to me. If you watch our next episode, you'll see a few surprise twists. One of them is that this man is my father." He gestured for Johannes to join him. "And he and I are going to take our family business and transform it in the coming years. Curious?"

A number of audience members nodded. "You bet," one shouted. A murmur of laughter spread through the room.

"Go, Base Camp!" someone else yelled.

"I've got a short film for you that will explain everything," Anders said. Avery tapped the keyboard and got the film going. They all stepped aside so the audience could see better.

When Hansen Oil's ubiquitous logo came up, Eve saw many people exchanging glances and shrugging their shoulders. They watched avidly as a narrator began to speak as images shifted on the film.

"Hansen Oil has powered America for generations."

Images of automobiles on highways, trucks on construction sites, farm machinery and factories crossed the screen. There was a clip of a much younger Johannes receiving a medal from a long-dead president.

"But now a new generation is forging America's future," the narrator boomed. "And Hansen Oil is becoming Hansen Energy." A portrait of Anders joined one of Johannes on screen. Among the audience members, people pointed at Anders and his father on stage.

Onscreen came images of wind farms, huge solar arrays, geothermal rigs and more. Surprised murmurs came from the crowd.

"Hansen Energy—a New Name for a New Mission."

As the film ended and the lights came up, Johannes Hansen took the stage. "My name is Johannes Hansen, and if you haven't guessed already, Anders here is my son. For a long time we saw the future differently. We're not the only ones at odds about it in this country, are we?"

Laughter and nodding heads greeted this question.

"I've seen the writing on the wall thanks to my son, though. Like it or not, change is coming. We can hide from it, or we can embrace it. I've been researching your town in the last few weeks because I wanted to see why my son was so adamant about staying here. Now I know. You folks are a lot like the people I know at home. Workers. Tradesmen. Ranchers. Farmers. The people who get things done in this country. And you aren't sitting around waiting for the world to pass you by. I've read about initiatives to change the way you're ranching, the way you're farming, the way you're building housing, the way you're doing most things. What strikes me most about Chance Creek, though, is the way you're doing it together. That's what this country needs. My son and I—"

"Hold on. Hold on!"

Eve craned her neck to see who was causing the ruckus at the back of the room. She cringed when she spotted Clem pushing through the crowd, holding something in his hand.

He barrelled his way up to the stage, climbed the steps, strode across it, shouldered Avery away from where she was reaching to protect the laptop, pulled out Johannes's memory stick and jammed a new one in.

"Don't believe a thing this man says." He pointed to Johannes. "Or that one, either." He jabbed a finger at Anders. "Hansen Energy isn't real. It's just a cover-up for all the damage Hansen Oil has done." He hit a few keys, and another movie started up.

Eve clapped a hand to her mouth as a familiar voice—her voice—narrated it. It was the first movie she'd made. The one detailing the intrusion of chemicals from the tailing ponds at Terrence field into North Run's water supply.

"See?" Clem howled as the images she'd stolen from AltaVista flashed onscreen. "Hansen Oil does nothing but destroy—hey!"

Clem reared back and covered his ears as fast-paced pop music suddenly blasted out of the speakers around the auditorium, and the familiar intro music to *Track the Stars* blared.

Eve met Anders's shocked gaze, then Avery's mystified one. Melissa, however, was biting back a big grin.

When a woman Eve dimly remembered joined her on the stage, Eve began to put two and two together.

That was Jana, Melissa's old roommate, a cute blonde with a pixie haircut. The one who was looking for footage of Clem—

"Hey, stop that! What the hell?" Clem shouted. On-screen, jerky, handheld camera footage showed him grab a woman, push her against a wall and rub his body against hers.

A collective gasp came from the audience as Clem lunged for the laptop, and Anders blocked his way. On the big screen over them, Clem continued to paw at the unfortunate woman, who was clearly trying to push him away.

Jana stepped to the lectern as Clem and Anders continued to wrestle behind her. "Hi, as long as we're doing introductions, I'll join in. I'm Jana Smith. That's my friend holding the camera." She pointed at the screen behind her. "And that's Clem Bailey assaulting a crew member from his show *Track the Stars*. You didn't hear about this incident because Clem settled out of court for an undisclosed amount, but it's why he isn't hosting *Track the Stars* anymore. I'd advise you to take anything he says with a grain of salt."

Applause greeted her announcement. Jana curtsied and left, taking the memory stick with her.

Melissa picked her way around the brawling men to reach Eve's side. "Took a hell of a lot of work to follow Clem and distract him while we stole his memory stick, overwrote his movie and got it back to him. Renata helped a lot. She was the one who tipped us off that he had your movie."

"Renata is a marvel." Eve hoped she got the whole story behind that escapade someday. "I wonder how she knew he stole our film?"

"She caught him. He's got extra crew members working for him—people you don't even know about. She's got extra crew members tracking his extra ones. Renata says your security is shit, by the way."

Anders wouldn't be happy to hear that. "The ranch is too big, and there's not enough men, I guess."

"Renata says their problem is they keep looking for outsiders instead of at the people who are already there."

They both watched as the sheriff arrived, handcuffed Clem for drunk and disorderly conduct, despite his insistence that he wasn't drunk, and took him away.

When they were gone, Johannes took the podium again. "Thank you to the brave men and women serving Chance Creek," he said and led a round of applause for Cab Johnson. Cab saluted him as he helped Clem out the back door.

"Clem Bailey wasn't wrong about Hansen Oil, however," Johannes went on. The crowd silenced again, and Eve stiffened. What was he doing?

Anders watched his father. Eve wanted to go to him, but she didn't want to distract from the moment.

"In order to fix problems, we have to admit we have them," Johannes went on. "Hansen Oil has a problem, and we mean to fix it. More to the point, we intend to

move to technologies we hope will cause fewer problems in the future. Now, we've taken up enough of your
time tonight. Let's get back to dancing. But remember,
you heard it here first. Hansen Oil is now Hansen
Energy, and we aim to be the leader in renewables for a
long time to come."

CHAPTER FIFTEEN

B OTH DIRECTORS WERE present in the room as Anders and the other men finished dressing for his wedding several weeks later. Clem had been locked up overnight, but he'd made a beeline back to Base Camp the minute he was out. Boone had called Fulsom to complain, but the billionaire told him to be patient. "He's coming in a couple of days to sort things out," Boone had told Anders earlier.

As usual, Alice Reed was on hand to make any last-minute alterations. They'd used these Revolutionary War uniforms so many times now, it was all old hat.

"New company, new job, new name," Curtis said as he adjusted his coat in the mirror. "It's like you're a whole new man."

"Same company, new direction," Anders corrected. "And the name isn't really new; I'm just reclaiming my old one."

"And all the money that goes with it." Curtis chuckled. "Anders Hansen of Hansen Energy. It's a shame you can't pump some of those funds into Base Camp. It certainly would take some of the pressure off."

"I won't have access to any part of Hansen Oil for months, maybe years, while my father cleans up the environmental mess he made in Texas. I won't sign on until everything is on the up and up. I don't want to be party to anything criminal. Besides, that would be cheating. I guess all I can say is that if we blow this, and get kicked off the property, a few years down the line I'd be able to help buy us a new one. But that's a ways off."

Curtis nodded slowly, then met Anders's gaze in the mirror. "Wouldn't be the same anyway, would it?"

Anders thought of the fields where the bison grazed and the Montana sky that seemed to go on forever. The bunkhouse where they had community meals and the tiny house in which he and Eve would start their life together. Chance Creek had gotten under his skin. It was as much a part of him as these people who had become his family.

"You're right," he agreed, "it wouldn't be the same."

"Where's Boone and his straws?" Alice asked while tightening a button on his jacket. She knotted the thread, snipped it with a pair of shears and surveyed her handiwork.

Right on cue, Boone burst into the room waving his fist.

Only three straws poked out of it.

"You know who you are," he called. "Step up and take your chances."

Angus, Greg and Walker did so. Slowly, Anders noticed. Angus hadn't wanted to deal with the matter of marriage since his former intended had walked out on him some months ago. Walker still hadn't cleared up the matter with his family that held him back from being with Avery.

And Greg—

Greg was just being squirrely these days.

Walker drew first, lifted the long straw for all to see and went back to getting ready.

Angus groaned. "Better get this over with."

Anders didn't know if he was referring to drawing his straw—or getting married. He shut his eyes, drew a straw—

And let out a whoop.

"Yeah—forty more days!"

Greg's shoulders slumped. He drew the last straw for form's sake and stared at it glumly.

"Guess it's my turn," he said.

"Cheer up. It's worked out for everyone else," Boone pointed out.

"Pretty sure it's not going to work out for me," Greg said. "Go ahead and find that backup bride."

"Will do."

"WELL, YOU AREN'T going back to school, and you're not living in our backyard, but I guess we can forgive you for changing plans—again," Eve's mother joked when she and Eve's father bustled into the room where she was getting ready. "At least we made it here in time to see you walk down the aisle!"

"Guess I'm not so bad at relationships, after all," Eve said.

"I guess not. Although I didn't expect you to run off and find a husband on a TV show. Still, I have to admit you found a handsome one, and Anders seems like a man with a good head on his shoulders."

"He is," Eve assured her. "You don't mind that I'm not going to live in Richmond?"

"I never said that," her mother said wistfully, "but sometimes you have to go where life takes you. I'm so proud of everything you've done. I didn't like it when you were racing around the world, putting yourself in so much danger, but you did a good thing standing up to Hansen Oil."

Eve thought she must be glowing. It took a lot to earn her mother's approval.

"We're both proud of you, honey," her father said.

Alice Reed popped her head into the room. "It's time."

Eve's parents hugged her, and her mother hurried to take her seat. Avery and Melissa, who'd agreed to be her bridesmaids along with Renata, entered the room with the bouquets they'd gone to fetch. They'd been a huge help organizing the wedding on such short notice.

"All the vendors in town know we're going to have a wedding every forty days," Riley had explained. "They keep things ready for us at this point. We have a standing deal with Mia Matheson, the wedding planner."

Thank goodness for that, because Eve had wanted everything to be perfect—and it was so far.

Her dress was a stunning gown with an empress waist, a beaded bodice and a long, trailing skirt. The flowers were lovely, as were the decorations in the ballroom at the manor, where the wedding was to be held.

Everything was ready. Almost everything. "Where's Renata?" Eve asked.

Avery put a finger to her lips and gestured to the doorway. Eve spotted Renata down the hall talking to Greg.

"…really something in that dress," Greg was saying. He held both of Renata's hands out wide, as if to see her better.

"Don't get used to it," Renata said, snatching her hands back.

"You're not as tough as you try to look," Greg said, taking one again and apparently holding on while Renata tried to tug it away.

"I'm tougher," Renata promised him. "And if you think—"

"Well, look at this," Clem said loudly, coming around the corner from the direction of the stairs. "What a pretty picture."

Renata gave one last tug and stepped away from Greg, her color high. "Haven't you left yet?" she asked.

"Who said anything about leaving?" Clem leaned in and leered at her. "When Fulsom gets here, I'll straighten up this whole mess. You'll be the one taking off."

"I doubt it."

"People, it's time!" Alice pushed her way into the

hall and clapped her hands. "No more arguing. We've got a wedding to get underway."

"Whatever." Clem disappeared back down the stairs. Greg moved closer to Renata, took her hand and, if Eve wasn't mistaken, squeezed it.

"Don't let him get you down. You're not going anywhere," he said. He turned and headed for the stairs, too, leaving Renata to look after him.

"Renata?" Alice called. "Let's go. Eve, are you ready?" She made a last-minute adjustment to the folds of Eve's skirt. "You look beautiful."

"I'm ready," Eve said.

"I'm ready, too," Renata said, suddenly all business. She plucked at the long skirts of her bridesmaid dress as if she had no idea how she came to be wearing it.

Alice shooed the other women into place, and they led the way down the stairs. Taking her father's arm, Eve followed. Boone was standing at the bottom of the steps. Melissa, Avery and Renata stopped at the entrance to the ballroom, waiting for their cue.

"There's someone who wants to speak to you," Boone whispered to Eve. He backed away, and Johannes stepped forward from where he'd been waiting in the hall that led to the kitchen. Her father sized the man up but kept his opinions to himself.

"I wanted to thank you again for bringing Anders back to me."

"I'm glad I could help—and I'm really glad you two found a way to work together."

"Guess I wasn't ready for the world to keep changing so much. I wish Anders's mother was here today to see him marry you. She would have been so happy. She was a true romantic."

"I wish I'd gotten to know her."

Music swelled in the ballroom.

"It's time," Alice said, gesturing for Melissa to begin walking toward the altar.

"I'd better go," Eve said to Johannes.

"Of course." She expected him to take his seat, but he lingered.

"I hoped—I mean, I don't expect your help, but—if you could see your way clear to forgiving me—I hope you and Anders will allow me to be in your lives. I've… missed my son."

"Of course," Eve heard herself say. "Of course you'll be a part of our lives." Johannes's smile was all the reward she could hope for.

She stood straight and tall at her father's side and waited for her cue to walk down the aisle as Johannes slipped off to take his seat. She knew her husband-to-be would be a far happier man now that he and his father were back on speaking terms. He'd missed Johannes as much as Johannes had missed him. Meanwhile, she was moments away from starting her new life here at Base Camp with the man of her dreams.

"Here we go," her father said. "Ready?"

"Ready."

When Anders caught sight of them, his smile lit up his face, and the butterflies in her stomach dipped, swirled and then settled down to flutter happily. Anders always took her breath away. Now she'd never have to leave him.

This was the future she'd always wanted.

This was home.

EVE WAS SO stunning Anders didn't think he could ever take it in that she was his forever. As Eve approached on her father's arm, Anders said a prayer of gratitude for whatever it was that had made him hesitate that night at the end of the lane, look down the road and see her coming toward him.

Fate had brought him a wife. A better wife than he could have found if he'd spent years looking. Together they'd grown. Learned about each other—and themselves—and their place in this community. Their place in the world.

He looked forward to years with Eve. A lifetime of discovery—

And nights together in their tiny home.

It was finally finished, ready for them to move in. He couldn't wait to go to bed with her every evening and wake up to her every morning for all the years to come.

Anders took Eve's hand when her father delivered her and went to take his seat.

"Dearly Beloved," Reverend Halpern began, and as they said their vows, Anders grew sure that all his prayers had been answered.

He spoke his lines with a surety he'd rarely felt in his life and was confident he could keep them. This was the woman for him. The woman he'd cherish forever.

The rest of the celebration passed in a blur until it was time to slip away and celebrate their marriage night together. Back in their new home, he carried her over the threshold and kept on carrying her right up the ladder and into bed.

"You're going to have to get me out of this dress," she told him.

"I'm pretty good at that." He was. He'd been practicing for weeks on the Regency gowns she normally wore. He turned her around, looked at the row of tiny buttons running down her back and said, "That's not fair."

Eve chuckled. "Get going, or we'll be here all night."

"I fully intend to be here all night," he informed her.

"You know what I mean." She looked at him over her shoulder. "Of course, we don't have to take the dress off. After all—I'm only going to wear it once."

"What do you have in mind?"

Eve shuffled forward, braced herself on the carved wooden headboard of the loft bed and lowered one hand to lift up the skirts of her gown.

Underneath it, she wore a tiny satin thong and a set of garters and stockings.

Anders had never seen anything more delicious.

"Pretend we're in that supply closet again."

"Good idea." He quickly followed her, loosening the belt of his Revolutionary War uniform. Settling behind her on his knees, he braced her with a hand to her waist and let the other hand go exploring.

She was ready for him, he soon discovered. Slick and hot to the touch, a dizzying combination. He meant to spend hours making love to his new wife—and he would, he promised himself—but this first time was going to go fast.

Not bothering to undress, either, he got into position, nudged against her—

And slid inside.

Both of them moaned.

"God, that's good," Anders said.

"Mm-hmm." She bent forward, pushing back against him. Inviting him deeper.

Anders let instinct take over from there, his thrusts even and strong, measured until he couldn't hold back anymore. When he sped up, Eve's knuckles whitened on the headboard, her back arched and she thrust back against him.

Her need fueled his, and soon there was nothing he could do but give himself to the experience as Eve cried out and cried out again, her abandon equal to his own.

When it was over, Anders wrapped his arms around his wife, buried his face in Eve's hair and kissed her, never wanting to let her go.

"I love you," he breathed.

"I love you, too," she panted. "Do it again."

They tumbled into a heap of laughter and bedclothes, and this time Anders undressed her before making love to her a second and then a third time.

"WAS IT PERFECT?" he asked her some hours later when they'd made a nest of the covers and snuggled together inside it.

"Yes," she said. "It was absolutely perfect. But I've got one more surprise for you." Her heart rate kicked up a notch. She'd been waiting to do this all night.

"Oh, yeah? What is it?"

"This." She reached down behind the bed and pulled out a package she'd stored there earlier. Opened it and lifted out a pregnancy test.

Anders sat up. "But—"

"I guess we've done our part several times over now."

He searched her face. "Are you okay with this?"

She nodded vigorously. "I'm great with this. How about you? A new job, a new wife—and now a child. Are you ready for all this?"

"Are you kidding?" He was beaming, but then his face clouded and he looked away.

"What?" Eve held her breath, terrified this dream day might turn into a nightmare.

"What if I'm like my dad—too stubborn for my own good? What if I mess up?"

"You won't," she assured him. "Besides, I'll be here."

Anders gathered her into his arms. "You are the best wife ever, you know that? You are everything I ever wanted."

"Keep telling me that, and everything will be okay." She snuggled closer, thinking she'd never been happier.

Meeting Anders's kisses with her own, she wondered what kind of record they'd set tonight. Surely no one had ever—

A loud thumping on the front door froze them both in place.

"Who is it?" Anders called, already reaching for his pants.

"It's Boone. Sorry to disturb you. Just wanted you to know—we're heading for the hospital. Savannah's baby is on the way!"

To find out more about Curtis, Hope, Boone, Clay, Jericho, Walker and the other inhabitants of Base Camp, look for *A SEAL's Desire*, Volume 8 in the *SEALs of Chance Creek* series.

Be the first to know about Cora Seton's new releases! Sign up for her newsletter here!

www.coraseton.com/sign-up-for-my-newsletter

Other books in the SEALs of Chance Creek Series:

A SEAL's Oath

A SEAL's Vow

A SEAL's Pledge

A SEAL's Consent

A SEAL's Purpose

A SEAL's Resolve

A SEAL's Desire

A SEAL's Struggle

A SEAL's Triumph

Read on for an excerpt of
A SEAL's Desire.

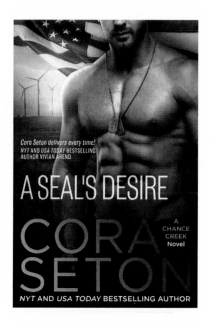

Cora Seton delivers every time!
NYT AND USA TODAY BESTSELLING
AUTHOR VIVIAN AREND

A SEAL'S DESIRE

CORA
SETON

A
CHANCE
CREEK
Novel

NYT AND USA TODAY BESTSELLING AUTHOR

Read on for an excerpt of
A SEAL's Desire.

10 years ago...

GREG DEVON THOUGHT he'd seen the worst of it until the school bus rolled up and parked not thirty feet away from where he stood. He'd been struggling to help erect one of the tents meant to house the survivors straggling down the mountain. The bus was as covered with mud and grime as everything else in the area, the fine drizzle still falling not up to the task of washing any of it clean.

Eight hours ago, before sunrise, when the drizzle had been a deluge, a mudslide had wiped out most of

Colina Blanca up the mountain. Rescue operations were based here in Mayahuay, a larger settlement more easily accessible from the capital. Now it was well past lunch and everywhere he looked people had gathered in knots and family groups. Babies crying, overburdened mothers swaying and crooning to them tonelessly, more people arriving every minute, all of them soaked, exhausted—

Devastated.

Rumor had it other aid groups were on their way, which was good because the one Greg had latched onto wasn't prepared for a disaster like this. He'd been woken by sirens in his dorm room back in Lima, nearly two hours away on the winding mountain roads. Never a heavy sleeper, he'd pulled on a pair of pants, stuck his feet into his hiking boots and a minute later was out on the street. He'd recognized another student who'd come here to Peru for the semester. Both of them were a little older than most of the college kids who came to study abroad and they'd hit it off. They hung out frequently, talking about their future plans.

"What's going on?" he'd asked Renny.

"Mudslide. Big one. It's taken out one village at least. We're going to help dig out."

Greg had piled in a truck with him and a bunch of other students, some he recognized, others he didn't. They'd driven straight up into the hills, the rain sluicing off their vehicle's windows until he thought the real question was whether they'd have to swim the rest of the way.

They quickly learned getting all the way to Colina

Blanca wasn't an option. Mayahuay was the end of the road—literally—and Greg and the others were put to work setting up tents and shelters, hauling boxes of supplies and stacking bottles of water for the victims when they arrived.

They'd started straggling in almost at once, and the snippets of conversation he'd heard—and understood—had left Greg chilled. Hundreds must be dead. Almost everyone in the village, maybe. A sound he'd never heard before pervaded the camp, a low keening that traced up and down his spine, telling him he knew nothing of true despair. All around him people were grieving loved ones they knew they'd never see again. Homes that were buried under tons of debris.

Mid-morning, Renny had tugged his arm, taken him aside, showed him photos forwarded from the village, and Greg began to understand the scope of the damage. They showed a moonscape—a flat plain of mud with only rock outcroppings and tufts of greenery sticking out from it here and there—former hills and trees now buried under the flow. It was amazing anyone had made it out and walked the miles down to Mayahuay.

Now Greg grabbed a water bottle, took a swig and watched as the school bus idled. He'd come to Peru for the adventure of it, champing at the bit to expand his horizons after a lifetime in Oregon, first at Greenside, the large agricultural commune he'd grown up at outside Portland, then at Lewis & Clark college where he'd been studying engineering. Nearly five thousand miles away from the farm that once had comprised his world, it represented a break from his childhood. He wanted to become his own man. Greg had already decided what he'd do next, just as soon as he had his diploma in his hands. Keep traveling around the world. Chase adventures.

He wasn't going to live a settled, small-town life ever again.

He sure as hell wasn't going to live in a commune. He'd had enough of that. He was done with the kind of hot-house atmosphere that can develop in such an insular situation. The way proximity could let a bully ruin a person's life while all their relatives and friends stood by and didn't even notice it happening.

The drizzle tapered off and tepid sunshine tried to break through the clouds. When the bus's door swung open, Greg was surprised to see a young woman exit. Dressed in crisp black slacks and a snowy white blouse, she had raven dark hair, a slim build. She wasn't soaked like everyone at the camp. Wasn't even damp. A man exited behind her, dressed more casually in cargo shorts and a T-shirt, portable video camera in hand.

A news crew?

He didn't think so. Several of those had arrived from Lima already, and these two didn't quite look the part.

"Get all of this, quick. Set up the shot for the reunion," the woman ordered the man holding the camera.

Reunion? Greg stepped closer, nudged Renny as he passed him. "Who's in the bus?"

Renny straightened from his task stacking pallets of

water bottles, turned and frowned. "I don't know."

"Where is everyone?" the woman was saying. She turned and looked over the camp again. "What's going on here? Is it some kind of fair?"

Dread twisted Greg's gut at her misreading of the situation. This sure as hell wasn't a fair. Who on earth did she expect to meet here? He watched the woman's gaze light on the huddled groups on the far side of the area in their mud-spattered clothes. The crying babies.

He saw the moment she realized something was wrong—the same moment the first of the passengers got off the bus.

The cameraman, who'd been panning the camp and getting a shot of the line of Red Cross vehicles that had just turned up the road, spun around at the woman's oath. He pointed his video camera at her, then at the bus where a girl—*a girl in a school uniform*—had just stepped down.

"Mama?" the girl said, scanning the area.

Hell, Greg thought.

"Fuck," Renny echoed beside him. "Are they from—?" He broke off, but Greg knew exactly what he meant to say. Where they from Colina Blanca? Had they arrived back from somewhere else expecting a welcoming committee here in the next larger town? Perhaps the charter bus operator had refused to make the run all the way up to their hillside village. Greg wouldn't blame him, given the usual state of the roads that far up in the mountains.

Wouldn't the driver have heard the news, though,

and turned back?

Maybe not.

The woman was conferring with Diego Alvarez, the man who had organized the convoy of student volunteers from Lima and had taken charge of the disaster aid operation so far. Greg had met Diego at a party just last week hosted for all the foreign exchange students at the university and the men and women who helped organize the exchanges. From the way Diego was gesturing up toward Colina Blanca, first pointing, then flattening his hand and making it swoop down like the wall of mud had just hours ago, he was informing her of what had happened.

Greg watched her take it in, her face a mask of shock. She stood still a moment. Behind her, girls kept spilling out of the bus, all in pristine uniforms, ranging in age from five or six to teenagers. Suddenly he knew exactly who they were. He'd seen a news story about the girls from the San Pedro School of Excellence who were celebrating the twenty-year anniversary of the founding of their institution with a trip to the capital. The school had been set up to help female students from this rural area to achieve an education that would leave them ready to attend a university, serve in government positions and excel in the private sector, too. The idea was that a generation of highly educated women could help bring this entire rural area out of its depressed circumstances. The girls stood alertly, maintaining the decorum they'd been taught.

Two more women stepped off the bus after the last

of the girls had scrambled out. One was tall with sharp, hawk-like features, her dark eyes quickly taking in the scene. The other was shorter, older, her hair going gray and her round face, which Greg somehow knew was normally wreathed in smiles, was grim. These two had seen at a glance that something was horribly wrong. They conferred in rapid Spanish before the tall one clapped her hands twice and barked an order at the girls. They lined up immediately in front of the bus.

That was when the first woman, the one with the cameraman, turned around. Her gaze rested on Greg for only a moment before it slid to the girls, but that moment stopped his breath in his chest. The pain in her eyes pierced him. She'd laid a hand over her heart unconsciously, as if trying to hold in a riot of emotions struggling to break free. She was young. His age, he figured, or a year or two older. She'd heard what had happened up in Colina Blanca. Knew what the girls standing next to the bus didn't—yet. That most of their families were probably gone—their homes destroyed—

Greg didn't realize he was moving until he found himself by her side. He took her arm. Steadied her. "Tell them fast," he said. "Make it clean."

She swallowed. Opened her mouth. He could feel the tears in her, but she didn't cry, her attention solely on the students. "Girls," she said in Spanish. Her voice wavered, but she steadied it. "Girls, I have something hard to tell you. Last night in the rain a mudslide was loosed. Colina Blanca was in its path. Many people were hurt. Died. You are safe here and we will do everything we can to reunite you with your families, but you will have to be patient and very, very brave."

Greg didn't leave her side through all the long hours of that afternoon, evening, night and into the next morning as Renata Ludlow, as he learned she was named, helped Mayra and Gabriela, the tall and broad-faced women, respectively, keep the girls together, feed them, keep them warm and search through the chaos of the camp for their relatives. Renata worked tirelessly, never looking at him, focused single-mindedly on finding the girls' parents, asking aid worker after aid worker if they'd seen any of the missing adults.

As a new day dawned, the truth sunk in. The twenty-three girls who made up the student body of the San Pedro School of Excellence were now orphans. Greg, who until 24 hours ago had little on his mind except catching a flight home to Oregon at the end of the semester in time for graduation in June, felt as if he'd donned some kind of robotic exoskeleton overnight, leaving him lumbering and unsure in his own body. It took him more than an hour to recognize that the feeling stemmed from a shift inside him: a restructuring of the framework of his mind.

No longer a carefree boy looking for an adventure, his aspirations had hardened overnight into something weightier. This was the work he wanted in the future— work that mattered. He wanted to accomplish things. Change things. Help people.

Something else—he wanted to share his life with a woman like Renata. Someone who could work so stoically, but who was so beloved by the girls of the San Pedro school that each of them had sought her out at one time or another during the long, dark hours of the night for consoling words and a shoulder to sob on. He'd known another woman like her once. A girl, rather, whose heart had healed all those who'd come in contact with it—those willing to be healed.

He'd let that girl down in the worst of ways and he was determined not to make the same mistake twice. A new protectiveness had taken hold of him. A desire to patrol the space around Renata and keep her safe while she tended and comforted the students she obviously cared for so much. He'd learned from listening to the people around them that she was from London, a recent film-school graduate here to do a documentary about the San Pedro school and the girls who attended it. He'd learned little else about Renata so far. Nothing at all from the woman herself, who kept moving, kept searching, refused to give up finding the girls' missing parents.

And that was his problem in a nutshell. Because Greg was falling in love with Renata.

And she hadn't even noticed he was there.

End of Excerpt

The Cowboys of Chance Creek Series:

The Cowboy Inherits a Bride (Volume 0)
The Cowboy's E-Mail Order Bride (Volume 1)

The Cowboy Wins a Bride (Volume 2)

The Cowboy Imports a Bride (Volume 3)

The Cowgirl Ropes a Billionaire (Volume 4)

The Sheriff Catches a Bride (Volume 5)

The Cowboy Lassos a Bride (Volume 6)

The Cowboy Rescues a Bride (Volume 7)

The Cowboy Earns a Bride (Volume 8)

The Cowboy's Christmas Bride (Volume 9)

The Heroes of Chance Creek Series:

The Navy SEAL's E-Mail Order Bride (Volume 1)

The Soldier's E-Mail Order Bride (Volume 2)

The Marine's E-Mail Order Bride (Volume 3)

The Navy SEAL's Christmas Bride (Volume 4)

The Airman's E-Mail Order Bride (Volume 5)

The SEALs of Chance Creek Series:

A SEAL's Oath

A SEAL's Vow

A SEAL's Pledge

A SEAL's Consent

A SEAL's Purpose

A SEAL's Resolve

A SEAL's Devotion

A SEAL's Desire

A SEAL's Struggle

A SEAL's Triumph

The Brides of Chance Creek Series:

Issued to the Bride One Navy SEAL
Issued to the Bride One Airman
Issued to the Bride One Sniper
Issued to the Bride One Marine
Issued to the Bride One Soldier

The Turners v. Coopers Series:

The Cowboy's Secret Bride (Volume 1)
The Cowboy's Outlaw Bride (Volume 2)
The Cowboy's Hidden Bride (Volume 3)
The Cowboy's Stolen Bride (Volume 4)
The Cowboy's Forbidden Bride (Volume 5)

About the Author

With over one million books sold, NYT and USA Today bestselling author Cora Seton has created a world readers love in Chance Creek, Montana. She has twenty-eight novels and novellas currently set in her fictional town, with many more in the works. Like her characters, Cora loves cowboys, military heroes, country life, gardening, bike-riding, binge-watching Jane Austen movies, keeping up with the latest technology and indulging in old-fashioned pursuits. Visit **www.cora seton.com** to read about new releases, contests and other cool events!

Blog:

www.coraseton.com

Facebook:

facebook.com/coraseton

Twitter:

twitter.com/coraseton

Newsletter:

www.coraseton.com/sign-up-for-my-newsletter

Made in United States
North Haven, CT
30 June 2022

20834466R00198